PROTECTOR
THE VIGILANTE CHRONICLES™ BOOK SEVEN

NATALIE GREY

MICHAEL ANDERLE

Protector (this book) is a work of fiction.

All of the characters, organizations, and events portrayed in this novel are either products of the author's imagination or are used fictitiously. Sometimes both.

Copyright © 2018 Natalie Grey and Michael Anderle
Cover by Jeff Brown, http://jeffbrowngraphics.com/
Cover copyright © LMBPN Publishing
A Michael Anderle Production

LMBPN Publishing supports the right to free expression and the value of copyright. The purpose of copyright is to encourage writers and artists to produce the creative works that enrich our culture.

The distribution of this book without permission is a theft of the author's intellectual property. If you would like permission to use material from the book (other than for review purposes), please contact support@lmbpn.com. Thank you for your support of the author's rights.

LMBPN Publishing
PMB 196, 2540 South Maryland Pkwy
Las Vegas, NV 89109

First US edition, December 2018

The Kurtherian Gambit (and what happens within / characters / situations / worlds) are copyright © 2015-2018 by Michael T. Anderle and LMBPN Publishing.

THE PROTECTOR TEAM

Thanks to our JIT Readers

Jed Moulton
Jackey Hankard-Brodie
John Ashmore
Keith Verret
Diane L. Smith
Angel LaVey
Paul Westman

If We've missed anyone, please let us know!

Editor
The Skyhunter Editing Team

From Natalie

For M and T

From Michael

To Family, Friends and
Those Who Love
To Read.
May We All Enjoy Grace
To Live The Life We Are
Called.

CHAPTER ONE

"We're close!" Kelnamon scrambled up the rocky incline and took a deep breath of fresh air. Happiness was brimming in his chest, and he could not keep back his smile—or the tears that were gathering in his eyes. He had come out here twice since he'd returned, but walking on his homeworld again was still unusual enough to provoke strong emotions in him.

It had been years since he had seen the gray and ochre rocks of Kordinev, his homeworld. He had spent eight of those serving on one of the big cargo freighters, saving up for the ship he now owned—the *Srisa*. He'd been its captain for over a decade now.

It had taken a tragedy and incredible danger for him to consider coming back to Kordinev. As much as he loved his homeworld, there was very little opportunity here. It lay far from any trade routes, and he was the seventh child. Had he stayed, he would have just been another mouth to feed. Rather than be a burden on his family, he had left to find work elsewhere.

But he had missed this place, and he had missed his family. He'd been so busy he hadn't realized how much.

He turned to look behind him now, and gave a wondering shake of his head as his companion clambered up the slope after him. Ferqar was a captain in the Jotun Navy. He had been born, as far as Kelnamon could tell, into incredible privilege, but had given up everything to become a ship's captain.

Then, due to political machinations, he had been demoted and sent to work on the Jotuns' border patrols—where he'd stumbled on the same conspiracy Kelnamon had become embroiled in.

Kelnamon was trying not to be bitter about that. Ferqar had found out that a fellow Jotun captain, Huword, was abducting and torturing alien civilians. Disgusted, Ferqar had helped arrange for Huword's assassination...aboard Kelnamon's ship.

The problem was, Huword had been part of something far bigger than Ferqar knew, and the *Srisa* had nearly been destroyed by a Jotun black ops team that was trying to cover up Huword's misdeeds. When they showed up, Kelnamon had taken the *Srisa* and fled to Kordinev.

Now he, along with the Brakalon government, was trying to figure out what to do about the angry civilians who had been on board his ship. Kelnamon was hoping that no one was going to come after them here, but every passenger had witnessed far too much. He was sure that the Jotun government wanted his ship destroyed, as well as everyone who had been aboard.

As much as the civilians hated it, they had to stay here until the coast was clear. He didn't know when that would be, though, and they were getting increasingly angry. After a long morning of arguing with a cloth merchant who was threatening to involve his guild, Kelnamon had gone out for a walk to clear his head, and Ferqar had come with him.

Which was when they'd seen a strange object hurtling out of the atmosphere to land nearby, firing thrusters as it went.

"We should probably have called for a hopper," Ferqar said when he reached Kelnamon. He wasn't winded, of course, since he was using his biosuit to move, but it was clear that the rough terrain of Kordinev was difficult for the Jotun to navigate.

"The point of a walk is that you *walk*," Kelnamon remarked. He still wasn't quite sure if Ferqar understood that. They had gone for walks several times recently, and Ferqar tended to ask where they had been going and what the point was.

"Yes," Ferqar agreed, somehow managing to imply that Kelnamon was completely insane, "but now we're searching for something, and a search is best done with technology—like scanners."

He did have a point, as much as Kelnamon hated to admit it. "Your suit *has* scanners, right? Have you been using them?"

It was hard to tell, but the faint movements in Ferqar's suit suggested that he was faintly embarrassed. "Well, yes. But I haven't found anything."

Kelnamon rolled his eyes. "So...using technology hasn't been any better than being on foot, then." He looked at the horizon and squinted as he slowly swung his head side to side.

This part of Kordinev, just outside the capital city of Herod, was hilly and weathered by the constant winds. The soft sandstone had been shaped beautifully, and the only vegetation was hardy scrub that nestled in the alcoves and cracks of the rocks where it was protected from the wind.

"I'm amazed that life ever took hold here," Ferqar stated, after a moment.

"Why?" Kelnamon felt almost offended.

"There's no *water*."

Kelnamon laughed. "Of course, there's water. Come, I'll show you." He knelt near a long crack in the top of the rock. "See those plants, how their leaves are so thick? They hold water inside. When it rains, the water pools here in the crack and the plant sucks it up through the roots, which are under the ground. If you're lost out here, you pull the plants up one by one and eat them for the water inside."

"And if you're an aquatic life form?" Ferqar asked, somewhat prickly.

"Well..." Kelnamon scratched his head. "No, there's no water like *that*, I suppose."

"Mmm."

Kelnamon stood up and brushed the dust off his knees, then realized something. "One of the trees over there has been knocked over."

"Those," Ferqar said, "do not count as trees. They are much too sad and small."

"No, just pay attention—there were five trees there yesterday. I remember seeing them. Now one of them has fallen over." Kelnamon waited for Ferqar to understand, then rolled his eyes. "Like it was *hit* by something."

"Oh!" Ferqar concentrated on the horizon. "Yes, I just got a burst of radio static."

"Come with me." Kelnamon was already running toward the hill, which was about a quarter of a mile away. "I'll show you the path!"

"This would be easier in a hopper!" Ferqar called after him, but he followed, each of his footsteps accompanied by a *clank*.

They were about halfway up the hill when a bolt of energy whizzed over their heads and both of them ducked. Kelnamon lost his footing and tumbled down the hill while Ferqar yelled something.

"Just get to cover!" Kelnamon called. He wedged himself behind a nearby boulder and peeked out. He didn't see anything—

Another burst of shots came from the trees nearby, and when the smoke cleared, he was able to make out a spidery shape. It was a turret of some sort.

"Ferqar?"

"I'm all right," Ferqar called back. "I said, it's not sentient—and it's of Jotun make."

"*What?*" More shots sounded, and Kelnamon looked around to see that the thing was advancing. "Get ready, it's coming our way! I don't suppose you have a gun in that suit?"

"Not one that can take *that* out!" There was muttered untranslatable swearing in Jotun, then Ferqar said. "Look, if I draw its fire, can you take it down?"

"I don't think we have a choice. Just tell me when to go!" As more shots zoomed by, one taking a chip off the boulder Kelnamon was hiding behind, the Brakalon yelled, "Go now!"

"Going!" There was a resounding *clank* as Ferqar leapt into action.

Kelnamon launched out from behind cover and charged at the turret. It must have had a proximity sensor, because as soon as he got close, its turret swung to point straight at him. He could see its laser sight staring at him like a baleful red eye.

There was no time to duck. With a roar, as much to keep himself brave as anything, Kelnamon grabbed the turret by the legs, whirled it over his head, and bashed it on the rocks. He kept slamming it on the ground, and was just starting to become satisfied that it was properly dead when something large and metal slammed him sideways.

He went tumbling down a nearby hill toward a drop off of a few feet and scrabbled for purchase on the rocks.

"No!" Ferqar yelled. "Drop! Do it now!"

Kelnamon obeyed, for which he was grateful a moment later when the remains of the Jotun bot exploded. From the boom, it had been a very high-grade explosive. If Kelnamon had been standing there—

He looked at Ferqar gravely. "What was that?"

"I don't know," Ferqar admitted. "It can't have been meant as part of an invasion or there would be hundreds of them, wouldn't there?"

Kelnamon wasn't willing to bet on that. "Come on. We need to get back to the capital and tell them about this. And..."

"And?" Ferqar asked.

"I think we should call on that human," Kelnamon said.

"He's good at finding out secrets. If anyone can figure out what this is, he can."

"How are things progressing?" Grisor entered the room with a nod to each of the analysts, and a deeper nod—although he hated to do so—for the other Committee members present.

Grisor was developing a very, very low opinion of the Committee members. The aides, analysts, and soldiers who supported their objective, however, had so far shown themselves to be exceedingly competent.

His vacation home on Jotuna D had been made over into a base of operations to advance the Committee's newest goals. A group of scientists and engineers was interpreting the schematics sent from the laboratories, and building conversion facilities. They would need equipment both here and to send to the Brakalon homeworld as soon as the invasion was complete.

Another group was assessing the homeworld. The Jotun government had preliminary data, of course—atmosphere, gravity, and a basic map. The information had not been collected with a small, targeted invasion in mind, however.

The Committee needed to know where it would be easiest to land near the capital city of Herod in order to take the government buildings and set up their conversion laboratory. The data they collected in the next few days would help them develop their plan.

Would they, perhaps, take over a specific building and convert everyone inside? Would they take the opportunity to accost a high-ranking Brakalon official on vacation and use that connection to lure others into the trap?

There was no way to know yet what the optimal plan might be.

Grisor was interested in the process. He went to the desk that held the newest maps.

"The probes are, by and large, surviving their descent," one of the junior analysts told him.

There was a round of hastily-cut-off hisses for her to be quiet. Grisor, intrigued by this, fixed her with a look.

"What does that mean?"

She faltered, but it was clear from her next words that she was answering him honestly. "One or two were destroyed upon landing. The terrain is very harsh. Another reported conflict and was summarily destroyed. I assume that was either hostile wildlife or that it was actually damaged during landing. It detonated, however, so anything nearby was destroyed." She paused, then added, "A certain number of losses are to be expected upon landing. We have had a very high success rate this time."

"So there was no reason to be worried, then?" Grisor asked. "About me knowing, I mean. You are all performing better than could be expected."

She nodded hesitantly.

Grisor looked around the room. "Remember that. I will hold you accountable for those things within your control. I will expect you to perform within the parameters you give me. If I find out you have lied, either about those parameters or about your performance, it will go badly for you. This will be your *only* warning."

They all gave terrified nods.

He left, one of the other Committee members dogging his heels. "You scared them."

"Good," Grisor replied. "They should respect us."

"There is a fine line between respect and—"

Grisor turned silently to observe the Committee member, who stammered and whispered an apology.

"I will not tolerate disrespect," Grisor warned him.

"You are only one member of this Committee," the senator blurted in a moment of rare defiance.

"Of course," Grisor agreed, lying with a flutter of a Jotun smile. "I seek only the respect one Committee member gives another. Our underlings, however, should understand that their honesty with us is required. Is that not so?"

"Oh. Oh, of course."

"Good. Now, let us go take some refreshment."

It would be poisoned, of course. This senator had shown his true colors, and they had reached the point in their plan where any weak link could be fatal.

It was time to begin culling the group.

CHAPTER TWO

"Barnabas?" Elisa's voice echoed up the stairwell.

"Up here," Barnabas called back. "I'll be down in just a moment."

"Oh, don't worry, I'm coming up."

"Don't do that." Worried, Barnabas dropped his tools and hurried down the stairs, nearly colliding with her on the landing.

She laughed at him, one hand cupping the very faint curve of her belly. Her pregnancy was just beginning to show, and she found it hilarious that everyone kept trying to do things for her. "You don't need to worry, you know. I'm fully capable of handling the exertion of stairs."

"Er..." Barnabas refrained from asking if she was sure about that.

Elisa held up a hand, palm out. "I solemnly swear that when I get too pregnant to walk up the stairs, I will admit it and have you all wait on me hand and foot."

"Ah. Good." Barnabas could work with that.

"What are you working on?" Elisa asked him.

"Hmm." Barnabas scratched his head. "Well, it's not that the stairs aren't structurally *sound*, you understand—"

"Say no more." Elisa was chuckling. "Can I look?" She peered around Barnabas and gave a gasp. "You're redoing *all* of them! Don't you have...I don't know, *criminals* to be hunting down?"

"Yes," Barnabas said, "but Shinigami needs to figure out where we should go first, how to get us past certain security protocols, and...well, a bunch of stuff."

It turned out that rescuing a friend who was determined to assassinate you was not an easy task—especially when said friend was trapped in a highly fortified base, protecting other people you were trying to bring to Justice.

Barnabas waved a hand and hoped she wouldn't ask about it. He led the way up the stairs. "You can see that I've made the steps a bit more level, and sanded them smoother. I'll apply varnish tonight. Tabitha said she would bring some."

"I can apply it," said Carter, who had come up the stairs behind them. "I mean, you could too, but Shinigami says it's time to head back to the ship."

Barnabas frowned. "She didn't contact me."

"She came in person," Carter told him. "She's trying to eat a sandwich. I'm guessing that won't screw up the cyborg body?"

"No, she can deal with it, but..." Barnabas had a lot of questions he wasn't sure he wanted the answers to. "Never mind. So, since you're here and I assume you'll be taking over on this, here's how I laid the boards. As far as I can tell, they won't creak anymore."

"Thanks." Carter scratched his head. "I have to tell you,

I feel a little bit guilty, making Ranger One do old-fashioned construction work."

"Don't." Barnabas' voice was emphatic. "First of all, I'm happy to help. What with another little one on the way and a bar to run, you have plenty of things on your plate. But I also like building things. If only you needed a hand in the garden!"

"Nuh-uh," Elisa cautioned, laughing. "The garden is *mine*. Although, I *was* hoping you might help me grow some herbs to use in beer…"

"I guess I know where you stand on the German-Belgian debate," Barnabas commented gravely.

"Huh?"

"Never mind. Beer is a delicate process, and I am happy to help. You know, the first beers I ever made were actually not made with hops, so I am well-versed in how different mixtures of herbs will affect the flavor."

"Wonderful." Elisa glowed. "I was thinking of trying to make a batch with orange peel." She led the way back down the stairs, elaborating on her various plans, and bemoaning how certain plants from Earth didn't seem to take well to the soil of High Tortuga.

In the bar's main room, they found Shinigami trying to take a bite of a sandwich while Gar and Tafa studied her with mild concern.

"I don't *know*," Gar was saying. "Oh, Barnabas, thank goodness. We couldn't remember the exact mechanics that humans use to eat. Will you demonstrate taking a bite for us?"

Barnabas stared at them all for a moment.

"I'll get you a sandwich," Carter said, trying to hide his

smile, and whisked off to the kitchen. He was back in short order with something Barnabas had never seen before, but once the smells of it reached him, he didn't hesitate to sit down and tuck in, oblivious to the aliens and Shinigami as they watched him chew and swallow.

It took about half of the sandwich before he could slow down enough to say, "This is *delicious*. What's in it?"

"There's a local bird the humans call a Tethran Fowl," Carter told him. "The rest of the species here apparently hate it enough that they never named it. Anyway, it has very fatty meat like duck. Add that to a nice cheese, some caramelized onions, a beer sauce..." He gave an artful shrug. "And there's a woman down the street who opened her own bakery, so we've been using her rolls. Good, yes?" He already knew it was good; his smile said as much.

"Amazing," Barnabas said, with feeling.

"I wish I could taste things," Shinigami remarked sadly.

"You *can* taste things."

"I can assess chemical composition. That's not the same." She looked glum. "Since I don't need food to live, there's no reason to make eating pleasant, per se."

"How *do* you power yourself?" Elisa asked curiously.

"I'm nuclear," Shinigami informed her blandly.

Elisa blinked like she didn't know if it was a joke and wasn't quite sure what to say in either case.

Barnabas polished off the rest of his sandwich in neat bites and cleaned his fingers on a handkerchief. There was a time when he would never have eaten anything so messy or so humble. He was glad that those days were behind him —and also glad that he no longer lived the *very* humble life of a monk. He could not imagine enjoying anything so decadent in the monastery.

He accepted a mug of beer from Carter with a nod and took a sip. His eyebrows went up. "This is *good*."

Elisa was glowing. "I brewed it!" She was practically bouncing in her seat. "I was very careful with all of the weighing and the temperature and everything, and I made beer! It's a proper beer, isn't it?"

"It is." Barnabas opened his mouth to mention that he'd spent a lot of time brewing beer, but decided that might intimidate her. He was looking forward to all of the combinations she'd told him about and wanted to make sure he got to taste them. After this introduction to her brewing skills, he was anticipating the new beers a lot more. He settled for saying, "I'm quite enjoying it."

"You know," Carter stage-whispered, "that's Barnabas-speak for 'this is one of the best things I've ever had in my life.'"

Shinigami snorted as the rest of the team laughed, and Elisa blushed happily.

"He's not wrong," Barnabas admitted with good grace. "I won't take your entire stash, but I will definitely be back for more. You *are* making more, right?"

"Yes." She was grinning.

"Excellent. We'll see you soon, then. Shinigami, you said we needed to head back to the ship?"

"Yes." Shinigami dropped the mangled remains of her sandwich and gave them a disappointed look. Apparently, she hadn't remembered how strong her cybernetic fingers were and had crushed the thing into paste. She cleaned her hands and stood up with a sigh. "Maybe I could program myself to enjoy food."

"As long as it doesn't violate the Skynet Protocol, do what you like," Barnabas told her.

Carter followed Barnabas out and drew him aside. "Can I talk to you for a moment?"

"Certainly." Barnabas inclined his head. He had sensed a certain reserve in Carter earlier, and it was more pronounced now. "Is something wrong?"

"Yes. I said... Well, you'll have noticed that Aliana's gone."

"Elisa told me what happened," Barnabas replied. "Carter, how long did it take you to settle down? A long time. You had to find something that kept that excitement and adventure alive—as well as having the right person by your side." He thought of Aliana, and could only wish that she *did* have someone to match her. She liked to laugh, Barnabas sensed, and she wanted to make something of herself. She was just a little bit aimless right now.

"Yes, but did Elisa say *why* she left?" Carter pressed. He looked miserable. "It was because she heard us talking. She heard me tell you what happened with Harry, and then with Lawrence. So, you see..."

"Ah." Barnabas ran a hand through his hair, careful not to disturb its arrangement. He groaned. "Well, there's not much you can do beyond apologizing."

"I know. I just want to know she's safe."

Where are you? Shinigami asked in Barnabas' head.

I'll be there in a moment. I'm helping Carter with something. And can't you locate me?

Yeah, but Tabitha has informed me that that's, and I quote,

"Stalker-y."

I suppose she's not wrong. I'll be along soon.

Fine, but I make no guarantees about what happens to this juice you left me to carry.

You have no actual muscles! It costs you nothing to carry things!

That is not *the point.*

Barnabas hid his smile as he laid a hand on Carter's shoulder. "You want me to keep an eye out for her?"

"Would you?" Carter looked grateful. "I don't know if you'd even see her. Space is big, after all."

"I have a feeling we might run into one another again," Barnabas told him blandly. It was even true, although in a far different way than Carter was probably imagining. It wouldn't be a chance encounter in the hallway of a space station. No, if Aliana had left to work for her former employer, she was likely still planning to steal the *Shinigami*.

Barnabas had to admit he was looking forward to seeing what she came up with as a strategy.

"I'll also ask other people I know to keep an eye out," he continued. "Not interfere or anything, just give us an update if they see her."

"Thank you." Carter gave him a relieved smile. "Get going—I've kept you long enough. I'll go finish those stairs."

"Tabitha said she'll be along at dinner time with the varnish."

"I'm guessing she'll be along early and have a long dinner," Carter corrected with a grin. He waved and disappeared back into the building.

It didn't take Barnabas long to get back to the *Shinigami*, and he went immediately to the conference room. He was pleased to see that Shinigami had managed to evade the detection programs for the satellites on Jotuna D. The defense system was multi-tiered and very aggressive and had caused them trouble before.

This time, however, Shinigami seemed to have no worries. There was a holographic map of Jotuna D hovering, with connections between each satellite, and Gilwar was poring over a set of code with her in the corner.

They looked up as Barnabas entered.

"So we can get onto Jotuna D?" Barnabas asked.

"We can," Shinigami said. "And even better news, I managed to get a bug into their systems."

"What? How?"

She gave him a deeply smug smile. "Oh, it is *such* a good story. Gather 'round, everyone."

Kelnamon and Ferqar had made good time back to the city. Ferqar, of course, was fine within his biosuit, but Kelnamon would normally have stopped for food and water.

This time, he made no stops. He'd scrambled over rocks and leapt gullies, with Ferqar struggling behind him. They did not have time to take the longer winding paths. If there were Jotun devices landing on the planet and shooting at innocent bystanders, they needed to get to the military *quickly*.

Once he was back, Kelnamon wasted no time sending a

message to a military liaison he knew, as well as the contact who was helping him figure out the situation with the *Srisa's* passengers. Both of them, he was sure, would know who to pass the word to. He let them know he would be available to discuss what he had seen.

Then he waited.

And waited.

And waited. That afternoon and evening, he assumed that word was winding its way through the appropriate channels. The next morning, he considered that perhaps many others had reported the same thing and they did not need his information.

Still, he was uneasy about it.

By the next afternoon, he was done waiting. He showed up at the government offices…only to find them empty.

"What's going on?" he asked a passerby. "Do you know? Why are the buildings empty?"

"I guess they've been told to go to remote offices," the Brakalon female said with a shrug. "It's some kind of drill. Don't worry, you can reach them all by message." She continued past him without another word, likely thinking that Kelnamon was simply curious.

Kelnamon's sense that something was wrong had intensified.

He was willing to bet that some messages *were* getting through. He was also willing to bet, however, that his had not. *Someone* had arranged for the military and government personnel to be out of reach while this plan unfolded.

He had to get word to Barnabas. The only question was, of course, how to do that without tipping off the people orchestrating this.

CHAPTER THREE

Zinqued trotted down the hallways of the *Palpari*, his nose twitching with excitement. He couldn't wait to find out what plans Aliana had for stealing the *Shinigami*. For months now, he had been able to think about nothing else. The ship was beautiful, sleek, and absolutely perfect in every way.

He could just see himself sitting in the captain's chair, ordering its all-powerful AI to guide missiles or find him anything he wanted. Tik'ta liked to tease him and roll her eyes, but when she had a ship like *that* to pilot, she wouldn't be upset with him anymore.

He had been dispirited when Aliana, their human crew member, had decided to stay on High Tortuga with her family—and then intrigued and pleased when she had contacted him and said she wanted to sign back on. He didn't know what was behind her decision, and he didn't care. She had been honest with him about their chances of stealing the ship, and he was glad to have her aboard.

A human, after all, could understand Barnabas in a way

no alien could. The nuances of human society, especially the fabled Ranger Corps, might help them come up with a con to sneak the ship right out from under him.

Zinqued was halfway up the corridor to Aliana's bunk when he heard a strange sound like a breath dragged in so quickly that it squeaked. A sound of pain.

He broke into a run and came around the doorway to find her wiping the heels of her palms across her eyes hastily. She hid her face as she did it, but when she turned to look at him, he could still see the redness around her eyes and the sheen of tears. She had been crying.

Zinqued was a Hieto, and Hieto did not cry. He had come to learn that some species did, however, and they did so when they were hurt or—sometimes—sad.

"Is everything all right?" he asked urgently.

"I'm fine," Aliana assured him, sounding a bit prickly. Her voice came out oddly, though, and she still wasn't breathing quite right.

"Are you sick?"

"I'm not *sick*."

"Is there anything—"

She swiped through the air with her hand, almost angrily. "I really don't want to talk about it. Er. If that's all right with you, Captain."

Zinqued waved both his hands. Unlike many other captains he'd met and worked for, he didn't feel the need to stand on ceremony. "Just 'Zinqued,' please. And I do not mean to distress you. I only wished to know if there was a problem."

"No," Aliana said. Zinqued wasn't familiar with human tells, but he was almost certain that she was lying. "There's no problem. In fact, I have a few preliminary plans for the theft of the *Shinigami*, if you have time to go over them."

"Always." Zinqued could not stop his stomach plating from rippling with pleasure. He liked nothing more than planning this heist. Even the attempts, while occasionally terrifying, gave him a rush that he could find no other way.

Aliana gestured for him to sit on the bed and unrolled several large sheets of reusable paper, which she stuck to the walls of her tiny cabin.

"This is the first idea. We bribe a station administrator at a smaller station to do two things. First, when the *Shinigami* docks, they disconnect the cables that control the mechanism. Someone would have to go outside and manually undo each in order to let the ship go. Second, they would close off the rest of the station so that there was no possibility of civilians getting hurt."

"Barnabas does not hurt civilians," Zinqued assured her gravely. It was something he appreciated about his opponent. Honor was important, after all.

"Exactly," Aliana agreed. She jabbed a finger for emphasis. "So when he sees that we, too, are taking precautions, he will deal with us as honorable opponents. *Trust* me, we do *not* want him to think we're dishonorable or that we're putting civilians in the crossfire. If we do that, our lives are forfeit. If we do it this way, we may still not take the ship, but he will not consider it imperative to teach us a permanent lesson."

"Ah." Zinqued looked at her shrewdly. "So you think there is a good chance that we will fail?"

"I've been very open with you about that," Aliana told him. Her voice was blunt. "My goal is to get us a foolproof plan, but I know that this will be very difficult, and that our chances are better if he isn't furious with us. Hurting civilians, or even putting them in the way of danger, will make him absolutely furious."

"Mmm." Zinqued looked at the other plans. "Yes, I see your point. What's that?" He pointed to a piece of paper she hadn't put up.

"Oh, it's— That's nothing. Nothing important." Aliana snatched it off the desk.

But not before Zinqued saw the name and last ports of call of a human ship and the name of the current and former captains.

"Ah," he said blandly. He nodded at the other plans. "So you say you have three potential plans?"

"Yes." She looked relieved…and she kept the piece of paper behind her back. "I think what we may be able to do is build a plan out of pieces of each of these. Run a series of cons, I mean. Maybe our earliest attempts aren't designed to *steal* the ship, just to learn certain things or test their responses."

"Ah." Zinqued was pleased by this. "Well, I will have you present these to the whole crew after dinner, then. I will go begin preparing it now. Remind me—do humans enjoy eating live snakes, or is that Yofu?"

Aliana gave him a queasy look. "That's Yofu. *Definitely* not humans."

"I won't make any *vlatesh'ka* for you, then."

"Thank you."

Zinqued waved to her cheerily and left, but he didn't go to the kitchen. Tik'ta was cooking tonight, and she was up to date on what each species aboard enjoyed eating. Since she didn't need any supervision, Zinqued would work on a side project.

He had done some research on Aliana after she came to work with them the first time. Her ship, the *James*, was a piece of junk, and she hadn't bothered to pay her dues before leaving the station last time. She seemed to be hoping the ship would be stolen so she wouldn't have to deal with it anymore.

Before that, she'd had a ship named the *Melisande*, and *that* ship had been the sort a good captain dreamed of. It wasn't flashy, not by a long shot, but it was deceptively quick, in good repair, and had a solid suite of components that would last a very long time.

As far as he could tell, it hadn't been stolen in an *illegal* way. Instead, someone she trusted, a man named Lawrence Hardy, had taken it from her. It had all been legal.

But from the look in Aliana's eyes when she mentioned it, and from the hurt he had just seen, Zinqued knew it hadn't been *right*. Although he hadn't known her very long, she was part of his crew, and he did not want her to be upset.

He was going to help her get her ship back.

He knew this was, in some ways, a very ironic plan from a ship thief, but he comforted himself with the fact that he was, after all, using his skills in larceny to help her get the ship back, and that his actions would technically be illegal. His reputation should remain secure.

He tried whistling as he walked to his cabin. He liked the sound of it when humans did it, but he hadn't mastered the technique yet. He was still cheerfully trying and failing as he sat down to work and pulled out his documents on the *Melisande.*

Somehow, some way, they would get the ship back.

"Lawrence," Ria began timidly. Small and delicate, she was absolutely swimming in her dark blue coveralls. She turned a wrench over and over in her fingers as she waited for him to look over.

At the desk, Lawrence paused to look at the ceiling in an exaggerated way that meant he was fighting for patience.

Ria realized her mistake. "Captain Hardy, I mean. I'm very sorry."

He turned to look at her at last, and she gave a little shiver. Lawrence was one of the most beautiful men she'd ever seen, with wavy brown hair, a sharp jawline, and blue-gray eyes set over high cheekbones. It was the sort of face that made you ignore every instinct that whispered that this man could not be trusted.

"Ria." His voice was grave. It was just as lovely as the rest of him, smooth and slightly burning. "You do good work as a mechanic, but you need to be careful to respect your captain."

"Yes, Captain Hardy." She swallowed.

Yes, Ria knew *exactly* why Aliana had fallen for Lawrence.

She bit her lip. "We need—the ship needs—some repairs."

"Make them." He looked annoyed.

"I need parts," Ria explained. "The engine is leaking coolant, and a new cap on the—"

"Make it work," he said, his voice dangerous now.

"I've made it work as long as I can, sir." She stood her ground. She knew her business when it came to engines. She'd recognized this problem months ago, and Aliana had set aside money to deal with it.

Money that Lawrence now had.

"Then do better. I don't want you coming to me every time you want a shiny new part."

"I don't." Her voice was angry. "I came to you because we *need* it, not because I want it." His look chilled her, but she didn't waver. "This is a valuable ship because it was kept in good repair," she said finally. She was trying to sound as icy as he looked, but she knew she wasn't doing a good job. Recklessly, she pushed onwards: "*Aliana* knew—"

He was across the room in an instant and she flinched away from him, seeing the flash of pleasure in his eyes. In that instant, she realized he wasn't going to hit her—he had just wanted her to understand that he *could*.

"Aliana is not in charge of this ship anymore, is she?" Lawrence asked. "*Is she*, Ria?"

"No." She kept her face turned away from him and said the word she knew he wanted her to say. "Sir."

He held the silence for a long moment.

"Make it work," he repeated, then went back to his desk.

Ria left, her boots ringing on the metal floors and her eyes narrowed. The *Melisande* was a good ship, and it hadn't been right, what had happened to Aliana. At the time Ria hadn't done anything about it, of course. When you played with fire, you got burned. Aliana should have known better than to marry Lawrence and put everything in both their names.

But if she were honest with herself, she would have to admit that she hadn't spoken up both out of cowardice...and because she had wanted Lawrence for herself.

She knew better now. He wasn't any prize.

A plan was beginning to take shape in her head to get back at him. She just needed to find out where Aliana was.

CHAPTER FOUR

"Excellency." Senator Qarwit, one of the senior members of the Committee, directed his biosuit to bow low as Grisor came into the room. "I wondered if I might have a moment of your time before you speak to Captain Jeltor?"

Grisor was surprised but nodded his head graciously. "Certainly, Senator." To the other two senators with him, he said, "Excuse me, please."

His guards opened the door to a nearby room, checked it, and stood back to allow Grisor and Qarwit inside. Qarwit stood by the door and waited while the door was closed. He was unusually worried, his tentacles rippling.

"What is the matter?" Grisor asked him. He liked Qarwit. Always respectful, Qarwit did not behave as if the others were mere steps on his rise to power. It was rare to see him question any of Grisor's decisions; what questions he asked were phrased respectfully, and never seemed designed to show off his intellect.

Unlike some Grisor could name.

"Excellency, I have concerns," Qarwit said finally. He kept his voice neutral. "I have not mentioned this before because I know it is not in your nature to be careless." He paused. "I am torn, you see, between my trust in your capabilities and what I see in Captain Jeltor."

Grisor considered this but said nothing.

"I worry that the captain's conversion is not complete," Qarwit continued. He was vibrating with tension now, unsure whether Grisor's silence was a good sign or a bad one. "He acted nobly and without hesitation to save you when the human attacked. I reviewed the holo logs. I hope that was not forbidden. I did clear it with—"

"I knew you had requested to see them." Grisor had been curious, but with so many things to oversee, he had not worried about such a request from a trusted member of the Committee. "You did so to seek evidence for your suspicions?"

"To see if my worries were well-founded," Qarwit said. "Jeltor's actions favored you. At the beginning of the fight, he had no doubts at all about his loyalty. The scientists did a commendable job."

Grisor felt a surge of annoyance. The scientists were long dead, and one of his personal guards had overseen Jeltor's conversion. He had not shared news of the infiltrated laboratory with the rest of the Committee, however, fearing that it would make him look weak.

So he only nodded, pushing away a stab of worry. These ideas had been conceived decades ago, and years of work were now threatened because the Committee had become known earlier than expected. Huword's death and the interference in Jeltor's conversion were complications that could doom Grisor's plans.

He could only hope now that they were not the first in a cascade of complications.

The Committee *had* to find a way to get the Jotun fleet to Kordinev before other species knew what was going on, and Jeltor was integral to that plan. They could not afford to be unable to use him.

No, Grisor reminded himself, what they could not *afford* would be to pin their plan on Jeltor and have him fail them. He should listen to Qarwit's concerns and adjust accordingly.

"It is simply that he has seemed less than devoted in recent days," Qarwit said. "When I reviewed the video and saw the human appealing to his *past* loyalties. I fear that those words have taken root in Jeltor's mind, so we should be very cautious before trusting him with any more of our plan."

Grisor nodded quietly and sighed. Qarwit was right to be worried, and he had chosen a private venue to air his worries rather than sowing seeds of doubt in the others. It had been well done; he could hardly fault Qarwit.

But to be so close, to have so little time to implement the plan, only to be held up by such a concern—

"Nothing ever stays done," he stated bitterly. In dawning horror, he added, "What if all of those who have been converted are vulnerable?"

"They may be," Qarwit replied after a moment.

Grisor gave him an annoyed look.

"It will change our plan," Qarwit assured him, "but surely it will not stop us. We will simply need those who are converted to be subtle and stealthy. We will need to make sure they are regularly brought in to have their conversion strengthened, and we will need to expand as quickly as we can on any occupied planets."

"Is that all?" Grisor asked bitterly.

"Better these problems," Qarwit replied, "than the ones that come from whole *species* failing to acknowledge our place as their rightful leaders."

Grisor had to admit that he had a point. "In most cases," he said drily, "sentience was a mistake."

"A test, perhaps," Qarwit countered with a gleam of a smile. "For us, I mean. For the rest...we will simply guide them. Help them."

Both of the Jotun males stared at one another for a moment, then Grisor laughed.

"You don't care in the slightest about helping them."

"Not at all," Qarwit agreed. "But it makes it more palatable to the rest of our people, doesn't it?"

Grisor sighed and nodded. "It does. It does. I wish they had more resolve."

"The world is often not as we wish it to be," Qarwit observed. "From the cold seas of Jotuna, we built our society. Perhaps from these trials, too, something greater will emerge."

Grisor fluttered with pleasure. "You speak truly. Now, let us go speak with Jeltor. Together, you and I can determine if he is to be trusted with this new part of our plan."

"Yes, Excellency." Qarwit followed him out of the room and past the other two senators, who murmured vaguely in annoyance when Grisor left them behind.

Grisor did not care. They had demanded to see the new

phases of the Committee's plan but had not been helping with implementation. Qarwit, however, had been running many departments of their makeshift headquarters, and he was doing so with quiet efficiency.

He deserved to be here.

In the rooms beyond, they found Jeltor. He had been housed in what appeared to be a very light, airy set of chambers. There were multiple pools for him to sleep and relax in, and there was a great deal of light filtering through the windows.

The place was highly secure for all its comfort. Grisor had taken precautions, even though he had been sure of Jeltor's conversion. The glass could not be broken except by extreme, repeated applications of force. Jeltor could not break out without the guards having ample time to get to him, nor could anyone break *in* easily.

"Jeltor," he called heartily. "How are you today?"

"Stir-crazy," Jeltor answered without preamble. "I want to be *doing* something, not..." He looked around. "Not being told to *relax*."

"Ah, I do beg your pardon," Grisor said. "Given the injuries the human inflicted, the doctors thought it best that you not be put under strain."

Jeltor gave a little snort to show what he thought of this. "My suit repaired me quickly, and I did not need very much recovery time."

"In truth," Grisor admitted, "I felt guilty. I had not intended for you to be involved. Seeing such an ugly side to your friend—"

"He is not my friend," Jeltor stated flatly. "He wishes to destroy the Committee. He would see us removed from our rightful place in the universe. He believes in petty freedoms above stability and order."

Grisor nodded. He did not look at Qarwit as he went to sit, but he left a silence and hoped that Qarwit would know it was an opportunity.

Qarwit took the opening without hesitation. "It must have been a shock. He had previously been a good friend to you. You thought you could trust him."

Jeltor laughed bitterly. "One can never trust Barnabas. He cares only for himself."

"Not his petty freedoms?" Qarwit probed.

"Fighting for those petty freedoms makes him a hero," Jeltor stated dismissively. "He likes being a hero. He wants everyone to worship him. He cannot understand fighting for one's species." He paced to the window. "It is because of him," he said finally, "that I am here. Not because I needed to *rest*." He swung around to look at them. "That's it, isn't it? You worry that because we once worked together, you cannot trust me."

Grisor said nothing.

"How can I argue?" Jeltor asked quietly. "I attacked Biset. I fought against you all. I have no right to ask for your trust."

"Do you want our trust?" Qarwit asked.

Jeltor had gone still, and his voice alone betrayed the depth of his feeling as he said, "*I want to serve your purpose. For that, I need your trust, and yet I know it is a risk. Perhaps it will always be too much of a risk. If so, I will abide by that.*"

Qarwit stared at him for a long moment, then looked at Grisor. He gave a faint nod. He trusted Jeltor.

"Actually," Grisor interjected, "we have a task for you."

"A real task?"

"A real task. As you say, you were once Barnabas' ally. We would be fools not to verify your new allegiance—but now we have. And you saved my life, Jeltor." Grisor kept his voice level. It was true that Jeltor had saved him, and he did not like that memory. He had come closer to death than he'd bargained for.

Jeltor nodded. "I did what I had to, Excellency. Only what any of us would do to save you and your work."

"I thank you, Jeltor. What I need now is for you to help us make new allies. I need you to get in contact with someone for me; someone who can help us achieve everything we have worked so hard for."

Jeltor considered this. "Who?" he asked finally.

"Admiral Jeqwar," Grisor told him. "She suspects that you are loyal to us, and winning her over will not be easy, but— What is it?"

Jeltor shook his head. "It is nothing. Go on."

"Why don't you come with us," Qarwit suggested. "We will show you the plans."

"You did *what?*" Barnabas gave an incredulous laugh. "You said the bots had all been destroyed!"

"I thought they had been," Shinigami replied. "But I had programmed one of them to go to sleep directly after getting into the suit. The suit didn't detect it, so it didn't get zapped."

"Until just now."

"Well, yes. It powered up in stages, and when its location tracking turned on, the suit detected it and fried it."

"What came online before that?"

"Audio." Shinigami leaned against the wall carelessly, ankles crossed. For a moment, she looked almost evasive. "Then video, which was nothing because it was in the inside a freaking biosuit. Then basic diagnostics, and then a location ping. Honestly, I'm surprised we got as far as we did."

"Did Jeltor notice?" Barnabas asked urgently.

"I would think so," Shinigami said. "But I don't think they would realize that we got the signal. The suit zapped it *very* quickly. If the bot hadn't been made by us, it wouldn't have managed to ping anyone quickly enough."

"Are they still on Jotuna D?"

"Yes, but in another complex. Grisor must own more than one. I can lay in a course and get us there soon. We should be able to get in without the satellites knowing. I embedded a protocol in one of them to tell me when they were updated. They made some changes, all right, but nothing I can't get around."

"Shinigami, you're a genius." Barnabas gave her a grin. "Oh, and…did you hear anything interesting?"

Shinigami might be an AI, but she couldn't lie worth a damn. She was so concerned about keeping her face blank that she forgot how guilty someone looked when they had no expression at all.

"Nope." Her voice was clipped and strange.

Barnabas gave her a look. "Shinigami?"

She sighed. "Look. Jeltor is brainwashed right now,

okay? I didn't get any details on what they're planning. Let's just move past this, all right?"

"*Shinigami.*"

She gave him a worried look, but she must have realized he wasn't going to bend because she gave another sigh and cued something up on the audio system.

"I did not need very much recovery time," said Jeltor's voice.

"In truth, I felt guilty." Barnabas recognized Grisor's snide tones. "I had not intended for you to be involved. Seeing such an ugly side to your friend—"

"He is not my friend," Jeltor said flatly. "He wishes to destroy the Committee. He would see us removed from our rightful place in the universe. He believes in petty freedoms above stability and order."

After a pause, a new voice said: "It must have been a shock. He had previously been a good friend to you. You thought you could trust him."

"One can never trust Barnabas," Jeltor replied. "He cares only for himself."

"Not his petty freedoms?" the new voice asked.

"Fighting for those petty freedoms makes him a hero," Jeltor said dismissively. "He likes being a hero. He wants everyone to worship him. He cannot understand fighting for one's species."

"That's enough," Barnabas said quietly. He swallowed as the audio was turned off. They were all looking at him—Gar, Tafa, Gilwar, Shinigami. They were looking at him with *pity*.

He knew the words weren't real. They were a product

of the brainwashing Jeltor had endured. Still, they cut to the heart of what he was. *"He likes being a hero."*

"You said you'd laid in a course?" he asked Shinigami.

"Yes." She made a small sound as if clearing her throat.

"Good. I'll..." He saw the uselessness of making any excuse. They knew why he was going. He gave a brief nod, not meeting their eyes, and left.

"One can never trust Barnabas. He cares only for himself." He could not escape the words now that they were in his head. Barnabas pressed his lips together, took a deep breath, and went to finish his preparations.

CHAPTER FIVE

In a little conference room on the other side of the complex from the main hub, Jeltor was pacing as he stared at the information on the screen.

"What do you think?" Grisor asked finally.

Jeltor said nothing for a long moment. This was a risky plan. The Committee was planning to lure Admiral Jeqwar in by having Jeltor offer to speak to one of her aides to prove his loyalty. When she got there, they would kidnap her and bring her here to be converted.

Every instinct told him that Admiral Jeqwar would be difficult to abduct and convert. She was famously strong-willed, and he had learned that the original scientists who'd developed the program were dead, with only partial notes left behind. This certainly wasn't an ideal setup for a quick turnaround.

On the other hand, she was dangerous, since she knew what the Committee was up to and she had the support of her generals. Even if they did not convert her, they would rob the Navy of one of its greatest assets.

"She will know it's a trap," Jeltor mused slowly. "She's not stupid. She'll know that we're trying to—"

"*Help* her," Senator Qarwit emphasized. His voice was gentle, but there was an edge to it.

He was the one, Jeltor knew, who was doubting the conversion.

And he wasn't wrong to do so. Barnabas' words had haunted Jeltor. He had put himself in danger specifically for Jeltor. He had known where the laboratory was, and he had not just destroyed it but had gone inside to try to keep Jeltor safe.

It wasn't that Jeltor felt any loyalty to Barnabas. No, that was gone—wasn't it?—and in its place was the overwhelming rush of devotion that came over him when he thought of Grisor. It was the sweetest thing Jeltor had ever felt. It was intoxicating; he could not get enough of it.

But why would someone come to save him when he did not want to be saved? None of Barnabas' actions suggested that he'd meant Jeltor harm. In fact, they suggested that Barnabas was risking significant harm to *himself* in order to…

Well, Jeltor didn't know, that was the thing. He didn't understand.

When he'd spat those words about Barnabas caring for petty freedoms over his own species, when he'd said that Barnabas wanted to be a hero, it had all been true—in a sense. But what did it *mean* to believe so much in little freedoms that he would come to "save" Jeltor at great cost to himself? What did it *mean* that he wanted to save aliens as well as his own kind?

Jeltor had seen heroism in many wars. Usually, those

who wanted to be heroes turned and ran when they got their first taste of real battle. The fact that Barnabas hadn't, that he had been willing to pick up a torch and walk into the darkness, said something about him that wasn't all bad.

He didn't want to be *called* a hero. He wanted to *be* a hero.

"Jeltor?" Grisor's voice broke into his reverie. "Did you hear the senator?"

Jeltor was annoyed but struggled not to show it. "Yes, Excellency." It was easy to be polite to Grisor. He felt a rush of happiness when he did so. And so, because Grisor would want him to, he gave a respectful nod to Senator Qarwit. "My apologies, senator. It is not that I doubt what we do for Admiral Jeqwar, simply that I think we can all agree she will fight us. If she would simply come here of her own accord for conversion, you would not have made this plan."

Qarwit relaxed slightly. "That is true."

"What we need to do," Jeltor continued, "is make her think she can win me back to her side."

He felt a strange thrill at that idea. Was such a thing even possible? Since his conversion, he was not upset by what had happened. He understood that not long ago he had believed one thing, and now he believed another. They had needed to put him in a tank to make him understand the right way to think, because he had not understood on his own. He was ashamed of that.

He *liked* the way things were now. He felt happy whenever he thought of Senator Grisor. He felt happy when he did things that would please the senator. He remembered the time before as one of confusion and worry. He had worked willingly with aliens, which was clearly something that should not have happened.

Other species were *not* as good as the Jotuns. This was simply a fact.

Or was it? He was confused. He didn't like being confused. He thought about Grisor and felt calmer at once.

"Are you all right, Jeltor?" Grisor asked quietly.

Grisor was paying attention to him. Jeltor felt a rush of giddiness.

"I don't want to speak to her," he replied. It seemed very true when he said it, but it was also a lie. For some reason, he *did* want to speak to her, even though he was afraid she might bring him back to the way things had been.

Even though he wasn't sure "afraid" was the right word for how he was feeling.

Grisor and Qarwit exchanged looks.

"I *will* speak to her," Jeltor confirmed. "I just don't want to. I don't like sneaking around."

Grisor relaxed. "None of us do," he assured Jeltor. "And when we have done our work and we rule the Jotun and the sector, we will not need to sneak around anymore, Jeltor. Remember, we are sneaking around because of others—because they do not see the truth."

"As I did not." Jeltor was ashamed.

"Like so many do not," Grisor said. "We do not hate them. We convert them, Jeltor. Look at you. Once, you fought against us, and now you are one of the most honored members of the Committee. You saved my life. Why dwell on how things were before?"

Jeltor nodded. He still did not want to speak to Admiral Jeqwar, but he knew it would make Grisor happy.

"I'll do it. Open the channel."

The two senators exchanged looks, then Grisor used his personal comm device to murmur a command. In a small alcove of the room, a screen came to life. Jeltor went to sit in front of it so he would appear to be alone in a small, deserted room.

The Jotun who appeared was one of Admiral Jeqwar's senior aides. He was a deep blue Jotun named Gorsik, and he fluttered back against the wall of his tank in alarm when he saw who it was.

"Yes," Jeltor assured him, "it's me. I'm close."

"I cannot speak to you," Gorsik replied at once.

"Wait—please!" Jeltor filled his voice with pleading. "I need your help. I need you to come get me and bring me back somewhere you can lock me away. No, that's not right. I...I need you to kill me."

Across the room, Qarwit started, and Grisor gestured sharply for him to stay silent.

Gorsik was also shocked. *"What?"*

"I need you to kill me," Jeltor repeated. "They've done things to my mind, Gorsik. I recognize you, but things are different. There are...orders. That's not right. There aren't any specific things to do, I don't think, but they made me loyal to them. I can only break out of it for a few moments at a time, you see?"

"Jeltor—"

"You need to come get me!" Jeltor insisted, his voice rising. "You need to send someone to kill me. I'm afraid I won't ever get better. And what if I hurt you if you try to make me loyal again? You have to tell them not to get close. You have to tell them not to trust me. No matter what they do—" He broke off and stared at the screen, pretending to be angry. "Disloyal," he spat at Gorsik. "Alien-lover. You would see us ground into dust for the rest of them. You and her! She's a traitor to the Jotuns!"

He ended the call and turned to look at Grisor.

"It's done," he stated when Grisor and Qarwit said nothing. "I asked them to do the 'honorable' thing, which will make her want to save me. But she's too *honorable* to send anyone else when I might be dangerous, so she'll come herself, you see? And when she does…"

"Clever," Grisor admitted. "But what if—" He broke off and shook his head. "Nothing. Not important. We will wait. You have done very well, Jeltor. You know the admiral well. And do not worry, you will not have to speak to her when we retrieve her."

Jeltor nodded and wondered why he felt so disappointed by that. He almost wondered if he could sneak in to speak to her while they were converting her.

He wouldn't, of course.

But he *could*.

"Barnabas." Shinigami flickered into being as a holographic representation. "Admiral Jeqwar is on the line, and she says it's urgent."

Barnabas sighed and turned away from the window. He should have felt a jump of adrenaline when he heard those words, but he felt nothing. He nodded for Shinigami to open the holo channel.

"Admiral Jeqwar," he began. "It's good to—"

"I've had word from Jeltor," the admiral interrupted him.

Barnabas tried to keep his face flat. "Oh?"

"Yes. He wants…" She considered her words. "He asked us to kill him. I thought you should know, as a courtesy."

"As a—" Barnabas realized what she meant a second later. "You're going to *do* it?"

"Of course I'm going to do it," she snapped. "He's been converted. He isn't trustworthy. As far as we know, it *can't* be undone. Meanwhile, he knows classified information, and *far* too much about how the Navy operates. Not only that, he's beginning to contact people. We need him out of the way."

"It might be genuine," Barnabas snarled at her. "Did you ever think of that?"

"Yes." From the grief in her voice, she was telling the truth. "I have. And it is too big a risk. If this is a trap, which it almost certainly is—"

"If it's a trap, then he's working with them, and he can give us information!" Barnabas would have pounded his fist on a desk if there had been one. As it was, he clenched his hand and then flexed it, forcing himself to stop making a fist. "Let us go retrieve him. We aren't a Jotun ship, so he doesn't know our internal workings—and couldn't get into your ships via ours, even if he did. We have a brig we can put him in, and we know enough about him to ascertain whether he's being truthful."

"No." Admiral Jeqwar shook her head. "I've seen what your ship can do. I'm not giving him the chance to command it."

"He won't command it."

"You're not thinking logically," she told him. "He's your friend—or he was. That Jeltor is gone, human. The truth is that we have plans to execute, plans that involve getting our forces into position to head off the Committee—and we cannot risk a traitor in our midst. I should not even have told you about this."

Barnabas closed his eyes for a moment. "No. It was a kindness. I...thank you. Let me tell his wife. I will say it was an accident."

She hesitated, then nodded. The call ended.

Barnabas turned to Shinigami's projection. "We need to get there as fast as we can."

She looked relieved. "I'm glad you agree. I've put us up to...well, faster than we should be going. And if we skip the early checks against the satellites—"

"Skip them," Barnabas stated flatly. "We don't have time for any of that. We *have* to get to him before Jeqwar does."

CHAPTER SIX

The rest of the crew—including Gilwar, now housed in one of the *Shinigami's* many extra cabins—had withdrawn after Barnabas left the conference room. Now, however, summoned by Shinigami's alert, all of them arrived on the bridge at a run.

Barnabas nodded to each of them as they arrived, pleased by their obvious engagement. Even Gilwar, still grieving for his partner in Intelligence, seemed determined.

Then again, it was hard to tell with Jotuns. Barnabas had no idea if he was interpreting the jellyfish flutters correctly. He simply knew that Gilwar had once been leery of allowing Barnabas to know about the Committee, even going so far as to tell an assassin to take a shot at him if she got the chance.

He now seemed to believe that Barnabas would not hurt the Jotun species as he destroyed the Committee.

"He cannot understand fighting for one's species." Jeltor's

words rang in his head, and he closed his eyes briefly. It was not genuine, he reminded himself.

He had spent too long as a monk not to be aware of himself, and he knew exactly why Jeltor's dismissive words cut him to the bone. Once he had become one of the Nacht, Barnabas had no longer felt much allegiance to humanity as a species. The things he had done…

They still made him shudder.

It was Catherine—and the experience of loving someone—that had set him back on the path, and that had been snatched away. Since then, over his many very different lives, he had seen too much of the myriad foibles of humanity to have any particular allegiance to his species.

Humanity, like every alien race he had ever encountered, had the capacity for great feats of goodness, and great depths of cruelty and apathy. What Barnabas had loved about Bethany Anne, in part, was that she sought what was best for the universe as a *whole.*

Was it so wrong that he did not revere humanity the way Grisor revered the Jotuns?

Logically, he did not think so, yet being called disloyal was something he could not simply shake off. Being accused of hunting fame and hero status shamed him deeply. Surely he was more than that.

Oddly, it was Tabitha's voice that appeared in his head. *How fucking stupid do you have to be to think that?*

Barnabas gave a bemused smile. Tabitha was not here to know about any of this, but he was quite sure that she'd have said almost exactly that—only, perhaps, in more colorful language. The last time he'd seen her, she'd described a series of increasingly improbable acts with a variety of species in increasing detail.

And she'd only been discussing a sandwich at the time.

He collected himself and gave a little shake of his head. "Thank you all for coming so quickly. As you may have divined, we are heading back to Jotuna D with all speed. The reason is that Jeltor has contacted Admiral Jeqwar and asked that she send someone to kill him. She has apparently decided to accept his offer."

He had meant only to speak logically and get them to the planning phase, but Tafa gave a little cry and put her hand over her mouth. Her eyes were shiny with tears and Gar put an arm around her shoulders, glaring meaningfully at Barnabas.

Why did you have to say that?

I'm going to agree with Gar here, Shinigami chimed in. *Dick move, man.*

It's true! Barnabas repressed a sigh. "I don't think she's eager to do it," he said to Tafa. "Also, she doesn't know we're going in to disrupt her plans, so we have a window. We *will* get him to safety." He stopped short of promising it. He could not do so in good conscience, and he hoped she didn't notice the omission. "I called us here to discuss *how* we will get him out. And rest assured, I would not risk any of you if I thought this was a lost cause."

Tafa took a deep breath and nodded.

Barnabas decided to segue into facts before he could screw up on the emotional part again. "We will be going to Grisor's private estate, which I think we can assume will be very well fortified."

"We're going to kill Grisor while we're there, right?" Shinigami asked.

Gilwar nodded to show his agreement with the sentiment. "We should take our chance."

"I don't think so," Barnabas replied.

There was an incredulous silence.

"*What?*" Shinigami asked finally. "If we're there—"

Barnabas held up a hand to stop her, but it was another moment before he spoke. These thoughts were only just becoming conscious, but he had been fighting the sense in recent days that they were going about this all wrong somehow.

Now he knew why.

"In every society, those like Grisor rise in secrecy and silence." He looked at the vast expanse of space showing on the ship's viewscreens. "The fact that there *is* a Committee, and that they've risen so high, shows that there is something in Jotun society enabling this."

"*No,*" Gilwar exclaimed furiously. "They would brainwash the rest of us. They know we would not accept their ideas any other way. They are not an expression of who we are."

"No?" Barnabas looked at him calmly. "We had a man on Earth who was the embodiment of forgiveness and kindness, who died gladly as an act of redemption for the very ones who killed him. Centuries later, his followers were killing one another brutally for speaking slightly different words of remembrance about him. Some of those followers believed that the exact words were so critical that forcing people to say them out of terror rather than genuine belief was more important than letting them speak whichever words they chose."

Gilwar stared at him silently.

"I do not know a single culture or species that has not grappled with this," Barnabas continued. "And by this, I mean the belief that they are superior to all others. *And they are always wrong,* but they go through cycles of believing it anyway. When they do, people like Grisor rise. Grisor and the other members of the Committee are not alone in their beliefs. They are a symptom."

Gilwar turned away, his frustration clear.

"And because of that," Barnabas said, "killing him will do no good. If he attacks us and there is no other way to save ourselves, of course, we will defend ourselves. But the Jotuns must put him on trial for what he has done. *They* must deal with this, and do so publicly. Secrecy and vigilantism on my part will do nothing to help them."

There was a silence.

"But you *are* a vigilante." Shinigami sounded confused and frustrated. He could hear the question under her words: "If vigilantism won't help, why are we even here?"

"There are limits to what I do," Barnabas replied. "To what *we* do, Shinigami. We are here to help those who have no other recourse, but right now, there *is* other recourse. We will help as we can, but the Jotuns must do this for themselves."

"He's right." Gilwar gave an unwilling chuckle. He clearly did not want to admit that he agreed. "It was what we said, Wev and I, when Kantar wanted to involve all of you. We said this was a matter for the Jotuns. Of course, we wanted to deal with it without anyone else knowing."

"That would be a mistake," Barnabas said. "Without a public reckoning, the same thing will happen again."

"And so you propose to capture Grisor," Gilwar said, "and deliver him to…whom, human? Who do you think will give him the Justice you seek?"

Barnabas had been quietly self-assured, but that question took him aback. "I had not thought of that. The Senate…"

"Might be sympathetic. He might sway them. You say you want this taken care of publicly, but what if the Jotun public agrees with him? That is the risk you take."

Barnabas turned away, rubbing his temples.

"We don't have to decide now," Shinigami chimed in. Her voice was clear and cool. "Barnabas was right about one thing: a mission should have *one* objective. Ours is to get Jeltor out. *If* Grisor wanders into our hands, we will try to capture him, and if that is not possible, we will do whatever is necessary to get out safely. Is that clear to everyone?"

There was a round of nods and murmurs, and Barnabas gave her a grateful look.

"I have a request." Tafa's voice was very small. When everyone looked at her, she seemed to shrink into herself before very deliberately standing up straighter. She looked at all of them, but her eyes came to rest on Barnabas. "I want to be—upgraded."

"What?" Barnabas asked after a moment.

"Like Gar was." Tafa's hands were clenched.

"Like, for combat?" Shinigami clarified dubiously. She and Barnabas exchanged looks.

"*Yes*," Tafa said impatiently.

"You want to be part of our combat missions?" Barnabas asked her. Tafa had participated in a bit of espionage a few weeks back, but that was a far cry from actual battles.

"Well, no. I don't." Tafa took a deep breath. "But I'm not going to keep cowering here on the ship while all of you go into danger." She swallowed hard. "If I were already upgraded, if I'd learned how to fight, I would be there to help get Jeltor back. I've failed him, and I don't know if I'll ever forgive myself for that."

Barnabas looked at her for a moment, and then—gently—peered into her mind. He had been surprised by her request, but now that he saw her thoughts, he could see how desperately she wanted this.

She was scared. In fact, she was terrified, but she knew there were reasons to move past that fear, and she would do so in order to help her friends.

"All right," he agreed with a nod. "We'll have you assessed in the Pod-doc, and we'll figure this out." Briefly, he debated telling her she hadn't failed Jeltor, but he knew that she would never agree with him, so he only looked at the rest of them. "We know some of what the Committee has for resources. I want a plan for our rescue mission drawn up within the next hour. Any resources you have, now is the time to share them." He gave Gilwar a meaningful glance.

Gilwar laughed. "I'll get you what we have on Grisor's estate. I got a good map last time, including the utilities. We can probably work with that."

"Good," Shinigami said. "Come with me, and we'll transfer all that data."

Barnabas gave a nod and followed them out into the hallway. They would get Jeltor back.

Then they would figure out how to undo his conversion. They would find a way. Barnabas promised himself that.

There was a ding from her computer, and Aliana looked up from her book. She did not move particularly quickly as she put the book aside and went to the desk; after the storm of tears, she had little energy left.

She had skipped dinner, having neither the energy to face the rest of the crew nor the desire to see people eating live snakes. Someone had come and left a plate of a plain soup, though, that did not have any snakes in it, alive *or* dead.

(She'd checked. Thoroughly.)

What she saw on the screen made her eyebrows shoot up. She sighed, put her boots on, and went to find Zinqued.

He was in the communal room off the kitchen, and he spun around in a chair to greet her with a smile. "Ah, there you are."

Tik'ta gave her a nod from one of the other chairs. She'd been open about the fact that she thought Aliana was making a mistake, signing back on, but she had been perfectly nice about it.

"The *Shinigami* just passed one of our checkpoints," Aliana reported.

"Oh?" Zinqued sat up, deeply interested now.

"I don't think we can catch it on this round," Aliana continued. "It's going like a bat out of hell."

Zinqued and Tik'ta frowned, trying to parse this.

"Sorry—it's going really fast. And I mean *really* fast. There's no way we could catch it, but it's heading for somewhere near Jotuna." She shrugged. "Anyway, I thought you might want to know." She gave a nod to Zinqued and one to Tik'ta—who looked frustrated that Aliana was helping Zinqued with this—and headed back to her room before anyone could ask her any more questions.

Steal the *Shinigami*, or not. She couldn't find it in herself to care very much either way. She'd been trying to forget meeting Barnabas on High Tortuga. Something about the memory unsettled her.

The sooner they were done with this job, the better, in her opinion. And if she needed to flee deeper into this sector to get away from human society, that would be just fine.

CHAPTER SEVEN

"Any luck?" Ferqar called.

"Shh." Kelnamon inched along a tiny ledge on the outside of the building. This was one of the tallest buildings on the outskirts of the main city, and it had a very tall radio tower on top of it.

He needed to hook into that tower.

As the days passed with no word back on his discovery, Kelnamon had become completely convinced that there was interference, either within the upper ranks of the government or in the buildings that held them.

He was hoping for the latter, of course—some trickery, a false signal that the Jotuns had learned of and sent out. But there was the possibility that someone in the Brakalon government had turned traitor, and Kelnamon would be a fool not to acknowledge that and plan for it.

Which meant he was calling in someone very different, and he had to do something unusual to get his message out.

So he was climbing the outside of this building in the dead of night in a desperate attempt to get a message attached to the weather data being sent to orbiting satellites. Ferqar had helped him work out a way to make the satellites send the message on, and hopefully it would arrive soon at a place he knew Barnabas had gone once: Victory Station.

He heard a strange skittering in the darkness and froze, but then pressed on. He didn't see anything moving, and he needed to get this message up to the antenna.

Once he hauled himself over the edge, he moved quickly. He attached a small device to the bottom of the antenna and waited while it ran through its warmups, then slightly changed the positioning of the dish and embedded transponder.

"Come on," he murmured. "Come on. Come on."

The message ran through once, then twice.

"You need to get back here," Ferqar's voice said in his ear. "Someone's coming, and it sounds odd. More of those bots, maybe."

Kelnamon grabbed the device and raced to the edge of the roof. He took one sweeping glance over the city before lowering himself over the edge and beginning to walk down the side of the building, holding the rope and bracing his feet on the wall.

The city looked normal, he thought. In a sense, everything *was* normal. People were going about their daily business with no idea anything was wrong.

Perhaps he should be making a big deal of this, making sure that everyone knew the government had been abducted. He feared hysteria, however, and a swift reprisal. Who could say what other forces were on Kordinev already, waiting to strike?

No, it was too risky.

He had just reached the ground when he saw them: turrets gleaming in the moonlight, their barrels swinging as they searched for targets.

"Ruuuun!" he hissed to Ferqar.

They pelted along the streets with the click-clack of the spidery Jotun turrets echoing behind them. The laser sights swung this way and that, but the street was deserted. Kelnamon and Ferqar were long gone.

A few streets away, the two of them slumped into the shadow of a doorway.

"Do you think the message got through?" Ferqar asked dubiously.

"I hope so." Kelnamon had never been one to delude himself with false hope. "I can only hope Victory Station manages to find Barnabas or we'll be shit out of luck."

"He might find out about their plans from somewhere else," Ferqar pointed out. "I worked with two members of Intelligence. They might know what's happening."

"And if they don't?" Kelnamon sighed. "Then we'll need to take care of this ourselves. And they have the jump on us, and we're divided."

CHAPTER EIGHT

"Ma'am?" Gorsik was in the doorway. "We're ready."

Admiral Jeqwar hadn't heard him come in, but he was fastidious about keeping his suit oiled and in perfect repair. She knew he had once been in the secret service, and sometimes—like now—she wondered just what skills he had that she did not know about.

Jotun assassins were rare, but those who existed were very, very good.

She nodded at him. "I'm coming."

"I—" It was rare that he was surprised. "I'm sorry? I thought you just wanted to give the launch order."

"No." She took a look around her office and did a quick status check of her weapons and defensive mechanisms. "I'll be the one going."

"*What?* No." He recovered almost immediately and moved to bar her path. "Ma'am, I would not disobey orders lightly, but this is madness. You correctly assessed that Jeltor is dangerous. Your order to kill him on sight was correct, and your current plan, to kill him from a distance, is also correct. But you should be nowhere near him."

"Gorsik, I know what I'm doing."

"*Do* you?" he pressed. "Or rather, do you *really* think it's a good idea?"

After a moment, she muttered an oath. "Dammit, Gorsik, why couldn't you just let me do this? You're the worst aide I've ever had."

His tentacles twitched in amusement. "If I thought you meant that I'd be devastated. Ma'am, why are you doing this? This isn't the admiral I know."

"Don't give me a sly set of compliments. You know I hate that." She stalked back to the window and stared out into the black. The proximity sensors in her suit told her that he had come to stand next to her, but he let her stand in silence before speaking.

In truth, she did not know what to say. She knew that this was folly. Her first assessment had been correct: Jeltor was dangerous, and the wisest course of action was to kill him before he could worm his way into the defense networks. When she had seen the recording of his conversation with Gorsik, she had been sure of her path. She had made her decision quickly, as she was wont to do, and had begun to execute it at once.

And yet…

"He asked me to do it," she told him finally. "He asked me to send someone, but he sent word to *me*. I'm not a judge, Gorsik. I don't choose who lives and dies, not that way. It feels wrong to send someone else. He reached out to me as a gesture of trust."

"If he was telling the truth," Gorsik replied softly. "I wonder about that, ma'am."

She turned to look at him with interest. She had caught the double meaning in his voice—he doubted Jeltor, yes, but he wasn't *sure* of the lie. And from a former member of the secret service, that meant something.

"So you think that too," she stated, testing.

He looked over. "Think what? Now is not the time for misunderstandings."

He had a point. "You think he's not sure what he wants anymore. That it might have been designed as a trap, but he still wants us to succeed."

"Yes," Gorsik admitted. "I think he is conflicted. It is difficult to brainwash someone without destroying their mind. Since he still seems functional, that means he might still think his way out of this. But I think it would be foolish to trust him; for *anyone* to trust him. Even them."

"*That's* why," Admiral Jeqwar said. Her voice was low. "I have to believe this can be undone, Gorsik. I *have* to. If we have to kill every innocent person they've brainwashed…" Her voice trailed off. "I can kill soldiers who stand against me in battle. I don't like it, but I can do it. I will even sacrifice my life if need be. But to kill civilians—ones who were chosen *because* they were allies? That's different. I'm not sure I can do that, so I have to hope this can be undone."

"They aren't your allies anymore, though," Gorsik countered after a moment. "If they're trying to kill you, it doesn't matter *why*. You have to defend yourself—and the others who are depending on you."

Admiral Jeqwar looked away.

Footsteps pounded down the hallway, and an aide burst through the door. "Ma'am? Ma'am! There was a flicker on one of the buoys, then our surveillance inside Senator Grisor's estate saw footage of the *Shinigami* landing there."

Dammit. And yet, her heart soared. She had never been one for running from choices…until now.

Now she was glad to let Barnabas take this choice from her.

"What do we do?" Gorsik asked her.

"We let Barnabas try," she told him quietly. "The humans have good medical technology, we know that. Perhaps they can undo what was done."

"And if they cannot?"

She wanted to run from this choice, but she must not. "Then I will offer to do what must be done," she said quietly. "For now, send in our ship and hook me in remotely. If I can aid them, I will."

The *Shinigami* landed lightly, as far as ships went. Its touchdown on the edge of Senator Grisor's estate was incredibly delicate.

In terms of more normal concerns, it flattened a huge number of carefully tended flowers.

"Oops," exclaimed Shinigami in studied innocence.

Barnabas sank his head into his hands.

"Well, it's not like they're *not* going to realize we were here," she pointed out. "They'll be missing Jeltor, so I *think* they're going to figure it out."

Barnabas tried to keep from laughing. Laughing, he

knew, would only encourage her. Like with a toddler, he thought whimsically. He straightened up and wiped his eyes surreptitiously. "Right. Let's get out there and abduct our friend. Now *there's* a sentence I never thought I would say."

"Right behind you," Gar said, nodding.

In the corner, Tafa watched from her chair. She gave a wan smile when they looked at her.

"Do you remember last time, when you were helping with surveillance?" Barnabas asked her. "You helped immeasurably. Shinigami will hook you in so you can do the same this time."

Tafa nodded, looking a little better. She waved at them as they left.

The gardens here seemed to have been designed for land animals, with the exception of the very large and very clear ornamental pools. Barnabas suspected there were many plants, rocks, and other elements underwater that he could not appreciate, but that Jotuns would find very relaxing.

Grisor, he thought, did not deserve a place like this. He would have stepped on the plants as he passed, but they didn't deserve that. He settled for toppling a large pergola.

"My hand slipped," he explained when Shinigami looked at him.

She rolled her eyes and they continued. It became almost a game to see who could do the most damage. Gilwar sent a silenced shot from one of his arm guns to take out a statue at the opposite end of one wing of the garden, and Shinigami used one of the benches to drag a deep trench where one of the walkways should be. She looked absurdly pleased with herself.

Gar, meanwhile, was moving rocks out of their carefully aligned places. He had an evil grin as he worked, which turned out to be particularly terrifying on a Luvendi.

Jeltor is in one of the inner rooms, Shinigami said, *but it's closest to this side.*

Any chance that we've been detected? Barnabas asked.

No, Tafa said. *I'm monitoring their security response teams both in network traffic and a live feed of their offices. They haven't noticed you. You're giving me an awful lot to change on the security feeds, though.*

Whoops. Gar sounded guilty. *Sorry, Tafa.*

No, it's good. Gives me something to do.

They continued to the edge of the building and, when Tafa gave them the all-clear, scaled the side of it. Jotun suits in general weren't made for climbing, so they hauled Gilwar up with a makeshift pulley.

This is undignified, he complained. Shinigami had hooked him into their Etheric communications stream.

Better undignified than on the ground floor facing down a bunch of soldiers, Barnabas advised cheerfully.

Why are those my only two choices?

Laughing, they crept across the roof and made their way to the edge of the courtyard that held Jeltor's rooms. A quick analysis confirmed the layout that Gilwar had found last time. The glass on the windows would be almost impossible to break. There was a way in through the ceiling vents, however, and they set to work getting in.

They dropped into the large, open main room, and only

just avoided going into the tanks. Stumbling and steadying themselves, they looked around. It was a beautiful room—if you managed to ignore the fact that it was a prison. Quiet and calm, it was filled with pale light that filtered in through the translucent glass of the windows.

"Hello!" Jeltor called from behind them.

CHAPTER NINE

Barnabas didn't have to wait for events to kick off. Without hesitating for an instant, Jeltor threw a bolt of energy with his Committee-made biosuit. Barnabas flung himself sideways and rolled, feeling the heat on the side of his face.

Lasers. That's new.

The Luvendi cut in. *That wasn't precisely a laser, it was—*

Not now, Gar!

And you're sure about this plan? Shinigami asked. On Barnabas' instructions, none of the others had drawn their weapons, and they had spread out.

Yes, Barnabas told them all. *I'm sure.* He brushed himself off and stood. Jeltor had moved right after he fired, and now he was crouched behind a large pedestal that held a statue of a Jotun in a biosuit.

When he peered out, Barnabas was standing quietly. His weapons were not drawn.

"It isn't going to work!" Jeltor exclaimed. He sounded

both furious and terrified. "It won't *work*, Barnabas, this act you're putting on."

"The part of the hero?" Barnabas asked. He tried to keep his voice level, but he knew that the words carried bitterness.

Jeltor said nothing. He did not come out from behind the pedestal, either.

"You're right," Barnabas continued. "Do you know what I was on Earth? I was a monster. That was what the Nacht were. Parents told children stories of us, and said if the children weren't good, the Nacht would come and take them away."

Still Jeltor did not speak, but he came out to stare at Barnabas.

"And you?" Barnabas asked. "You're the same, in some ways. Becoming a Nacht—it changed you. The Nosferatu, more so. You're neither one nor the other right now, are you? And the uncertainty terrifies you. That was why you asked Admiral Jeqwar to kill you."

Jeltor's biosuit went rigid.

"She spoke to me about it," Barnabas said.

"What was she going to do?" Jeltor asked, a bit wildly.

Barnabas hesitated. "*She* was going to do it. That is why I came for you."

Jeltor laughed. It was a hysterical sound, echoing off the stone and glass. "She was going to do it. I tried to lure her in with honor, and she was going to kill me. I shouldn't have thought she would be so easily trapped."

"Or perhaps you *did* think she would honor your request," Barnabas snapped, striking as fast as a snake. His voice was hard now. "And that was *why* you asked, Jeltor.

There's enough of you left in there that you're afraid of hurting the people you love, aren't you? You're afraid that the Committee might successfully use you as a weapon, and you don't want—"

That was all he got out before Jeltor shot again. The Jotun gave a yell of fury and advanced, sloshing through one of the pools of water as he shot...and kept shooting. Barnabas hurled himself around the room. His reflexes were good, more than equal to any other species'—but the Jotuns used auto-targeting in their suits, He was hard-pressed to get away from that, forced to change directions often in order to confuse the system.

Along the sides of the room, Shinigami and the others watched. He caught a glimpse of her face, which was set and determined, her hands clenched. She didn't like this plan. She had suggested simply overpowering him and abducting him, but Barnabas was afraid that doing so would be confirmation of the biases the Committee had implanted.

He sensed that Jeltor was wavering, and he wanted the Jotun to break on his own.

"Fight me, damn you!" Jeltor yelled at him.

"No." Barnabas stared him down before another bolt forced him to seek shelter. "I'm not here to fight, Jeltor, and I'm not here to kill you, either. I'm here to bring you home."

"Home? Where I could do as much damage as I pleased?" Jeltor's voice was ugly. "You hid Jelina and the children from me."

Barnabas crouched behind another pedestal. It was true. As soon as they had received word that Jeltor had been compromised, he'd had Jeltor's family moved somewhere he did not know, with no communications in or out.

Jelina hadn't asked for anything when he left. Not for him to bring Jeltor back alive, and not for him to kill Jeltor rather than put her and the children at risk, either. In some ways, that had been harder to bear than silent pleas.

She was only one person, and she knew she was caught up in something much larger than herself.

This, Barnabas thought, was the cost of empires. It was a cost he'd seen extracted from Bethany Anne, paid again and again by her and by her closest companions. He liked to think that it had been worth it, but it was heartbreaking to see the fallout.

No, he would not let Jeltor go home—not as the Jotun had understood it.

"Your home is in your mind, Jeltor." He kept his voice level and soft—nothing loud to startle the Jotun. "I have known madness. I have known the sense of being unmoored from myself like a ship in a storm. That is where you are now, and you know it."

"You are wrong," Jeltor called back. "For the first time, I have certainty."

"Do you? If so, you would not have offered what you did. You would have found some other way to lure the admiral in." Barnabas stood now. "Jeltor, you made your offer *hoping* she would take it, but there is no need for that. When you do their bidding, you feel good, yes? They've made sure of that. But there is a moment of sickness, too, isn't there? There is a moment of knowing that it is wrong. *I know you.* That will drive you mad. You were never one who could ignore something that was wrong."

He looked at Jeltor, whose gun was still pointed at him. There was no shot being charged.

"Jeltor," Barnabas repeated. "Come *back*."

Jeltor stared at that familiar face and felt his world flipping.

Barnabas was right. The rush of pleasure he felt when he did Grisor's bidding was strong, but even the overwhelming strength of it could not wipe away that one moment of knowing he was betraying himself.

When he had first come here, the little voice that told him so had been quiet, but after seeing Barnabas come for Grisor the first time, the voice had gotten stronger.

Unmoored like a ship in a storm. Jeltor struggled to make sense of himself. He longed for the certainty that he'd been promised when they'd tortured him, and yet he knew it was false.

Either way.

"You don't know that it can be undone," he told Barnabas. Speaking those words was terrifying, and the fear filled him with the urge to run back to Grisor and seek refuge in the lies.

"I have faith," Barnabas assured him after a moment. "I can't offer you certainty or a way out, Jeltor, but I have faith that we will find one together."

"What do *you* have to do with it?" Jeltor asked cruelly. "Taking credit for someone else's work again?"

"No." Barnabas winced at the words but then smiled reassuringly. "I cannot do the work for you. I can only be your friend. But, Jeltor, I pulled myself out of madness alone—for self-preservation and nothing more. That is not something I would wish on you. I want you to have friends by your side as you do this; friends whose belief in you will see you through the dark moments."

"We're here, Jeltor," Gar chimed in.

Jeltor looked sharply at him and saw Gar's instinctive desire to reach for his weapon, but the Luvendi held himself steady and did not do so.

They were not going to kill him. Jeltor was not sure if the feeling in his chest was relief or hopelessness.

"I can't do this," he told them all. "It can't be undone; it's too much. I'll always be a risk."

"Jeltor—" Barnabas began.

"No! Listen. They're going to take Kordinev first."

"Jeltor—"

"*Listen!* I don't know how much time I have, how long I can hold onto this, before the conversion takes over again." Already, it was calling him. A false refuge was still a refuge, and thinking of decades of struggle was too much to bear. He fixed his mind on the one objective he had: to tell them what the Committee was planning.

Once he had told them, he could rest.

"They'll go for Kordinev," he said again. "The Brakalon homeworld. They're still deciding on a plan, but their first thought is to take over the government with a few high-level officials and begin converting people before anyone knows they've been taken over. Once the army is converted, they'll have a fighting force few could defeat."

"Infantry isn't the most useful thing these days," Barnabas mused.

"No, but the Jotuns don't have them," Jeltor countered.

"At the same time, they'll be working to convert our admirals and work their way into the programming of the ships. Right now, there are failsafes—if an admiral loses control, individual captains can take back control of their ships. It's never been used, but they all know the protocol. The Committee is working to undo that. They'll have Brakalon infantry and strike teams, and the Jotun Navy. With those, they can do almost anything they want to."

Barnabas gave a quick nod.

"They're arguing," Jeltor continued. "They have the technology and they know they need to move fast, but with the first team of scientists gone, they aren't certain how often they'll need to refresh the conversion or how many they can convert at once."

The Jotun they had brought with them made a small, satisfied noise. *"Good."*

Jeltor could feel his sanity starting to slip. "That's all I know," he told Barnabas desperately. "They're still making the plan for Kordinev. You'll need a resource on the ground there if you can get a Brakalon. I don't know—"

He was having trouble concentrating.

"Jeltor, stay with me." Barnabas' voice was urgent.

"I can't; it's too much." He was so afraid. So afraid, and so weary. He could not do this for the rest of his life.

"Just for a moment," Barnabas urged. "Then another, Jeltor. Moment by moment. The more you practice, the easier it will become. *I've done this before.* I know it's possible."

"I—*can't!*" Barnabas began to step forward, and he was overcome with terror. They would try to help him, keep him in this absolute hell, and he couldn't bear it. Jeltor shot, this time with his gun. Bullets sprayed around the room and his former crewmates dove for cover.

When they were no longer looking, Jeltor ejected himself from his tank and dove into the water of the pools, darting for safety in the small alcoves where they could not follow.

"Fuck!" Shinigami yelled as she threw herself sideways.

"Are you hurt?" Barnabas called. He had every faith in the structural integrity of her cybernetic body, but who knew what might get jostled or disrupted by a hard hit? "Is something broken?"

"No, but he ruined my jacket. I *really* liked this one!"

"*Focus.*" Barnabas scrambled up and saw the suit standing oddly still. It took only a split-second to note the empty tank. "*Filius canis.* He's in the pools."

"How do you catch a jellyfish that doesn't want to be caught?" Shinigami asked philosophically as she came to stand beside him.

"I'm going to be honest; I don't think you do," Barnabas admitted. "At least, not without a great deal of time that I'm guessing we don't have."

Guys, he tripped something, Tafa reported in the same moment. *There are guards converging on your position.*

"Yep." Barnabas rubbed his head. "That sounds about right."

"Come on," Shinigami urged. "Let's get out. You were right; this *was* the way to get through to him, but we'll need to come back." She stopped when she saw his facial expression. "What?"

"We're *not* leaving," Barnabas told her. "Not empty-handed, anyway. Progress with Jeltor is good, but we are *not* leaving until we have something more."

"So, what are we trying to get?"

"You know," Barnabas told her, "I'm not quite sure." He took out his Jean Dukes and primed them, giving her a beatific smile. "I'm thinking of just letting the moment guide me."

"Oh, good," Shinigami replied. "You've decided to wing it. I'll have you know we rely on you to be the buzzkill who makes sure we have a plan."

"You *used* to, you mean." Barnabas strode to the door. "All right, motherfuckers, let's have some fun."

CHAPTER TEN

Barnabas yanked on the door and sighed when it was locked. "Of course, they had him in a prison. Of course, they did." *Tafa? Shinigami? Can either of you open this door?*

I've got it, Tafa said. *Locating you and working on the grid, one moment.* A few interminable seconds passed while everyone twiddled their fingers and Shinigami edged closer to the door, looking uncertain, then a click sounded. *You should be good to go.*

Thank you. Barnabas added privately to Shinigami, *Thank you for letting her handle it.*

Shinigami nodded with a faint gleam of a smile and held the door for the rest of them to head into the corridor.

Tafa, what's the layout of the soldiers?

They're spreading out across the gardens to block all exits, Tafa reported. *They still don't seem to know you got in from the roof. Do you need any particular kind of exit? Is Jeltor coming with you willingly?*

Barnabas and Shinigami exchanged stricken looks.

Oh, no, Shinigami said quietly to Barnabas.

It's a long story, Barnabas replied. *But knowing where the soldiers are is a big help. You should see us soon!*

All right, Tafa said after a moment. Her tone said that she knew something was wrong, and she was trying to keep herself calm.

They didn't have any time to lose. Barnabas turned toward the bulk of the building and took off at a run. He was going to try to strike a delicate balance between getting something good out of this before anyone knew where he was going and getting enough of the guards to follow him that their path to the ship would be clear.

An idea came to him. *Everyone think: what would we do if we were planning to take this place out now? I'm not saying that's what we're doing, I'm just saying that's what we want them to* think *we're doing.*

Take down the automated defensive systems, Shinigami shot back promptly.

Close any electronic doors and lock them to keep people partitioned, Gilwar added.

Go straight for Grisor and hold him hostage, Gar suggested finally. *It's not necessarily the best thing to do, but it's one of the things that signals the intention.*

Good. We'll do all of that. Barnabas shot them a grin.

I'll get the doors, Gilwar offered. *If someone can find me Grisor's last known location, I can just leave open the doors that lead us straight to him.*

Working on it! Tafa sounded glad of the distraction. *I'll let you know.*

I'll get the defensive systems, Shinigami said. She detoured to something that looked like a totally normal wall panel and popped it open with a gentle touch on a specific point. It lifted and slid up into the ceiling to reveal a large control panel. *Cover me.*

What is it like to be you? Barnabas asked rhetorically. He nodded at Gar, and the two of them took up flanking positions to protect Shinigami and Gilwar. Barnabas was anticipating that as soon as the soldiers realized they'd stopped at a control panel, things would escalate very quickly.

Gilwar, I've sent Grisor's last known location as a ping to your biosuit's scanner, Tafa said. *I'm tracking him visually on the security feeds. He's going to his chambers, alone, and he has a lot of shields and so on in there. A panic...pod-thing, it looks like.*

Good, Barnabas said. That had given him an idea. He was pretty sure his grin was the one Shinigami called his "evil-sneaky smile." Apparently, even an AI couldn't come up with a good combination of those two words.

Are you going to tell us what you're planning? Gar asked curiously.

Not yet, Barnabas replied.

That's so he can claim whatever he does was his master-plan, Shinigami offered. *Don't believe him; he's full of crap.*

Yeah, yeah. Barnabas kept his gun half-raised and slightly unfocused his eyes on the hallway in front of him so he could react quickly when guards came into sight. He could hear their footsteps. *Tafa, how many are on the way?*

You have...ten or so coming from the gardens. They've left some there.

I was hoping they wouldn't be so smart. Ah, well. Any coming from the other direction?

Five.

Gar, you ready?

Of course, I am, Gar said. *Especially since I gain an extra second or two every time by them being surprised to see a Luvendi with a gun in armor.*

Barnabas snickered.

Defensive systems turned off, Shinigami reported.

Doors closing, Gilwar added. Indeed, doors started slamming down nearby, and there were concerned shouts.

All right, move! Barnabas stopped guarding the garden side and joined Gar, pelting down the hallway. *Let's see how many more we can get out of the garden and following us. As for these...*

They're around the next corner, Tafa reported.

Excellent.

The *Shinigami's* crew was already firing as they came around a corner. One of Barnabas' shots carried a Jotun guard back into another of its teammates. The two of them together clipped a third as they went over, sending a wild shot over Shinigami's head and leaving only two of the five up and firing.

Gar took out one of those two with a careful shot. At the beginning, he had been very impulsive when it came to combat, but he was learning to take his time.

To Barnabas' surprise, Gilwar took out the other. His shot was a bolt of energy similar to Jeltor's, and it was directed with immense precision at the biosuit's neck. Whatever internal mechanism it hit, the suit shut down almost immediately, jerking and flailing as the Jotun thudded to its knees.

Shinigami gave a whoop as she took two long, loping steps and launched into the air, to come down on the pile of three other Jotuns. She grabbed the first, who had been rendered very dead by the Jean Dukes round, and used it as a mace to take out the other two. Her human-sized body did not look capable of wielding the biosuit with ease, which made the whole thing much better.

She gave them a delighted grin when she was finished. Since she was an android she was not even panting, something Gar looked vaguely annoyed by.

"Come on!" she urged. "This way to Senator Scumbag!"

Gilwar seemed to find this hilarious. He was still chortling as they took off down the hall.

Grisor is now inside his panic pod, Tafa reported.

Very good, Barnabas replied. His evil grin was back. *I assume there are more soldiers mobilizing?*

They're trying, but Gilwar has the doors locked down. They can't seem to get them open.

If the biosuit'd had a human face, Barnabas assumed it would look very smug. As it was, Gilwar was fluttering inside his tank in a way that reminded Barnabas of jazz hands. He stifled a snort.

All right, we'll do what we can before they get through—if they do at all.

You're coming right up on the office, Tafa told them. *One more door, and...yep, that's it.*

Thank you, Tafa. Barnabas wrenched the door open. Privately, he added one more command to Tafa. From her amusement, he could tell she knew what his plan was.

He went into the room, holstering his guns, and was pleased to see that the panic pod was clear. Grisor could see them—and he looked quite smug.

"Look who it is," he began. "Barnabas...without Captain Jeltor."

"Mmm." Barnabas grunted noncommittally. He did not want to give Grisor anything to fixate on when it came to Jeltor. "And you're here in this piddly little glass thing. You know, there's a human colloquialism about glass houses. It might even be considered applicable, in a broad sense."

"You think you can get through it?" Grisor asked smoothly. "You can't. You could direct every ounce of firepower you have at it and you still wouldn't even be close."

"Really?" Barnabas drew his Jean Dukes.

This is a trap, Shinigami cautioned him. *He knows it can withstand firepower, so he's trying to tempt you into using all your ammo.*

I think so, too. But by playing along, we're just filling the time so he doesn't figure out our real plan.

What is *our real plan? Although I have to say, it's nice to know we have one.*

Yes, isn't it? And I'm not telling just yet. Everyone fire. Barnabas aimed and let loose.

For almost a minute, there was no sound except deafening roars as everyone's guns went off and kept doing so. When the smoke cleared, there were a couple of scorch marks on the box, but nothing else, and Grisor was wearing a smug smile.

"Now you see how outmatched you are," he announced. "Look at me, defenseless inside this pod...but you can't breach it."

"We'll find a way," Barnabas told him, schooling his voice to sound arrogant. "Your soldiers are locked out. We can pry it open and get you out."

Grisor's suit turned just slightly as if looking at something. Barnabas followed his glance and saw a strange device in the corner; something handheld.

Apparently, Grisor wanted them to think that thing could open the pod. Barnabas considered, then went over and retrieved it.

Shinigami?

Not sure what it does—or if it does anything, actually.

Safe to bring on board the ship?

I'd say so. We'll just— Then she realized. *Oh, you are* evil.

I know. Barnabas gave her a smile and then looked up as the whole room shuddered and the roof began to peel back.

Grisor looked up. "What are you doing?"

"You're right that we can't get you out of the pod," Barnabas said. "Not in short order, anyway. But what we *can* do? We can get the pod out of the room."

A large metal claw dropped through the now-open patch of ceiling and locked on. A current running through the claw managed to freeze Grisor in place when he put out an arm to steady himself.

Barnabas didn't want him using a self-destruct.

As the pod began to withdraw into the sky, he nodded at the rest of the team. "Get ready for extraction. We're not leaving empty-handed now."

He was still smiling when Tafa's voice broke in, high with worry.

Guys? We have a big *problem.*

CHAPTER ELEVEN

What's going on? Barnabas demanded. *Tafa?*

They've got ships warming up. Tafa was about five seconds away from full-on panic. *They're going to try to shoot us down.*

Fat chance, Shinigami said darkly. *Let me at 'em, and I'll burn this whole fucking place to the ground.*

There are too many! Tafa's voice was rising, fear vibrating into the Etheric. *Get back to the ship, please? PLEASE! We have to get out of here.*

Another claw descended from the *Shinigami's* belly, and the whole team darted over to grab it. Shinigami ordered it to ascend. Her cybernetic face was utterly blank as she focused on scanning the area around them to figure out where the ships were, and on making sure they would be safe inside before any ground forces got to them.

They barely made it. They were just being drawn into the ship when a scatter of gunfire burst out below them. The hatch slammed shut under their feet, and they dropped onto the deck with sighs of relief—only to feel the ship shudder as Shinigami directed a few shots back.

Radiating fury, she stalked over to Grisor. "You know what happened just now? Your guards decided to shoot at us; pick a fight for the sake of picking a fight. They started it—and I finished it. That's how this whole fucking thing is going to go, just so you know. You decided to start something, and we are *not* going to be nice in how we shut it down."

Grisor glowed with smugness as Barnabas came to stand beside Shinigami. He smiled blandly into the panic pod.

"She's right," he told the Jotun. "So all those dreams you're having right now about dying gloriously and sparking a movement that brings the Jotuns to ascendance? *That's not going to happen."*

He couldn't read Jotun expressions perfectly, but from the sudden stillness of the jellyfish body, he knew he'd hit a nerve.

"Gilwar," He nodded at the other Jotun, "Gar will stay here to assist you in locking down this pod however it needs, and Shinigami will be available to make a plan." *Don't let this cretin overhear you*, he added. *Use the Etheric to communicate.* When both Gar and Gilwar nodded, he glanced at Shinigami. "Let's go to the bridge. Tafa needs us."

She nodded as the ship shuddered again, and both of them took off. It was hard to believe that Shinigami had once been unable to take even a single step. Her competence had come along by leaps and bounds, and her running form was eerily perfect, especially on the smooth decks of the ship.

The artificial gravity assisted them in keeping their feet, so elegant that it was a dizzying surprise to come onto the bridge and see the horizon dipping and swerving crazily on the screen. Tafa, wide-eyed and looking absolutely terrified, had her hands off the controls.

Barnabas could only pray that meant Shinigami was controlling the ship.

"How many ships?" he asked Tafa, keeping his voice businesslike. She needed to learn to focus on facts and keep moving through dangerous situations, or he was not going to feel comfortable putting her in combat.

She gulped and looked at the screen. "Twenty…six? No, twenty-seven." There was a storm of beeping, and she gave a little wail. "Thirty-two."

"All right." This was admittedly not a great situation, but he wasn't going to make things worse by telling Tafa that. *Shinigami, tell me you have a plan?*

You're the one who makes plans! Shinigami swerved out of the way of a whole wing of Jotun fighters. She determinedly did not look at him. *Just tell me your objective*, she said grimly.

Take out as much of the science facility as you can and get us out of here. I want to keep him *alive for a trial, but I don't want to take the chance that someone else will deploy the plan in his absence.*

Roger that. She gave a small smile. *Missiles priming and locked— Oh, hell.*

What? What is it now?

More ships. A lot more ships.

Shinigami—

And they're shifting the protocols in the satellites. Clever buggers—they had a whole new set of programs ready to go and loaded it in once we got here. We have to get out of here before everything comes online, which means going very fast in one direction, which means not taking evasive maneuvers, which means...

Barnabas waited for a long moment. *Which means we're screwed?* he asked delicately.

She gave him a look. She'd clearly calculated the odds already because there were no ships on the viewscreen and the color was getting progressively darker as they shot toward open space. *Yeah. Little bit. I'm not saying we can't do it, I'm just saying they've stacked the deck* real *well.*

Then the alarms burst fully to life and Shinigami swore in several languages Barnabas didn't know.

"What the hell was that?" Tafa yelled.

"Keep it together," Barnabas told her crisply. He met her eyes and gave a brief nod. She could do it—if she was willing to. He looked at Shinigami.

"They came out of *nowhere.*" Shinigami's face was screwed up with determination. "We were getting out of range of the rest, but this one— Oh, wait."

"'*Oh, wait?*'" Barnabas gave her an incredulous look. "Now is not the time for 'oh, wait!'"

"No, no, it really is." Shinigami started laughing. "All right, let me just say we're still heading into space and all that, but here's what's going on behind us." She swapped the viewscreens and sat back in her seat, still chortling.

The ship that had seemingly appeared out of nowhere

was a Jotun ship, but it wasn't on Grisor's side. That much was obvious.

Mostly from the way it was taking out ship after ship from Grisor's fleet. Missiles were streaking this way and that in a dizzying array, flying out in formations Barnabas had never seen.

"Holy..." He leaned forward, frowning at the screen. "What am I watching?"

"You are watching," said Gilwar from the door, "a thing very few people have ever seen: Admiral Yeneda Jeqwar at her finest."

"She's on that ship?" Barnabas demanded. Losing Admiral Jeqwar would be a blow they could ill afford. If they went up against another fleet—or, worse, if she were captured—

"I doubt it," Gilwar replied. He nodded at the screen as he came into the room. "Remember, an admiral is able to control a whole fleet at once. She's probably still on Jotuna. Hail her." After a moment of hesitation, he added, "Offer the passcode, 'clear waters.' It means she's being hailed by a member of Intelligence. I trust you won't misuse that."

Barnabas nodded, pleased by his trust. "I won't. Shinigami?"

"One moment, just zapping a few— Ow, son of a bitch!" There was a hollow boom on the side of the ship. "Fucking satellites. Okay, bringing her onto a channel. Jotun ship *Gedwaz*, this is the *Shinigami*, hailing you under clear waters."

A moment later an amused voice came back. "I don't mean to be rude, *Shinigami*, but I'm a little busy right now."

"I understand that, Admiral." Gilwar had switched to a

dialect of Jotun that was coming through slightly garbled in Barnabas' implant. "We have a prisoner on board—Grisor. He will be brought to Justice at an appropriate time and place."

That was, in any case, the gist of what Barnabas was getting. The admiral spoke back, half the words not translating, and Gilwar nodded at Shinigami.

"You can stop broadcasting."

"Would you mind rehashing that for me?" Barnabas asked wearily.

"She's taking care of cleanup and putting on a show, so they know exactly what they're dealing with, as well as broadcasting a message that Grisor was taken by this joint mission. They have bugs in the Naval networks, and she wants to throw them off by making them think this was planned and they didn't know about it."

"And Grisor?"

"She's pleased that we have him and that we didn't kill him. She wants what you want," he added wryly, "though perhaps not from a place of kindness. She was displeased that Jeltor was put on trial. I think she wants the same done to Grisor to drag his secrets out in the open and ruin him."

Barnabas gave a small smile. "I'm not saying I *don't* want to ruin him, just that I also have other motives. I take it he's secure, by the way?"

"Yes. We can't disable the pod yet, but he can't send any signals, or get out of our cage even if he opens his."

"Good."

"*This* is interesting," Shinigami commented.

"What is?"

"We have a pending notification from Victory Station. There's a message waiting for us, and it's tagged, 'One-floating-motionless.' I'm going to guess that's Kelnamon. It seems like a good way of indicating the *Srisa* and how we first met him."

"Why is he sending a message that way?" Barnabas asked, frowning.

"Oh, I think I have an idea of why." She gave him a look. "Don't you? Remember what Jeltor said? Remember where he said they were going to strike first?"

Between their capture of Grisor and their escape, Barnabas had, in fact, managed to forget that. His mouth dropped open. "They're *already* on Kordinev?"

"I don't know," Shinigami said, "but I do know that if so, we have a source on the surface and any keys to thwarting them will be in that message. I'm setting a course for Victory Station."

Barnabas gave a single nod. "Do it."

The ship was turning.

Aliana looked up from her book with a frown and then got up to pad down the corridors in her stockinged feet. The *Palpari* was an exceedingly clanky ship, and she had gotten tired of sounding like a drum solo when she walked anywhere.

Zinqued was alone in the cockpit, humming to himself, and staring out the window…

"Is this Victory Station?" Aliana asked in confusion.

"Yes," Zinqued affirmed. He gave her the Hieto version of a smile, scrunching his nose. "You should put on shoes. We need to disembark and take our places, yes, before our target shows up."

CHAPTER TWELVE

"So...why are we here?" Aliana turned sideways to slip past a group of Leath missionaries. "Also, who were they? They're religious now?"

"Defeat tends to do that to people," Zinqued told her philosophically. "Were you there for that?"

"Er, not precisely. I mean, everyone was, kind of. It's a long story." Aliana waved a hand. "Look, you keep dodging the question. What's going on?"

"Just a bit farther," Zinqued told her. "You'll see."

Aliana scowled as she stomped along behind him. "I hate surprises. You know, you could just *say* you found the *Shinigami* and it's here, or we're going to see someone *about* the—"

She stopped dead in her tracks a moment later.

A woman was standing on the loading docks, staring at them. Small and fine-boned, she had dark hair and wide, long-lashed black eyes. Hers was the sort of delicate beauty that was set off well by an evening gown and diamond jewelry, but instead, she was wearing blue coveralls with plenty of grease stains, and her hair was drawn back in a careless bun.

She met Aliana's eyes, then went up the ramp to a beautiful ship. Her fingers hovered over the keypad next to the doors, and she entered a few keystrokes before heading back down. She looked back, gave a single nod, and disappeared into the crowd.

She had unlocked the ship—or, rather, she had changed the codes to what they had been when Aliana first owned it. Because this ship was the *Melisande,* the ship she had scrimped and saved to buy with Harry; that she had fixed up with scrap parts and elbow grease until it ran like a dream. The ship she'd hired Ria to be the mechanic for.

The ship Lawrence had stolen from her.

Aliana realized she was shaking. She wanted to run away.

"We have to move quickly," Zinqued said. "Ria agreed to unlock the ship and make sure it was unoccupied. She requested clearance for it to undock unexpectedly, so you'll be able to get on board and get it off the station if you go *now.*"

"*What?*" Aliana gaped at him.

"Not everything has to be deep-space traps and ambushes," Zinqued told her with a smile. "Go. Get the ship, and I'll get in touch with you soon."

He made to disappear back into the crowd, but she grabbed his arm.

"Wait! You can't just go—"

"You don't have time to wait. The emergency clearance will expire soon."

"I don't care about that." Aliana held onto his arm. "You... Zinqued, you arranged for this? Why?"

He considered. "You were sad," he said finally. "I know what it is to miss a ship."

"I don't miss the *ship*," Aliana snapped. She saw the look on his face and sighed. "Okay, yes, I do. I miss it—a lot. Harry and I were married there—"

"Do you have time for this?"

"Just listen." She could hear the pleading in her voice. "What's been hurting so much is what Lawrence *did* to me, what he took—and that they all just went along with it. I hired them and they were my family, and they just let him kick me off my own ship and fly away and strand me in the middle of nowhere with no money. No nothing. It wasn't about the ship, it was what they did."

"That one—" Zinqued jerked his head in the direction Ria had gone, "is trying to make it right."

"Yeah, well, little good it does now!"

"It restores to you what should be yours." Zinqued gave her a look. "Is that not worth saving?"

"I don't—" Aliana turned away, hands buried in her hair. "I don't *know*. It isn't just Harry; now I have all these memories of Lawrence, too. I don't want to, but he's part of that ship, and I kind of never want to see it again."

There was a pause.

"Should I not have done this?" Zinqued asked finally. "I thought it would help."

Aliana began to cry. She wiped her nose angrily, then used her sleeves to dry her eyes. "No, it was nice. I just— It's *so* nice. Why did you do it? We had a deal."

The Hieto hunched his shoulders and rocked from side

to side as he thought. "I didn't like our deal," he said finally. "You were only going along with it because you had this to hurt you. You wanted to get even. I *thought* you wanted your ship back. I wanted you to help me because you wanted to, not because you had to just to get this ship."

Aliana stared at him. It felt like someone had torn her chest in half, she thought with a strange detachment. This alien, who didn't even know her all that well, had done this for her because he didn't want her to be sad.

She settled for saying, "You know, you're going to go broke with that attitude."

Zinqued burst out laughing. "Ah, that I am. You're not wrong. Tik'ta despairs of me."

"Oh, no." Aliana shook her head, still laughing. "What did she say about this?"

"Actually, she approved of this." Zinqued was nodding appreciatively. "I think she mainly thought it would keep me occupied."

Aliana shook her head with a smile. "Well, thank you, Zinqued."

"Yes." He gave her a smile. "So are you going? I think you have about ten minutes to get aboard and begin getting out of here."

"I suppose, yes." Aliana stared at the ship. "This wasn't how I pictured it. I wanted revenge, Zinqued. I wanted Lawrence to suffer the way I suffered."

"Ah." Zinqued shook his head. "Never wish for suffering. That is what my—what do you call them?—my mother's mother used to say."

"'Grandmother,'" Aliana said. "Grandmas are always wise. They know when to whup you upside the head, too, and tell you to stop being stupid. I wonder what mine would be saying right now." She considered. "She would probably say that I had been very stupid to let Lawrence steal the ship in the first place, and to make sure it couldn't happen again—*then* worry about revenge."

"That is good," Zinqued replied dubiously, "and maybe it will give me time to explain to you why not to seek the suffering of your enemies."

"You steal ships for a living."

"Yes, but I do not actively wish for pain." He flapped a hand at her when he saw that his careful distinction wasn't meeting with approval. "Go now. We will talk later. Why are you looking like that?"

"Zinqued," Aliana began slowly.

"Yes?" He gave her a bright smile.

"Er." Aliana looked out the window behind him. "So, uh—you brought me here to steal back my ship?"

"Yes," Zinqued told her proudly.

"That was…the whole reason?"

"Yes." He looked a bit baffled.

"Nothing else?"

"No." He sounded worried now. "Why?"

"I mean, it just seems weird to me," Aliana mused, struggling to keep a hysterical laugh from welling up in her chest, "that after so long spent setting up alerts and so on, we should get here for some totally unrelated reason, and suddenly…" She put her hands on Zinqued's shoulders and turned him so he could see the docking bay. "There's the *Shinigami*, docking at the same station we're at."

Zinqued had always been honest with her, and yet some

part of her had believed he was telling her a lie about why he'd come. That was, until she saw the look on his face.

There was no way he would have been able to keep all of his emotions in check if he'd known the *Shinigami* was going to be here. There was also no mistaking the shock she was seeing.

"Oh, my God," he burst out. The Hieto version of that term didn't exactly translate, but the sentiment was similar. "Quick. Back to the *Palpari*. We have to talk to Tik'ta and—"

"Aliana," a new voice called.

Aliana froze. Slowly, both she and Zinqued turned, and even though she steeled herself, she felt the familiar flutter in her stomach when she saw Lawrence's handsome face.

Damn him.

"Lawrence." Her mouth didn't work properly.

He smiled, fully aware of what that look was doing to her—seeing all of the longing, the shared laughter, and the hatred.

"Fancy seeing you here," he said. "Why are you on Victory Station?"

CHAPTER THIRTEEN

"Barnabas." Shinigami's voice came over the speakers. "Are you in your room?"

Barnabas looked up from his book. "You...you don't know?"

"Right." Shinigami sounded evasive. "Okay, wrong, I did know. I remembered Tabitha saying it was stalker-y to follow you around the ship, so I tried *not* to know where you were, but it turns out it's really hard *not* to know something when you've got this many diagnostic readouts. I tried, though."

Barnabas smiled at one of the cameras. "And I appreciate the effort. What was it you wanted to talk to me about?"

"We've been granted clearance to dock at Victory Station, and I should have the connection to decrypt the message shortly. I'm intrigued as to why they didn't contact us directly. I'm sure the message will explain it. In the meantime, is there anything you want me to do about Grisor?"

"Ah, yes." Barnabas felt a moment of amusement. He'd decided to let Grisor stew for a good while and was pleased that he'd managed to forget about the Jotun entirely while reading his present book. The search for a rogue submarine commander was surprisingly gripping, even when he knew no such thing had ever happened.

He considered.

"No, let Grisor wait. A few days will do him good. I trust he hasn't gotten out or created any havoc?"

"No. He's tried to send several messages using all different sorts of encryption methods and signals. Sometimes I zap him, and sometimes I pretend they've gone through."

Barnabas burst out laughing. "Shinigami, you're an evil genius."

"Excuse me." She sounded prim now. "I'll have you know this serves an important purpose. He's trying to win at a game he's not actually playing instead of using his technology in a way that might actually do damage."

"Ah, yes. But was that why you did it?" Barnabas carefully marked his place and put the book on a side table. "Shinigami?"

"I think we both know the answer. Goodbye." She signed off as the docking clamps grabbed at the ship.

Barnabas was still chuckling as he walked down the corridor toward the blast doors. *Gar? Tafa? We're at Victory Station. If you'd like to get anything, we can certainly pause here briefly—depending on what's in Kelnamon's message, of course.*

I'll let you know as soon as I get through the decryption, Shinigami broke in.

You haven't broken it yet? Gar sounded worried.

I second the question, Barnabas added. He'd stopped in his tracks and was frowning at the ceiling.

Long story short, Kelnamon appears to have encrypted it with a passphrase instead of an algorithm, so now I have to figure out what sort of asinine clue he thinks we could all get. I swear, organic life forms are the worst.

Does anyone have suggestions? Barnabas asked delicately. He could hear footsteps, and he turned to look as Tafa came around the corner with Gilwar.

Srisa, Gar suggested.

Tried it, Shinigami said.

Huword? Barnabas suggested.

Ferqar, Tafa chimed in. *Or—what was the section of the legal code that meant he had to float in space?*

Oh, good thought. Shinigami sounded impressed. *Keep sending ideas. I'll let you know as soon as I—oh.*

Did you get it? Barnabas held up a hand to stop the others from going to the door. He'd rather they just leave now for Kordinev if they were needed.

No, Shinigami reported. *You'll never guess who's here, though.*

Barnabas had an immediate thought, discarded it, and then decided it was the only thing that made sense. Still... *You cannot possibly be talking about Zinqued.*

Bingo.

Barnabas tipped his head back with a groan.

Oh, come on, Shinigami said. *You've enjoyed that battle of wits.*

"Battle of wits" *is a very charitable term. It's like playing chess with a deranged ferret.*

Tickets to that, please.

Gar had arrived, and he and Tafa were snickering. Barnabas gave them a severe look. They shut up, but he noticed that Gilwar was not bothering to hide his amused flutters. He probably assumed that Barnabas could not interpret Jotun mannerisms.

Barnabas decided he was just going to sit on that piece of knowledge for now. A different thought had occurred to him.

Shinigami, is there any possible way they could have known we were coming here?

It is possible, Shinigami said. *Anything is technically possible. I know we went past at least one checkpoint on our way to Jotuna. As far as I know, we passed none on our way here, and I did not notice anyone tailing us—which I definitely would have noticed if they'd sped up to pass us or if they'd been in front of us the whole time.*

Interesting. Barnabas turned to look as Shinigami came around the corner in black pants, a tank top, and a bolero jacket that reminded him strongly of Bethany Anne. "Now that everyone is here, we might as well speak out loud. As far as we know, Zinqued doesn't know we're here, and I'd be incredibly surprised if he'd managed to—"

"To…" Shinigami prompted.

"You don't think Carter told Aliana about the *Srisa* and this message from Kelnamon is a trap?"

Shinigami blinked. A moment later, she reported, "If it's a trap, it's an incredibly good one, and also incredibly stupid."

"Well, that would track."

"Agreed, but what Hieto or human will have access to a

waypoint on Kordinev? The message definitely originated there."

"Hmm. Just a thought. Let's assume they don't know we're here, then. If anyone starts following us, we'll report it silently and regroup here *immediately*. Is that clear? Whatever you're doing, come back."

Everyone nodded, and Gilwar raised one mechanical hand. "Just a question. Who is Zinqued?"

"It's a long story," Barnabas said.

"He keeps trying to steal the ship," Shinigami reported.

"And he's still alive?" Gilwar asked dubiously. "You never struck me as one to suffer fools."

"I've come to be quite fond of these fools," Barnabas told them honestly. He buttoned his suit jacket. "So, shall we?"

Gar was explaining their repeated run-ins with Zinqued and Tafa was chiming in about Aliana as they all walked out of the ship. Shinigami smiled at Barnabas.

"I like to think that no one here can tell I'm an android."

"Most organic life forms probably can't," Barnabas agreed. "You've come a long way from when you first got that body."

She shuddered. "Learning to walk was terrible."

"I have no doubt. Now, is there anywhere you want to— Wait. Look." Barnabas nodded to the docking area next to them.

There, not entirely unexpectedly, was Zinqued. With him was Aliana—and both of them were arguing with a tall man who was wearing far too many concealed weapons and an infuriating smirk.

"Who's that?" Shinigami asked.

"That," Barnabas said, "is Aliana's ex-husband. And Carter *did* tell us to look after her."

Shinigami gave him an incredulous look. "We're going to get involved?"

"Did you have any other specific plans for this trip?" Barnabas asked her. When she said nothing, he gave a nod. "Precisely. All right, here's my plan…"

"So, why *are* you on Victory Station?" Lawrence's gaze sharpened as he looked at Aliana.

Stay calm, Aliana told herself. *He doesn't know what happened with Ria. There's no possible way he could know.*

Of course, there were *plenty* of ways he could know, and even a second of going down *that* rabbit hole threatened to make her insane.

Lawrence was smart, and he didn't care about anyone but himself—unless he thought someone had crossed him, in which case he became obsessed with making them pay. He would use the letter of the law to string Aliana up on charges; drag everything she'd ever done into the light—

Her eyes focused abruptly on a man with reddish-brown hair coming up behind her ex-husband. The *Shinigami*, she thought in despair, and she had the urge to laugh hysterically.

But Barnabas only gave her a wink before disappearing into the crowd. "Trust me," that wink said.

Or maybe she *was* going insane.

Lawrence had turned to follow her gaze, but Barnabas was lost in the swirl of people. The man looked at Aliana again, his eyebrows drawing together. "Are you trying to con me?"

By now, Aliana had recovered her composure. She should have gone for it when Zinqued told her about the plan. She could see that now. It would have been worth it to see the look on Lawrence's face or even just imagine it.

She hadn't stolen the ship, though. She was here, and that was that—and she was *not* planning to give Lawrence anything to work with.

"I'm not trying to con you," she told him honestly. A little bit of honesty might go a long way here. Lawrence was good at sensing lies. "You're not why I'm here, and I don't actually want to see you."

Lawrence looked at her suspiciously, but he could hear the ring of truth in her words.

And then he smiled, and something in Aliana's stomach turned over. Why did someone so evil have to be so freaking good-looking? It was unfair. It was more than unfair, really; it shouldn't be allowed.

"You don't want to see me?" he asked her. "Why not?" He was standing far too close now. "Aliana, we had some good times together."

Keep it together, woman. "Yes, we had some good times, which may or may not have been an elaborate con on your part." Aliana gave him an icily pleasant smile. "After which you stole my ship—no, please, I am not interested in hearing you recall the legal technicalities—and left me nearly penniless on a remote station. And all because... Well, I have to ask now. *Was* there a reason? Why me? Why any of it?"

Lawrence gave her a blank look for a moment, then lifted one gorgeous shoulder. "Because I wanted to."

She wished she hadn't asked.

"Please go away," Aliana told him.

He smiled meltingly at her again. "No."

"Fine. *I'll* go away."

"Don't." His hand shot out and closed around her arm. "I've missed you. You've missed me."

"No. No, I haven't."

He saw the lie at once. "Yes, you have. You missed the way we used to laugh together. You missed…" He gave her a meaningful look. "And you missed thinking you were better than me. That you were *settling* for me."

The change in tone came so fast that she was still blinking when she felt the pain in her arm. His hand was clamping down tightly.

"You're a con artist, Lawrence." She didn't cry out. She wasn't going to give him the satisfaction. "You like preying on people. Yes. I thought you weren't right for me." The fingers tightened, and she tried not to wince. "All right, this is what you want to do? *Fine.* I *was* settling for you, but it wasn't because *I* was better than you. It was because *Harry* is better than you. That's right. He's dead, and he's *still* a better man than you. The memory of him makes me happier than you ever could have. I am going to miss him every day for the rest of my life, and when you die, no one is going to miss you."

The look in his eyes was truly terrifying, but Aliana wrenched her arm out of his grip and smiled recklessly at him. "You can puff up and get threatening all you want, asshole, but you took everything. There's nothing more you can do to hurt me."

"Excuse me," a new voice interjected.

Aliana glanced over…and her jaw dropped. A gorgeous woman was standing in front of them. Tight black pants showed off legs that gave the impression of going on for days and her black silk tank plunged nearly down to her navel, showing a carefully-curated hint of what lay beneath. Dark hair cascaded over her shoulders, and her lips were painted red.

She looked familiar…

But Aliana couldn't quite place her.

The woman looked at the *Melisande*. "I'm looking to buy a few more ships." There was now a faint accent in her voice. Had she had an accent to start with? Aliana wasn't sure. "I asked the station manager. I said, 'Whose ship is that?' And he told me to find you—I think." She looked at him and Aliana, and her eyes raked dismissively over Aliana's cargo pants and ponytail. "Are you in the market, maybe? I will give you a *very* good price. Severance for all your crew, of course. Or perhaps you could all come work for me."

Her smile held a *lot* of promises.

Aliana knew what was coming in that instant, but it seemed to take forever to play out as Lawrence started to smile.

"Of course," he said. "You know, she *is* a good ship, and if you say you're offering a good price— Well, and of course I would be delighted to discuss future employment." He was good at giving promising smiles too. "In fact, can I buy you a drink?"

She gave him a pleased smile. "Of course! A drink with a handsome man. And…your crew?" She waved a bored finger at Aliana.

"*Former* crew," Lawrence specified, twisting the knife. "Aliana didn't do well with the new management. You know how it is." He put his hand in the small of the woman's back and guided her away, pausing only to throw a glance over his shoulder at Aliana. "Oh, by the way, you told a convincing lie, but I know you were lying. Ria told me everything. I had her thrown in the station jail. Don't worry, all those codes have been reset again."

And he was gone—gone, with the woman in black swaying seductively in her heels as she walked. Aliana stared after him, trying to keep it together. She could do this. She'd survived his cruelty once. The *Melisande* wasn't hers anymore, and she wouldn't let him hurt her with it again—

"Is he gone?" Barnabas' voice asked. He smiled when Aliana whirled to face him. "Good." His eyes traveled over her and Zinqued. "Let's talk, shall we?"

CHAPTER FOURTEEN

I hate this, Shinigami commented as she strutted away from Aliana and the others. *I mean, don't get me wrong, I love how my ass looks in these pants, but this sucks otherwise. Why did I get stuck with the douche-nozzle and the rest of you get to do the fun parts?*

The real question, Barnabas asked drily, *is why you started having a Russian accent halfway through that conversation?*

I had to amuse myself somehow!

Well, I hope you know you're going to have to keep it up or he'll get suspicious.

Please. He's dazzled by this shirt. He's not going to notice if I start speaking in actual *Russian.*

That is depressingly true.

Shinigami grinned and tossed a smile at Lawrence. Her assessment of attractiveness, based on the media she had been able to evaluate, showed that Lawrence had many features others might consider attractive.

He was, however, an irredeemable douche.

"Tell me about yourself," she said to him. "How does a man with such *manners* come to run a cargo ship?"

His chest puffed up, but she noted from his faint evasiveness that he wasn't quite sure how to play this. She would bet that the real question was whether he wanted to play an honest, blue-collar craftsman who would impress women with his down-to-earth attitude and callused hands, or if he wanted to pretend that he was a gentleman having a lark captaining a ship.

She started composing a douche bingo card in her head.

"How does a lady of such class come to be interested in having a fleet?" he asked her.

Sounding her out. Clever. Of course, that would make sense if he were someone who liked to con people.

"Oh," she waved her hand, "I am sure you are too busy to hear about it."

"No, no." He stopped and drew her to a halt, swinging her to face him. His touch was very gentle on her elbow.

As if she hadn't seen how hard he had been gripping Aliana's arm. She busied herself with a new bingo card: karmically appropriate ways to hurt Lawrence. Breaking all of his finger bones was *definitely* on there.

"Has anyone told you how enchanting you are?" Lawrence asked winningly. "I think I could listen to you talk all day."

Shinigami gave him a smile and ignored the urge to punch that smarmy expression off his face. She added punching to the karmic punishment card and checked off, *absurd over-the-top compliment* on the douche card.

"Well…" She looked around. "I'll *certainly* need a drink

if I'm to tell you all of it. Although I might go through *several* drinks, I warn you."

"Oh, that would be just fine." His smile was smarmy in the extreme. "And Victory Station has some truly spectacular bars, did you know? Here, let me introduce you to Gianni. He's the bartender at Endless Reach, and he makes divine cocktails." He kissed Shinigami's hand.

"Oh." She dimpled at him, not quite sure what to say. "Well, if you insist—if you think you have time—"

"I have all the time in the world for you," he assured her.

It was a good thing for Lawrence that Shinigami didn't have a normal stomach. If she did, she would have puked all over him. As it was, she waited until his back was turned and followed him with a massive eye roll.

It was a pity she couldn't get drunk because this was going to be a *long* hour or so.

Still... She perked up. Barnabas and the rest were *really* going to owe her after this one. Maybe she could get them to give her a second body. Or more flamethrowers.

Yes. More flamethrowers.

And she'd test them on Lawrence.

Thoroughly cheered up, she followed him with a wide smile.

"So." Barnabas looked at Aliana and Zinqued. "Zinqued, it's good to see you again. You know, after the battle with the Jotun fleet, I was worried about you. You came very close to being vaporized."

Aliana glanced between the two of them, open-mouthed.

Barnabas decided to have a little bit of fun. "You won't know about this, of course," he told Aliana, "but Zinqued once tried to steal my ship. More than once, in fact. Isn't that right, Zinqued? I'm sure he's quite reformed now, though. He must be if he's taken up with you."

Aliana gave him a deer-in-the-headlights look.

"Just messing with you." Barnabas gave a grin. "He's still trying to steal the ship, and you're helping him."

Now they both gaped at him.

"So here's my deal," Barnabas said. He wasn't going to explain the mindreading just yet. "Carter asked me to keep an eye out for you. He, of course, does not realize why you wanted to meet me on High Tortuga."

Aliana gave a groan and dropped her head into her hands. "I didn't *want* to meet you," she said, her voice muffled. "That was the worst."

"I beg your pardon?"

"No! I didn't mean…" She picked her head up, now blushing furiously. "*You're* not the worst, it was just the worst to— Oh, never mind."

Zinqued was looking back and forth between them curiously.

"I'm sorry, I'm still messing with you." Barnabas could feel his lips twitching. "This is *fun*. However, we have somewhat limited time. The woman you just saw distracting Lawrence was Shini—Shannon, my associate." As far as he knew, Zinqued was still unaware that Shinigami was an avatar of the AI, and he didn't want to spill the beans on that. "She's agreed to keep him occupied by stringing him along and making him buy very, very overpriced drinks for her while *I* help you steal the ship. To clarify," he added, "steal *Lawrence's* ship, *not* the *Shinigami*."

There was a long pause.

"We weren't trying to steal his ship," Zinqued explained finally.

"Yeah, why would you think that?" Aliana asked.

"For one thing, the two of you currently look like two children who've painted the dog and are trying to keep their mother from finding out, and for another, stealing ships seems to be how Zinqued solves problems. And Lawrence did take *your* ship, didn't he? We did some research, Shinigami and I."

"The AI," Aliana murmured to Zinqued. She added meaningfully, "They're famously loyal."

Barnabas, peering into her head for a moment, found several memories of her telling Zinqued that it would be impossible to steal the *Shinigami*.

He found himself hoping that she tried anyway.

"The people who say that haven't met Shinigami," he told them blandly.

Hey! I am busting my ass for you guys right now!

"I meant Achronyx," Barnabas corrected.

That's better. However..."Shannon?"

We'll talk about this later.

Aliana and Zinqued looked at him like he was a grenade that might go off at any moment.

"Shinigami and I discussed it," Barnabas continued, "and decided that there was no way you could have known we were going to be on this station. Despite past interactions, it seems that this meeting happened genuinely by chance. So, for that reason—and also because the man you were speaking to seems to be a terrible excuse for a human being—we are going to help you steal his ship. Or, rather, steal *your* ship *back*. Then we will all go our separate ways. I can't imagine we'll cross paths again, after all." He gave Aliana a bland smile.

Her internal monologue was fairly consistent swearing.

BINGO! The interjection from Shinigami was so unexpected that Barnabas jumped. Aliana looked at him with a frown and he shook his head.

Bingo? he asked Shinigami.

Oh, sorry. I was playing bingo with all of the douchey things he was saying. And I won!

Yes, yes, very good.

He looked at Aliana. This was going to be *fun*. Well, it was going to be fun if she said yes. Barnabas slid his hands into his pockets, tilted his head to the side, and waited for her to remember how to speak.

He really was hoping she accepted his help on this one.

This was bad. It was very, very bad. In fact, it was probably a trap.

"Excuse me." Aliana gave Barnabas a polite smile and dragged Zinqued a few feet away. "All right, level with me. You've run into him *how* many times?"

"Four," Barnabas offered.

"It's rude to eavesdrop," Aliana told him with great dignity.

"Indeed." His mouth twitched. "I'll go a few feet farther away."

"Thank you." She watched while he strolled away, looking elegant and entirely unconcerned, then looked at Zinqued. "So?"

"He was right, you know." He was still looking at the *Shinigami*.

"Yes, yes. Focus." Aliana took him by the shoulders. "Do you have *any* idea how dangerous he is?"

"Oh, yes." Zinqued looked both amused and terrified. "I once saw him and two friends work their way through hundreds of mercenaries."

"Okay." Aliana felt a bit queasy. She stole a glance over her shoulder. "Wait, really? Him in the suit right there?"

"You said—"

"I know, it's just hard to believe." She blew out a breath. "My point is, if he really wanted you dead, you'd be dead right now."

"Yes. I suppose so."

"So he's toying with you," Aliana said resignedly. "With *us*, I guess. Well, let him. If he wants to get his jollies helping screw Lawrence over, I say we take the deal."

"And steal his ship," Zinqued said.

"One thing at a time," Aliana advised him. She marched back over to Barnabas. "All right, we'll take the deal. The first thing we have to do is get Ria out of jail. She screwed me over, but she did try to make it right. It wouldn't be good to leave her here. Let's go."

"Incorrect," Barnabas told her. "We have to rewrite the ship's registration so it's solely in your name, then you'll be able to get her out as the captain of the *Melisande*."

"Oh, that *is* better."

"I thought you'd say so." He smiled at her. "Let me just ask Shinigami." There was a pause. "Your middle name is Lilly, yes? Two Ls?"

"I—yes."

"Place of birth approximately in the Betoger Nebula, yes?"

"That's about where the *Meredith Reynolds* was, yes, but—"

"Approximate is fine. Bethany Anne has great respect for the power of bureaucracy. Anyone trying to verify information on humans has a very, *very* difficult time doing so unless they can prove there's a need." He gave her a smile.

"I still can't get over the fact that you just call her Bethany Anne."

"It *is* her name. Now, come along, both of you—yes, you too, Zinqued, I see how you're looking at my ship—and let's get Ria out of jail."

As they walked, Barnabas pointed out some of the features of Victory Station and recounted his exploits here. Aliana gaped at him, laughing at some of the cons he'd pulled. She knew that in some ways, his actions were very similar to Lawrence's, yet—

"That's the difference," she murmured to herself.

"Hmm?" Barnabas looked at her with interest.

"I, uh…I was just thinking." Seeing his curious look, she took a deep breath for courage and explained, "Lawrence is a con artist too. It made me uncomfortable that I was applauding you for *your* cons, because *his* ruin people. Then I realized the difference: he finds a target, he learns everything he needs to about them, and he pretends to be the perfect person so he can take everything. You find a target and you learn about them, but you always give them an out. It's like you set a trap right in the middle of the easy way out, and if they do the right thing, they'll never know the trap was there."

Barnabas looked absurdly pleased. "Yes. Yes, that's exactly it." He didn't say anything more, but she could tell he was happy by the way he hid his smile.

It turned out to be very simple to get Ria out of jail. Aliana waltzed in with her chin held high, introduced Barnabas as her lawyer, and complained that they had imprisoned her mechanic on false charges without even speaking to her first.

"Ma'am, we verified that the accusations were being made by the owner of the human ship—" The Torcellan checked the paperwork *"Melisande."*

"Well, clearly you didn't," Aliana said, "since I'm the owner."

There was some hasty muttering as they ran her card. The Torcellan came back, hands fluttering.

"I am so sorry, Captain. I promise this will *not* happen again."

"I should hope not," Aliana said severely.

"Is there anything else we can do for you?"

"Yes." She gave an icy smile. "We'll want to leave shortly —to go to a station where this sort of thing *doesn't happen.* I'd appreciate it if you'd take care of all the notifications. You know who I am, so there shouldn't be any problems."

"Yes. Yes, of course." They waved her away, Ria trotting in her wake, and Aliana gave a disbelieving laugh.

"We pulled it off!" she said excitedly as they emerged into the docking bays.

"*You* pulled it off," Barnabas corrected. "And before you get all flattered, let me just say that you're rather too good at that for comfort."

"Says the man who proposed stealing a ship." Aliana flashed him a grin. "Now, how do we get back onto the ship? Lawrence said he changed the codes."

"Leave that to Tafa." Barnabas nodded toward a Yofu mechanic who was fiddling with the control panel. "We'll be on the ship in a jiffy."

"Who *is* this guy?" Ria asked dubiously.

"Oh." Aliana coughed. "Right, of course, you don't know. Hang onto your hat, because this is *good*…"

CHAPTER FIFTEEN

"How's it going?" Barnabas asked Tafa as he led their strange party up the ramp.

"To be honest, I'm just holding this scanner thingy here while Shinigami does the work." Tafa shook her head. "I'm a glorified pedestal."

Oh, don't say that, Shinigami cut in. *You're so much more than that, Tafa.*

Thank you, Shinigami.

You have thumbs! *Four of them!*

Tafa gave Barnabas a long-suffering look as he snorted with laughter.

To distract her, he asked, "I don't believe you've met Aliana, have you? She's Carter's niece. Tafa, Aliana; Aliana, Tafa. Tafa came to be part of our crew after we ran into a mercenary group that was taking hostages. And this is Zinqued, captain of the *Palpari*, who you may remember as the one who has tried to steal the *Shinigami* several times. Zinqued, Tafa."

Tafa looked curiously at Zinqued and Aliana.

"Where's Gar?" Barnabas asked Tafa.

"On board," Tafa replied. "Well, on board the *Shinigami*. He says he doesn't want to take the chance of Zinqued stealing it."

"Ha!" Zinqued exclaimed, pleased. "So he thinks it is possible."

Everyone gave him a look.

"Read the room, man," Aliana told him.

"We are all friends here," Zinqued said with great dignity. "For now. What benefit in pretending none of our history has occurred, eh? Often adversaries become friends."

"He's a philosopher," Barnabas told Aliana. "Less uncommon than you'd think amongst thieves."

"I...see."

Barnabas was enjoying this every bit as much as he'd expected. As Tafa gave a small sound of satisfaction and the doors clicked open, he grinned and stepped back with an artful bow, gesturing for Aliana to go first.

"Your ship, Captain."

"I *do* like the sound of that." She gave Zinqued a small smile. "And thank you, Zinqued. Thank you for setting this up and—"

"If I may interject," the Hieto said, "we missed our window last time. Let us not make the same mistake twice."

"Ah. Yes." Aliana nodded decisively and strode onto the ship. "All right, two major tasks, as far as I can tell. No, three. First, get all of the verification systems retagged to me instead of Lawrence."

"I can help you with that," Barnabas suggested.

"Excellent. Next, make sure there aren't any booby

traps anywhere, probably on secret caches of goods he's hidden away. Or in the captain's quarters."

"I'll call Gilwar to come scan for those," Tafa offered.

"Good," Barnabas replied. He was trying not to laugh at the idea of a high-profile Jotun spy assisting in a single-ship theft. "Wait, what was the third thing?"

"Put all of Lawrence's things in a pile on the dock and set them on fire," Aliana said sweetly.

I like her. Can we keep her?

We're getting her a ship, so I doubt it. He didn't hate the idea, however.

That's a shame.

Barnabas agreed and followed Aliana to the bridge. He used some of the tools in Tafa's bag, as well as Ria's knowledge of recent missions, to scan the area for booby traps.

There were several.

"You know," he mused, as he helped Ria disable one of them, "one might say it would be very fitting for Lawrence to be killed by his own booby traps."

"Yes," Aliana agreed. "Although I don't really want him *dead*. I just want him not to have anything he got by cheating it out of people. And I want him to stop being such an asshole."

"He's not going to stop being an asshole," Ria predicted from under the desk. "You, ginger dude—keep holding that."

"Sorry." Barnabas held the piece of machinery as he peered under the desk. "My hair is not *ginger*."

"It's basically ginger."

"She's right," Aliana weighed in. Seeing the look on

Barnabas' face, she added hastily, "But it suits you! It really does."

"Mmm." Barnabas looked back under the desk. "Almost done?"

"Not really." Ria sounded annoyed. "He didn't have me install these. He did them himself, which means they're all messed up and are a pain in the ass to remove. Once an asshole, always an asshole. I should have just clocked him on the back of the head with a brick the first time I saw him with a welding torch."

"Yes," Aliana agreed, "you should have." There was a pause, and she added delicately, "You also should have said something about it that time he stole my ship and left me penniless on a remote station instead of taking a job with him and letting him get away with it."

Ria scooted out from under the desk and looked up at her gravely. "Yes, I should have. I'm sorry." She heaved a sigh. "Thank you for just saying it. It was hanging there."

"Mmm." Aliana shrugged.

"Excuse me," Barnabas broke in, "but I'm holding a live booby trap."

"Oh! Right." Ria dove back under the desk. "Sorry. Oh. Oh! Okay, that came off easier than expected. Let me just get the fuse out and—okay, we're good. You can set it down." She came out with a smear of grease on one cheek. "That should be all of them. Let's reset the passcodes."

Barnabas handed Ria his handkerchief. "Oh, no, keep it. It's no trouble. And it sounds like Tafa and Gilwar are finishing up as well. I wonder how Shinigami is doing?"

"The AI?" Aliana asked.

"Oh. Right. Yes. She's, uh—she was crunching numbers for something. Also, I wonder how *Shannon* is doing."

You could have given me literally any name, Shinigami said, *and you chose Shannon?*

What's wrong with Shannon?

I don't know, it's just not very...you know. I want to be something really cool-sounding. Like Optimus Prime!

A name starting with S-H.

Oh. Right. Well, I don't know!

How's it going?

Ugh. This dude is a gigantic douche.

The problem with Lawrence, Shinigami reflected, wasn't so much that he was *a* douche.

It was that he was the *biggest* douche.

"Perhaps you'd like to see the ship now," he suggested. "The living quarters are *quite* nice."

Also, he was a sleazebag. Shinigami found herself wondering if she could put him in a room with Tabitha and watch the man get the living shit kicked out of him while being insulted in exceedingly indelicate Spanish.

In any case, while Lawrence clearly saw Shinigami as a new mark, he also wanted to hurt Aliana, and she did *not* approve of that.

She deflected his transparent offer as well as she could. "Oh, you should see my flagship." She'd been coming up with increasingly outlandish stories about her business and living situation. "Have you ever seen Yofu marble?"

Lawrence sat back, blinking. "I, uh…no, I don't think I have."

"It's gorgeous," Shinigami cooed, letting the fake Russian accent ripple through her voice. "Blue-green, and *so* beautiful. I decided to panel my shower with it, and I liked it so much that I put it in for the floor of my entertaining room."

"You have an entertaining room on your flagship?" Lawrence asked dubiously.

He was sensing that something was wrong. Shinigami covered her tracks by laughing.

"Of course! I'm not an animal." She nudged him with her elbow. "In my circles, a businesswoman *really* needs to make her partners feel special. Deals like ours—well, they don't come up every day, yes? The Yofu marble, I turned into a *very* select market. I've only sold it to a few. The rest are beating down my doors, but only I have the mines."

He was practically drooling as he tried to formulate a plan. "I…see." He seemed to have come to a decision. "I know I could never hope to buy any—you're so clever about that—but could I at least *see* it?" He leaned close. "I don't want to say Gianni has lost his touch, but these drinks aren't as good as they were last time. I can mix a much better martini than this."

"You think so?" Shinigami held her glass up in mock surprise. "I thought this was good!"

"It doesn't hold a candle to what I can make," Lawrence assured her. "Shall we?"

"Okay, just let me finish this one."

"I promise you don't want to drink anything lesser." He reached over to take the glass out of her hand.

Help! Give me some way to stall him!

I'll take their payment systems out for a few minutes, Tafa told her.

Ask him about the woman, Gilwar added. *Play the jealous potential paramour. From what I saw, he is clearly attempting to woo you.*

And I thought I was a buzzkill, Barnabas said drily.

Shinigami suppressed a snort of laughter as she looked at Lawrence gravely. "I would, but... Can I be honest with you?" She leaned forward, touching his arm lightly.

"Of course." He took her hand and played with it.

"It's...well, the woman I saw you with." Shinigami looked away, pretending to be resolute. "It seems as if there was something between you."

"Oh." She saw him consider what to say, then he threw Aliana under the bus with as much sleazy conviction as he could muster: "Aliana was a very valued employee, don't get me wrong. I quite care for her. I like to think of my crew as my family. You understand, I'm sure."

Shinigami nodded. If she spoke, she would tell him exactly what she thought of him, and she couldn't do that just yet.

"Aliana developed feelings for me," Lawrence continued. "Feelings I simply couldn't reciprocate. I had hopes that we could move past it, but she was determined to have a relationship. The whole situation got quite ugly, I'm afraid."

"Oh." Shinigami tried to think of something to say that would keep him talking. What did self-absorbed con-artist humans like to talk about? They tended to keep the *other* person talking.

She was going to have to out-con-artist the con artist.

"So…is there someone special in your life, then?" She gave him a look from under her lashes. "I don't want to misread the signals you've been giving me."

Something in Lawrence's eyes flickered. "And you haven't been. My life hasn't always been conducive to a settled relationship. I am always seeking someone special, however—for whatever life brings." He gave her a smile and kissed her hand again. "I will be right back. I have to settle the check."

Shinigami leaned back in her chair and considered her options as he wandered away. She saw him go to the back, where the manager had gone.

A couple of minutes later she realized what must have happened. Lawrence hadn't come back, but all the managers had.

Shit.

What is it? Barnabas asked.

Unless I'm wrong, Lawrence is on his way right now. Get that ship out of the dock!

CHAPTER SIXTEEN

"See, the thing is," Aliana maneuvered her way around a corner, sweating as she tried to maintain her grip on a trunk of Lawrence's clothes, "he was always so *charming*."

"I know," Ria said glumly. "And he is so good at stringing people along. I talked to the rest of the crew, and he'd been doing it to *all* of us. Everyone! Even John was in love with him by the end."

Aliana gave a snort of laughter, then dropped her end of the trunk. "Wait, what do you mean, 'by the end?'"

"Oh." Ria let her end down carefully and stood up, rubbing her back. She sighed. "He...he fired almost everyone two weeks ago."

"*What?*"

"Yeah, we hadn't gotten a lot of jobs lately." Ria hunched her shoulders. "Honestly, I think it was just too much work for him to keep finding them, you know? He wanted something easier."

"He's always looking for something easier," Aliana said darkly. "So why didn't he fire you?"

"He can't keep the ship flying without me," Ria explained. "He hasn't spent any money on repairs, even the repairs we were saving for when you left, and it's… It's fixable, Aliana, it is, but I need parts to do it."

Aliana groaned and tipped her head back against the wall. "Did he spend all the money, do you think, or was he just hoarding it?"

"I think he spent it all." Ria patted the top of the trunk meaningfully. "Sorry," she added.

"No, it's not…it's not your fault. It's just, why do awful people get to screw up, and nothing you can do will *undo* what they did, you know?" Aliana gave the trunk an annoyed look. "And this is all worthless junk, too. Well, setting it on fire will help me feel better about it, at least."

"Feel better about what?" Barnabas asked, coming around the corner.

Aliana blinked at him. She hadn't heard him approach. She shrugged. "Lawrence cleaned out all the accounts, because of course he did, and now there's no money for all the repairs he didn't do." She shook her head. "We'll make it work. There's always a way to trade labor or something for advance money, you know? And once we've gotten the ship purring like a kitten again, we'll be back to building up those reserves."

"Oh," Barnabas said neutrally. "We found the accounts he switched out of your name. There's still quite a lot of money in there."

"There *is*?" Aliana felt her heart leap. "Oh, thank God. That's amazing. Can you…can you get them back?"

"Banking systems are a bit complicated, but we did manage to transfer the money to new accounts." He gave her a smile. "I'll get that," he added. He picked up the giant trunk with relative ease and carried it off on his own.

The two women stared after him.

"Aliana," Ria said.

"Huh?"

"Those accounts were empty. I'd bet anything."

Aliana looked at her. Deep down, she knew that Ria was right. Lawrence was terrible with money—or, rather, he was very good at spending other people's money. There was no way her carefully-accumulated nest egg was still there.

Which meant that Barnabas had either given her money Lawrence stole, or...

She bit her lip. "I'll pay it all back." It was really the only thing she could do.

"Are you sure he's going to be okay with that?" Ria asked doubtfully. "He did it as a gift."

"Yes, but it's too big a gift," Aliana replied firmly. "He's already helping me get the ship back. I'll just tell him I appreciate it, but—"

"I don't think he'd give you money he couldn't afford to spend," Ria added. "And I bet you that if you ask him about it, he'll swear he doesn't know what you're talking about. Aliana, who *is* this guy?"

"I told you who he was."

"Yeah, I know, but...who *is* he?" Ria shook her head. "I mean, how do you know him? Why's he doing all of this for you?"

"He doesn't like injustice." Aliana marched back into the captain's quarters and loaded her arms with Lawrence's clothes. "So he's righting a wrong he saw. And my uncle asked him to look after me." She rolled her eyes. When Barnabas had said that, she'd wanted to sink through the floor.

Based on how successfully he was embarrassing her, Carter was going to make a spectacular father.

"Uh-huh." Ria didn't sound convinced, but she grabbed an armful of clothes as well and followed Aliana into the hall. "That sounds like it—because your uncle asked."

Aliana was about to tell her that if she kept giving sass, she could kiss her year-end bonus goodbye when they rounded the corner and ran smack into Lawrence.

"What. The hell. Are you doing." His eyes were burning. "You sent some stupid—actor—to distract me, and it nearly worked. You looked *so* hurt when I walked away, but you were just setting me up, weren't you?"

Aliana stared at him wordlessly. Her heart was going double-time now.

She had to think. She had to get him off this ship—

"Get off my ship," Lawrence told her.

"It's my ship," Aliana retorted. She wasn't sure where the confidence came from. Maybe she was pretending to be as self-assured as Barnabas. Whatever it was, she wasn't the slightest bit worried. She looked at Lawrence and wondered why she'd ever been afraid of him.

"It's *not* your ship," Lawrence spat, leaning close with a cruel smile. "You just left it out there for someone to take, and I took it."

"And I," Aliana said, "took it *back*."

He gave her a long look, then he pushed the side of his coat back and pulled out one of his pistols.

Ria gave a tiny strangled noise, and he shot her a hard look. "I know you helped her. Don't you dare try to run!"

Aliana blinked and then, overcome with some sort of reckless certainty, tipped her armful of clothes forward. He reached out automatically to take them and she took the gun out of his hands, dropping the magazine and throwing it over her shoulder whimsically.

"This ship," she said simply, "is in my name. You pulled some technically legal shenanigans in order to steal something that wasn't yours. Now you can try to prove the ship was 'yours,' but I'm going to tell you right now that you won't have much luck."

He stared at her, his arms full of clothes. "What?" he managed finally.

"She means," Ria said, "that you've screwed over so many people that when she says you stole her ship and changed the registration illegally and a bunch of other people come forward to tell the judge what you stole of theirs, no one's going to doubt her. Because you *did* steal it. You married her so you could steal it."

"Yeah, thank you, Ria; that's enough now." Her pride was taking a beating from this. Aliana looked at Lawrence. "So that's where we stand. You thought you could just keep conning people and they'd all run away with their tails between their legs, and you know what? I did." She smiled. "And now I'm back. So *you* get off *my* ship."

He almost growled at her, he looked so angry. "I should have you arrested. I could shoot you for trespassing, you know."

"Oh, I wouldn't do *that*," Barnabas murmured nearby. When all of them jerked around, he gave everyone a careless smile. He was leaning against one wall, arms crossed. "I think you'd find that was a *very* bad plan."

"Oh, yeah?" Lawrence asked. "And why is that? You think you're someone special in that suit?"

As tempting as it was to let the two men posture at one another, Aliana was done letting other people deal with her mess.

"Hey." She grabbed Lawrence by the shoulder and swung him around. "It doesn't matter. What matters is that you're on a ship registered in *my* name and you're pulling guns on *my* crew. Get. Off. My. Ship."

His chest was rising and falling quickly, and she could see the pulse beating far too quickly at his throat. He was *furious*, but he also didn't know what to do. She'd never stood up to him like this before.

She wondered if this was the first time he'd seen someone again after he'd screwed them over.

Aliana had a thought. "And by the way, don't try to find someone else and screw them over."

Ria and Barnabas tilted their heads to the side almost identically.

"You don't get to do that anymore," Aliana said. "You like to make up stories and con your way into people's confidence. If you'd put half of that effort into building your own company you'd have a few ships of your own by now, but you're lazy, and you're cruel. Stop *doing* that. If you do that again, I'll find out, and I'll make sure you give back everything you stole. Make you work off all of the debts you've *ever* acquired. So consider this your one chance. And *get off my ship.*"

He gaped at her for a moment, then looked at the others

with a little laugh. Aliana could see him getting ready to play off the whole incident: *look how crazy she is, overreacting like this.*

But when he saw the looks on their faces, he didn't even try. His mouth compressed to a thin, angry line and he turned and strode off, dropping shirts as he went.

It wasn't the most dignified exit, especially when he ran into the woman with the black hair. He stopped in his tracks for a moment, and she gave him an ironic two-finger salute before strutting up to Aliana and shaking her hand.

"You told him off *good*. I'm...Shannon." She gave Barnabas a look Aliana couldn't interpret.

"Hello," Aliana said nervously. This woman was incredibly beautiful, and something about her just *screamed* "don't fuck with me." "Thank you very much for helping me." She looked around. "Thank you all."

"Well, I, at least, owed you." Ria gave a shrug. "Don't know why the rest of them are here," she added meaningfully, "but I'll be doing a proper inventory, and I'll get back to you about the parts we need, boss."

"Sounds good," Aliana replied. She felt almost giddy as Ria walked away, and then she looked at Barnabas with a sigh. "Okay, okay, I know, he had a gun. It was stupid to just tell him off and throw him out, but—"

"You seemed like you had it under control," Barnabas explained simply. "I would have intervened if I had thought it was necessary, but I didn't." He hesitated for a moment. "How do you feel?"

"On top of the *world*!" Aliana burst out. "I told him off! I did! And he's not going to be a good person overnight, I know that, and maybe he won't ever be, but I told him off and I didn't let him intimidate me and I *meant* it—I'll make him own up to what he did if he's a jerk again."

Barnabas was giving her an almost quizzical smile. "I know. I know you will. Ah…" He cleared his throat and rubbed the back of his head for a moment before smoothing his hair and adjusting his cuffs. "Well, if everything seems to be good here, we'll head out. Tafa. Shannon."

"Oh. Right." Aliana nodded. "Thank you. So much."

He had been walking away, but he turned to give her a smile. He nodded once and headed off, stopping only when Aliana ran after him.

"Wait!"

He turned. "Yes?"

"I just, uh—" She wanted to hug him. She settled for sticking out her hand, but when he reached out to put his in it, still smiling bemusedly, she threw caution to the winds and wrapped her arms around him. He went rigid in surprise for a moment, then the dark-haired woman hissed at him and he hugged Aliana back. She sensed that he wasn't used to being hugged.

"Sorry," she said, flustered. "'Thank you' didn't seem like enough. Not that *hugging* you is enough, but, uh—you know." *Stop talking, you're not making any sense.* She sensed she was blushing. She gave him another nod, then turned and jogged away before she could say anything even more stupid.

Today had been a *very* unexpected day.

CHAPTER SEVENTEEN

Barnabas was still smiling when he made his way into the conference room of the *Shinigami* a few minutes later. He was so pleased by the general state of life, in fact, that it took him a few moments to notice that no one else was talking.

He looked up. Everyone was staring at him.

"What?"

Shinigami swiveled back and forth in her chair. She seemed secretly delighted by something, although Barnabas could not say what it might be.

"How ya *doin'*?" she asked.

"Is that the thing from that show? *Friends*?"

"No, that's 'how *you* doin'?' Totally different."

"Are you sure?" Barnabas asked dubiously. He waved a hand. "I'm doing fine, thank you. Very well, in fact." Everyone seemed to find this hilarious. "What? What is so funny?"

"Oh, nothing." Shinigami smiled. "It's just nice to see you so relaxed. In such a good mood."

"I…thank you." Barnabas stared at her with the growing feeling that this might be a trap of some sort. He sat back in his chair, looking around the room.

"We did some good work today," Gar piped up after a moment. Everyone stifled another laugh.

"What is *with* you?" Barnabas asked, exasperated. "Gar is right—we *did* do good work."

"You know who did good work…" Shinigami prompted.

"Yes, yes." Barnabas rolled his eyes. "I know. You had to deal with the douche. You did very good work."

"Oh, no, I wasn't referring to myself, although you're right, I *did* do fantastic work there. Well, kind of. He spooked and ran back to the ship. Apparently, I'm not a natural at making men think they're interesting."

"Gabrielle is of the opinion that it's quite easy," Barnabas mentioned. "You might want to ask her for pointers. Actually, I regret suggesting that; you're dangerous enough as it is."

"*Anyway*," Shinigami said, "I was *talking* about Aliana. She did some good work today."

"Oh! Yes." Barnabas sat forward, resting his forearms on the table. He nodded decisively. "I thought she showed great personal growth. You know, she ran away when she heard Carter speaking about her, and one could see how much she wanted to buckle and allow others to clean up the mess with Lawrence, but when the chips were down, she really— *Why is everyone laughing?*"

Gar was doubled over, one hand on his stomach, while Tafa stifled her glee behind both hands. Gilwar's tentacles were a swirl of dizzying motion, and Shinigami was shaking her head in mock protest as she giggled.

"Someone," Barnabas growled dangerously, "had better explain what's going on."

"Oh, it's nothing," Shinigami gasped out. "Just that no one's won the bet yet."

"Don't tell him about the bet!" Tafa exclaimed. "That throws it."

"I have to agree," Gilwar cut in.

"*What* bet?" Barnabas demanded.

"How long it would take in this meeting before you actually brought up the reason for it," Shinigami explained. She gave him a look that said she was going to burst out laughing again at any second. "It's been a *long* time for you, and you're still… Oh, what should we call it?" She studied the ceiling in an elaborate act, tapping her mouth with one finger. Then she sat up and looked him dead in the eyes. "*Smitten.*"

Barnabas blinked at her.

Everyone held their breath.

"I beg your pardon?" Barnabas asked finally.

Gar got the look of someone fearing his imminent death, but Shinigami had no such qualms. She grinned impishly.

"Oh, look, you've reverted to excessive politeness. I think we hit home."

"No, I—" Barnabas shook his head. "What are you talking about?"

"Oh, my God," Shinigami exclaimed. "He's serious."

"It's quite common for people to be blind to these

things in their own case," Gilwar weighed in. "Both parties, actually."

"*What are you talking about?*"

"Oh, man." Shinigami rested her head on the table for a moment. "It's like this, dude. You got it bad. Aliana's got it bad. You two got it bad. Do you see where I'm going with this?"

"No. I absolutely do not—*oh.*" Barnabas gave her a look. "No. No. No." He considered. "No," he added one more time for good measure.

"A strong rebuttal."

"No. This is ridiculous." Barnabas looked around the room. "You cannot possibly agree with her? Wait, *do* you?"

Every one of them nodded.

"No!" Barnabas said. "That is entirely—no. We stopped to help her because Carter asked us to look out for her."

"Mmhmm," Tafa murmured.

"Of course," Gilwar chimed in. Both of them sounded completely unconvinced.

"So, whenever you want to be just, you know, *polite* to someone, you help them steal a ship, hack databases to change registration, give them money for new parts for their ship, and then smile like an absolute loon for about half an hour because they hugged you?" Shinigami asked. "That's all because you're so happy that you were able to do a favor for…Carter?"

Barnabas looked at her serenely. "Yes. I'm happy that we righted a wrong *and* that we helped Carter. He'll be very happy to know she's okay. He's been worried sick."

"Right—which is why I'm sure you informed him at

once that we'd run into her." When Barnabas got a panicked look on his face, Shinigami gave a grin. "Gotcha."

"Look, just because I... It isn't as if..." Barnabas tried again. "She's my friend's *niece*," he explained. "It would be entirely inappropriate to, you know, court her."

"The stodgier he gets, the more you know you hit a nerve," Shinigami stage-whispered. "Also, I never thought I'd say this, but you're blushing."

"I am *not* blushing."

"You *definitely* are."

"She's right," Gilwar added.

Barnabas looked at him. "I see you've been taking lessons from the others on how to be a pain in the ass."

"I was already pretty good at it."

Barnabas groaned. "Let's not talk about this right now, shall we? We have business to attend to." It took him a good few seconds to remember what that business *was*, of course... "Shinigami, did you get the message from Kordinev?"

"Yes." Shinigami relented on the subject of torturing him. She brought up the message on the screen. "As you can see, Jotun bots are landing on the surface, and it's unclear if they've infiltrated the government or networks yet. He suspects that they *have* gotten into those."

"That would make sense," Gilwar said easily. "You keep any messages about what's going on from reaching their intended recipients. Word doesn't spread quickly enough, so people don't mobilize fast enough."

"We need to get in there," Barnabas said grimly, "and disrupt *everything* they're doing. I'll see if I can get any details out of Grisor on the way there, although I don't intend to tell him where we're going."

"Good plan," Shinigami replied. "Do you think we should send a message back?"

"No," Barnabas returned at once. "We have to trust that he knows what's going on. Gilwar, do you see any parts of the message that Ferqar might have embedded?"

Gilwar shook his head. "I doubt he would. He wouldn't want to put anything in Jotun in there. They would understand that immediately."

"That makes sense," Barnabas agreed. "Very well. Shinigami, get us to Kordinev. Gilwar, draw up a report on anything we might need to be careful of, as far as you know. And I'm going to—" He decided at the last second not to admit that he was going to send a message to Carter. He searched for something else. "Come up with an interrogation plan for Grisor," he finished.

He left before they could needle him any further about Aliana.

He was not *smitten*.

That would be ridiculous.

CHAPTER EIGHTEEN

Grisor was pacing around the tiny panic pod when Barnabas arrived in the brig. He did not become aware of Barnabas' presence until he turned to pace back toward him, at which point he stopped comically and went completely still.

"Good morning," Barnabas greeted him courteously.

Grisor said nothing.

"I came to check on you," Barnabas continued, "to see what you need. We're not familiar with the requirements for Jotuns. *Do* you need food?"

Grisor looked at him warily. "Will I be staying long enough for that?"

"I have no idea," Barnabas replied. He wandered over to one of the benches and sat down. "For two reasons. First, I have no idea how often you need to eat, or *what* you need to eat—"

"I am sure you could find out that information," Grisor suggested icily.

"I'm sure I could," Barnabas agreed. "But it's really not so much to ask, is it? After all…" He glanced at the panic pod. "It's not as if you have much to do."

There was a long pause.

"What was the second reason?" Grisor asked finally.

"Ah, yes. The *second* reason is that I'm not sure how long you'll be here."

Grisor went entirely still once more. "Is that a threat?"

"I have you locked in a cell aboard my ship," Barnabas pointed out. "I don't need to make threats, Grisor. You're already captured."

"Then why are you *here*?" Grisor spat at him.

"I told you," Barnabas said patiently. "To check on you and see what you needed."

"After leaving me here for days?"

"You seemed well enough on the monitors. Always pacing." Barnabas dug deep for his memories of various bored aristocrats over the eons and waved one hand to indicate the pacing. "What do you *do* all day?"

He didn't need to read Grisor's mind. He was fairly sure he could feel the absolute hatred radiating out of the tank.

All he needed now was to make Grisor think of the things Barnabas wanted to know. He had notorious trouble sifting through the memories of Jotuns. If they were thinking of the thing in question, however, he had fairly good luck interpreting their thoughts.

The process was somewhat like wading through grape jelly.

"Well, if you don't want to talk or tell me what I need to know, I can leave." Barnabas stood and adjusted his cuffs.

"Just don't think you can waste away and die tragically to fuel your little...what was it? What was the plan? Oh, yes. Take over the whole sector." He allowed himself a chuckle as he turned to leave.

"You have no idea," Grisor snapped hatefully, "who you're playing with, do you?"

Barnabas turned back. He could see visions in Grisor's head, but so far they were only visions of what Grisor wanted: armies trampling over fields, fleets darkening the skies, slaves bowed by their labor, and riches flowing to the Committee.

Amazing how little war changed over the years. Barnabas shook his head wearily.

Then, curiously, he decided to be honest.

"Do you have any idea how predictable you are?" he asked the Jotun. He strolled forward. "How long do Jotuns live?"

"Fifty cycles," Grisor said. "Give or take."

Same lifespan as a standard human at the turn of the twentieth century, Shinigami translated promptly.

Thank you, Shinigami. To Grisor, Barnabas said, "Do you know how long I've been alive? Over ten times that long, *Excellency.*" He let the title slide off his tongue like an insult. "Do you know how many of you I've seen over the years?"

Grisor said nothing, but he radiated wary surprise.

"*So* many." Barnabas sighed wearily. "And you're all the same. You dress it up in all different ways. Some of you are priests. Some of you are noble-born. Some of you are warriors. Some of them are even honest about what they want. That's refreshing in a depressing sort of way. It just gets so tiresome, how you keep cropping up." He paced around the pod, narrowing his eyes into it.

Grisor turned warily to watch him.

"I should have known when I came here that I'd only find more of the same," Barnabas continued. "I suppose I had some grand vision that we'd stamp it all out; that one day we'd be done with this boring, inane, ridiculous bullshit. And that's never going to happen, is it, Grisor? Because ten, twenty, thirty cycles on—maybe fifty, maybe a hundred—there will be another one like you. Just one more in a long line who will kill a bunch of people because they can, and eventually die in misery like all the rest of them."

He had shocked the Jotun, he could tell. There was a certain satisfaction in that.

"You have never," Grisor said finally, "seen anyone like me. I alone can bring the Jotuns to ascendancy."

"Oh, *please*. I've heard this speech a dozen times, and that's just in person. You're the *only* one who can achieve *whatever goal*, which is why you *have* to enslave a bunch of people—or torture them or kill them—for the glory of that wonderful *thing* you're trying to achieve."

"You think to judge me by the speeches of lesser *species*?" Grisor spat at him. "You have never met anyone like the Jotuns. You cannot comprehend the feats we are capable of."

Barnabas began to laugh. It was ridiculous. He had seen things Grisor could not understand. He had seen the effects of the Kurtherian war that had spanned sectors and millennia.

None of that mattered, however. It wasn't the point. None of what Grisor said was the point.

"You don't actually care, Grisor—admit it." He was grinning now. "You just want to rule the universe, don't you? You had a nice, convenient excuse with all of that business about the Jotuns being superior to everyone else—your words, not mine. You're jellyfish in metal suits. It's impressive, but not planet-shattering. But if you hadn't had that to believe, you'd just have come up with some other reason." Barnabas shrugged. "Maybe it wouldn't have been you, in that case. Maybe you'd have lived out your life in obscurity on some little backwater Jotun planet while another Jotun or a Torcellan or a Brakalon played all of this out. Who can say? There's always one of you, though."

"The Brakalons." Grisor seized on that as Barnabas had hoped he would. "Stupid, lumbering oafs. So concerned with their rules and their procedures. They could never take over the sector."

"You'd be surprised. It's the ones you don't expect who get the farthest." Barnabas inspected his nails. "Funny business, demagogues. Of course, they're not always demagogues. Sometimes they're just dictators. You seem to be going for both."

Being made to feel insignificant and uncreative, it seemed, was the key to getting under Grisor's skin, and he was going to milk that for all it was worth.

"For all you know," Barnabas went on carelessly, "the Brakalons will be your downfall. It could happen. You'll try to extend too far, and the next thing you know, it's Hitler and Poland all over again."

"What?"

"Nothing." Barnabas reveled in the stream of images he was receiving out of Grisor's mind: the names of Brakalon generals, parts of the defense network, ways to herd the soldiers onto ships for deployment—

He turned and made for the door, whistling.

"Wait!" Grisor slammed his mechanical hands against the wall of the pod. "Where are you going?"

Barnabas turned to look at him. "I told you, you bore me. I've heard all this before, Grisor, and I'll hear it a bunch more times after *you're* dead and gone, I'm sure. You're all the same."

He left with Grisor's shouts ringing in his ears.

Shinigami.

Yello.

That is a ridiculous colloquialism.

Man, you're still *stodgy. She's got you good, that one.*

We are not *talking about this right now. For one thing, I have the names of several generals the Committee intends to target. They've started receiving data from Kordinev, and they are in the message networks.* He turned a corner and took the stairs two at a time. *They've intercepted several attempts to get word off-planet. We're lucky that Kelnamon was clever enough to reach us, and God only knows how many tries it took.*

He considered as he walked.

I think they're speeding the timeline up, he said finally. *Their plan relied on the fact that no one knew what they were doing, and that no one would even think to look for it. Now they don't have the setup they want, but even if they go with ninety percent, they could still be dangerous.*

Agreed.

The best thing we can do, I think, is keep knocking the legs out from under them as they get things set up. We need to figure out what their plan is on Kordinev and head it off at the pass so that even if they have a fleet to use, God forbid, they aren't able to make use of anything on the ground.

I'll start assessing known data, Shinigami told him gravely. The teasing was gone from her voice. *Barnabas—you meant what you said, right?*

About what? Barnabas paused, looking up curiously at the cameras.

Shinigami projected herself in front of him, though she kept her discussion silent as she looked at him gravely. She was wearing her armor in the projection, perhaps to feel safer. *You said you'd still be hearing this speech from other people long after Grisor was gone. You think we're going to win, right?*

Of course, I think we're going to win. Barnabas smiled. *They always lose in the end, Shinigami. Sometimes it takes a lot longer than we want it to, but they always lose in the end. I promise, Grisor isn't going to win this one.*

Good, she said with feeling. Her humor returned as she added, *By the way, he's still yelling for you to come back. You got under his skin.*

Barnabas snickered. *Let's let him stew for a while, then.*

Agreed. Shinigami nodded and disappeared.

Barnabas whistled as he made his way back to his rooms. He definitely did not spend any time looking in the mirror once there, trying to imagine how someone new might see him after all these years. He was used to checking for dirt or stray threads on his clothing, not examining his features, but if someone were to meet him for the first time—

This was ridiculous. He went back out into the main room and resolutely opened his book. He was going to read about submarines. He was *not* going to think about Aliana.

Definitely not.

CHAPTER NINETEEN

A scattering of gunfire came from around the corner and Kelnamon grimaced in frustration. They had to get the government officials out of these bunkers. There was no telling what was being done to them while they were in there, and the knowledge they had could compromise the entire Brakalon infrastructure and population if it were tortured out of them.

He did not even want to think of the damage they could do as double agents, even unwilling ones, if they believed their families were held hostage.

Jotun turrets now surrounded all of the government buildings, and they had laser-targeting and almost instantaneous firing capabilities. There was no element of surprise when it came to them; one couldn't burst out of cover and elude them.

Under any normal circumstances, Kelnamon would have ordered everyone to retreat. He knew they were going to take heavy losses as they pushed forward. Everyone knew it, and the fear was plain on their faces.

Even Ferqar moved hesitantly in his biosuit and had been subdued lately.

Kelnamon was grateful for Ferqar's help. Ferqar had shown that when a member of his own species, even a highly respected one, was doing something sadistic and immoral, he would stop them. Still, it was one thing to carry out vigilante justice on a single Naval captain, and quite another thing to be fighting a larger Jotun initiative.

Kelnamon had broached the subject with him some days ago. He did not want to take the chance of Ferqar having a crisis of conscience in the middle of a battle, so the discussion needed to be had.

"Have you considered that this might be a government initiative?" he had asked Ferqar. "That you might have orders, if you were on your ship, to come take over Kordinev?"

Ferqar had become slightly agitated, but Kelnamon was beginning to know him well enough to see that he wasn't surprised by the question. He had thought about it.

"I wondered that," he admitted. "We knew Huword was involved in something big. What if the Senate really was planning something like this? Or…I hate to say it, but what if the Navy was? I can't see Admiral Jeqwar doing something like that, but it's possible, isn't it?"

Kelnamon didn't know what to say to that. He'd always found the Jotuns insufferable, absolutely sure they were better than everyone else. He didn't think it was in any way unlikely that their government would order another species subjugated.

Ferqar gave a mechanical sigh. Enough species had such mannerisms that the Jotuns had programmed similar sounds into their biosuits. "It doesn't matter," he said at last. "Whether this is some rogue faction or the whole government, it isn't right. The Brakalons haven't been our enemies; they haven't threatened us. I can't justify taking over Kordinev, even if the whole government is in agreement."

"You know you'll be branded a traitor," Kelnamon told him. "You aren't just failing to go along with it, you're actively fighting them."

This thought seemed to amuse Ferqar. "Everyone is being called a traitor these days," he said between mechanical chuckles. "The word is beginning to lose all meaning. Anyway, I am in good company."

"Well enough," Kelnamon replied cautiously. "I just wanted to check before you wound up fighting your own kind."

"I am hoping we can stop it before it gets there," Ferqar explained seriously. "Freeing your government would be a good first step. Then we can mobilize more effectively."

They had proceeded to do what they could, rounding up as many military personnel as they could find without going through the message networks, outfitting them in secret, and preparing an assault on the government buildings where the bureaucrats and officers were imprisoned.

It was amazing how resourceful they had been. People used any number of ingenious methods to spread the word throughout the capital city and out into the surrounding areas. Someone had offered a factory building as a base of operations, and weapons had been delivered to their makeshift headquarters, hidden under bushels of produce or wrapped in bolts of cloth.

Brakalons showed up in droves. They might not be military-trained, but they were ready to fight and die for their people.

The problem was, many of them *were* going to die. Even trained soldiers would have a hard time against the defenses the Jotuns had set up. Kelnamon clutched his weapon and tried to find the courage within himself to order an attack.

"You must do it," Ferqar told him. The Jotun had come to kneel next to him in the dust of the street. He had a gun as well since the rifles embedded in his suit's arms had run out of the specific ammunition they needed. His biosuit was battered and dented now.

"I know," Kelnamon told him. "But I don't want to give the order that kills them. They are civilians."

"More will die if we do not do this," Ferqar told him. "You know that. There will be a rebellion soon, and it will be bloody. Better it be now, before my people have landed infantry. Or…" His voice trailed off.

"What?"

"I have been wondering," Ferqar said quietly, "if they want to turn the Brakalons into their mercenaries? Press all of you into servitude."

"We would not fight for them," Kelnamon argued.

"How can you say for certain what you would or would not do? They may have ways to compel you." Ferqar shook his head. "But all of this is speculation. Better we go now, and—"

The gunfire came again, closer this time.

Much closer.

With an oath, Kelnamon looked around the corner—

and gasped in horror. The Jotun turrets were *advancing*. He had thought they were fixed, but they had extended spidery legs and were creeping down the city streets toward the attacking force.

"They're advancing!" he called back along the line. They'd been trying to keep quiet, but there was no benefit to stealth if it got them all wiped out. "Everybody run. Regroup two streets back!"

Their guerrilla force burst into motion and fled along the streets, some of the less fortunate dodging blasts from the turrets—which, sensing motion, had begun moving more quickly. Beside Kelnamon, a civilian stumbled and fell. He hauled the male up and kept moving, but a moment later another shot took the limping Brakalon in the head.

"Kelnamon!" Ferqar sounded horrified. "They're running; they're too fast!"

"Scatter!" Kelnamon yelled to the resistance fighters. "Confuse the targeting systems!"

He realized too late that he'd made a terrible mistake. With such quick targeting, the turrets could easily track multiple moving targets—and they did.

He knew what he needed to do. With a roar, Kelnamon charged back toward the line of turrets. They seemed to be either remotely controlled or possessing some basic intelligence. If he made himself a more dangerous target than his fighters…

"Kelnamon!" Ferqar yelled. "Stop! Don't!"

But there wasn't any other choice. Kelnamon knew that if he didn't do this, none of the other fighters were going to get to safety. Just like he had out in the brush, he grabbed one of the turrets and hurled it to smash against a wall.

The other turrets, sensing this new threat, abandoned the chase and swiveled to face him.

The turrets *did* seem to have prohibitions against shooting one another. That was interesting, and it gave him an edge. He grabbed another and bellowed in pain when it shot directly at him, catching him in the arm. He used it to bludgeon another—

Three shots hit him at once, and his whole world turned blood-red. He staggered, falling to his knees. He could hear Ferqar yelling something, but he didn't understand. A turret was advancing on him, and its laser sights gleamed like a baleful red eye. Kelnamon looked up at it and had the vague thought that this wasn't how he'd thought things were going to end for him. He'd made it through so much, escaped the Jotun death squad, and now, so suddenly, it was all going to be over.

Which was when the turret exploded. The rest of the turrets swiveled, trying to find the source of the new threat, but one by one, they were picked off.

"*GERONIMOOOOOOO!*" yelled a vaguely familiar voice.

Kelnamon heaved himself to his feet. He wasn't sure what "Geronimo" meant, but he knew a battle cry when he heard one. Someone was here, and they were clearly on his side. He must have lost a good deal of blood, though, because the world spun crazily around him and the next thing he knew, he was on the ground again. He couldn't feel his hands.

Then the human's face swung into his field of vision, blue eyes worried and black armor already streaked with reddish dust.

"Captain Kelnamon?" Barnabas asked. Behind him, Kelnamon could see a dark-haired woman gleefully pulling a turret apart. "Captain Kelnamon, stay with me!"

Kelnamon tried to speak and he tried to hold onto consciousness, but it was no use.

The world went dark.

CHAPTER TWENTY

Kelnamon lay in the Pod-doc, its dimensions almost outmatched by his brawny form. His vital signs had been failing fast by the time they got him to the ship, but the technology in the Pod-doc was unmatched and they had caught him before his life had faded from his body.

He was slowly but steadily improving. It had been the better part of an hour, and he was almost ready to be woken up.

Shinigami came to stand beside Barnabas, who was staring at the smooth white exterior of the Pod-doc. She linked her hands behind her back and looked at him.

"The rest of the mission was simple enough. The Jotuns had gotten into the building controls, as you would guess, so when the government officials tried to leave, they found out they couldn't. We only had to override that, and they were able to get out. Ferqar is briefing them now, but it looks like a couple of them are missing."

Barnabas looked at her worriedly.

"I know." Shinigami shook her head. "I don't know if

they managed to land any equipment to convert them yet. I'm guessing they haven't—that our attack on Grisor's compound interrupted that."

"They had a good plan," Barnabas mused, "but it hinged on secrecy. All of it hinged on people not finding out and not being able to organize until the military leaders and bureaucrats were already converted. Now, as with Jeltor, the rest of them will know not to trust them."

"There is that," Shinigami replied, "but it's not so simple. What's been going on here is still known only to a few people. There are huge parts of Kordinev that are still unaware anything was wrong—and the people who were taken were knowledgeable about the defense networks and some of the remote colonies."

Barnabas looked at her sharply.

"Even if it isn't something they do gracefully and secretly, they could still pull it off," she told him bluntly. "If they showed up today, they'd probably have enough information to march in and take over. They wanted to rule everyone with conversion, but they could do it the old-fashioned way for a while and convert people later."

Barnabas dropped his head into his hands.

This was a nightmare. The Committee had sat in the shadows for years, gathering its strength, and now, even being forced into the open before it was ready, it was still dangerous. It was a viper, he thought, lashing out at anyone who dared challenge it.

They had struck at the Jotun Navy and at Kordinev so quickly. They were taking advantage of the fact that the Navy and the Senate did not trust one another. They thrived on brokenness and mistrust, and even if they failed, they would take hundreds of innocent lives with them when they went.

Rage was burning in his chest.

"Barnabas?" Shinigami sounded worried.

"I should have burned the whole thing to the ground," Barnabas whispered. "I went to the Senate and told them to clean up their act, and I should have just locked them in there and dragged out every one of their secrets until we found out about this. If I hadn't been so concerned about—"

"*Don't* doubt yourself. You did the best you could."

"It wasn't enough!"

"So what? You're *not* going to do the best you can?" Shinigami threw up her hands. "Listen to yourself. You're not sloppy, Barnabas, and you're not vengeful. You're also not omniscient. You can't punish people *before* they've done anything wrong. That's Justice. It happens *after* something's gone wrong, and yeah, it sucks, but it's just how things are."

"They're going to kill people," Barnabas argued. "How many of that force Kelnamon organized did they lose?"

She hesitated. "Twenty-two," she said finally.

"And in the laboratories?"

"You're not doing yourself any good," she warned him. "You came here as soon as you knew something was wrong. You've been tracking the Committee, finding out all their secrets. What more could you have done? Not as some omniscient god, but as *you*? As a human being, Barnabas. What more could you have done?"

"I could have tortured Grisor until he told me everything," Barnabas ground out. "I could have bombed that facility to the ground instead of trying to protect Jeltor. How much time did I waste going back to get him out alive?"

"Barnabas." Shinigami wrapped her arms around herself and sighed. She was looking at the Pod-doc, but her eyes were focused somewhere far away. "If you get to the end of this and you've sacrificed every principle you hold dear and every friend you had, what's the point?"

"It's just a few people," Barnabas replied quietly. "Just us. If we do good things and take evil out of the world, will it really matter if we're dead—or if our consciences are stained?"

"You know philosophy has no answer to that," Shinigami told him. "You could argue it either way, couldn't you? The ends justify the means…or the means are equally important, if not more so. You have to choose which way you want to go." She gave him a hard look. "And in the time we've spent together, while we've been becoming friends, you've valued moral means. That's the man I want to work with. If you decide you want to go rogue and kill, torture, and sacrifice the people you care about? Well, I can't stop you, but you'll be doing it on your own."

Barnabas gave her a smile and looped an arm around her shoulders. "Thank you," he told her. "Perhaps it was foolish, but when I see that I have failed—"

"Nope." Shinigami cut him off with a shake of her head. "Don't go down that road. You can't save everyone. You'll go mad if you try. Do the best you can, and let that be enough."

Barnabas nodded, and both of them turned to the Pod-doc as it began to open. Its top tilted up and came, at last, to a stop. There was only the faintest whir of sound from the machine; it ran as smooth as silk, its workings hidden under the shiny exterior.

Kelnamon sat bolt upright a moment later, having woken suddenly. He was searching for a weapon, Barnabas could tell, then realized roughly where he was the next moment.

He looked at Barnabas suspiciously. "I did not think I would wake again, but I feel better than I ever have. Is this real?"

"Very real," Barnabas assured him.

Shinigami stepped forward to offer him a hand out of the Pod-doc, her cybernetic body not trembling when Kelnamon's weight rested on her briefly. He stretched and gave a wide yawn.

"I should get one of those," he said. Then he looked around the room. "The others... If you saved me, surely you could save them."

There was no easy way to tell him the truth. "My friend, I am afraid we could not," Barnabas said quietly. "You were still alive when we got you to the ship. The others had already passed on. Their injuries were too severe."

Kelnamon stood silently for a long moment. "I led them to their deaths," he said.

Shinigami gave a loud sigh. "Will everyone in this room stop being self-indulgent for a moment? Actually, for a damned long while. We have a lot still to do, and the universe can't afford to have everyone tying themselves in knots about their perfectly reasonable decisions. Look, I'm immortal. I *promise* when this is over, I will sit with you two for as many beers as it takes for you to get all the bitching out of your systems. Okay? Okay. Good. Now let's go do something useful."

Kelnamon looked like a massive deer in headlights. Barnabas laughed.

"I've found she's generally right about these things," he told the Brakalon. "Let's go speak about what needs to be done. Most of the military and government officials have been freed, and we'll need to get moving as quickly as possible to get the rest back and possibly quarantined."

He led Kelnamon to the conference room, where the Brakalon squinted at Gilwar. "Ferqar?" he asked dubiously. "Did you get a new suit?"

"I am not Ferqar," Gilwar told him. If he was annoyed, it did not show in his voice. "My name is Gilwar. I am presently assisting Barnabas. May I mention, your decision to attack the turrets directly was quite brave and saved countless lives?"

It was the right thing to say. Kelnamon's shoulders settled a bit, and he gave a nod.

"Ferqar is on the surface," Barnabas told him, taking a seat. "He is sending us reports as he gets the time. In the meantime, why don't you tell us everything you know?"

Kelnamon sat as well, taking a stool that would accommodate his much larger body.

"It began a week ago or so."

Their weeks are about the same as ours, Shinigami told Barnabas privately.

Thank you.

"Ferqar and I were out walking in the barrens beyond the city when we saw something fall, so we went over to see what it was. Ferqar said it was a Jotun device of some kind, and it shot at us. We managed to deactivate it, only for it to trigger a self-destruct. When we got back to the city, we alerted the military and bureaucrats.

"We heard nothing back." He shook his head grimly. "I suspected at once that the Jotuns had gotten into our networks and were blocking messages. It took me two tries to get anything off-planet to you.

"Not only that, they had used an obscure protocol to make the officials relocate to those buildings you stormed with us. The protocol is to keep them safe if Kordinev is under attack." From his tone, it was clear that the irony was not lost on him. "We created a fighting force by passing messages any way we could that wasn't on the networks. People sent weapons and came to help."

"You couldn't get the Army?" Shinigami asked.

"No. The Army is always housed at bases well outside any of the cities. There was an…incident. It was far in our past, but we have never allowed our Army to be near government buildings since then."

"Ah." Barnabas gave a wry smile. "It's a lovely idea, that one, until someone simply goes against it."

"Julius Caesar?" Shinigami asked him.

"That's the one." Barnabas frowned. "I wonder—do those bases have easy access to ports so that the soldiers could be transferred to carriers?"

Kelnamon looked horrified. "Yes."

Barnabas shook his head wearily. "I'd be willing to bet anything that the officials still missing can give the orders, and that no one on those bases is aware of the problems."

"Same," Shinigami agreed promptly. "They're hoping to

get the troops off-planet before anyone realizes what's going on and hold their families hostage for their good behavior."

"Ferqar said the same." Kelnamon pushed himself up to pace. "I can't believe this. It can't be happening."

"It *is* happening," Shinigami said. "So you should definitely believe it." She leaned back in her chair, pushed a little too far, and didn't have the instinctive reflexes to recover. There was the much-too-loud thud of a heavy cybernetic body hitting the floor.

Kelnamon watched quizzically, and the rest smothered their laughs.

Anyone who laughed at Shinigami had to spar with her. That was the rule, and even Barnabas was beginning to get wary of doing so.

"What do we do?" Kelnamon asked Barnabas. "Whatever we destroy to get our officials out, we then can't use against the Jotuns when they arrive. It's a nightmare. They'll have us bombing our own infrastructure."

"It's amazing," Barnabas said philosophically, "how much damage you can do if you just behave like a total sociopath. Realistically speaking, the Committee can't be more than twenty people. Even with their whole team of scientists and guards, it's probably under five hundred. And yet, here we are."

"So what's your plan?" Shinigami asked.

"We've infiltrated government buildings before," Barnabas said. "This will be not so much a smash-and-grab job as a don't-smash-but-do-grab job. We get in there, get the hostages, and get out. On the other hand, I'm seriously considering having you bomb every one of the launch pads at the bases."

Kelnamon made no protest, only considered this. "How long would it take you?"

"About an hour," Shinigami said. "Assuming I've found all of your bases, which I think I have."

Kelnamon groaned. "We're going to have to reset our entire defense infrastructure when this is over," he said, frustrated. "But that's not important. Hold off for now. We'll do it if we have to."

Shinigami nodded.

"Everyone get ready," Barnabas told the team. "And come up with some way to use Grisor better than we have been."

"We'll see what we can do," Shinigami replied.

The team left to get their armor on, and Barnabas gave Kelnamon a nod. "We'll nip this in the bud," he told the Brakalon.

Kelnamon nodded, but he didn't look convinced.

CHAPTER TWENTY-ONE

Qarwit stood in the center of Grisor's ruined office and stared at the portrait of the former occupant on the wall. Grisor did not come from a distinguished family amongst the Jotuns, but he managed to convey the same stern air of authority as the old noble lines did in their portraits.

"Excellency." One of the soldiers stood in the doorway, head bent to show deference. "We have acquired the target and are preparing to convert him."

"Do it as quickly as you can," Qarwit directed. He considered, then added, "Better we take the chance of breaking him entirely than they suspect what we've done."

It was true. On the heels of complication after complication, loss after loss, Qarwit had launched a desperate gambit. What could not be achieved by one means would be achieved by another. They had been thwarted, but he swore they would not be defeated. So help him, they would reach Kordinev with the Jotun fleet, and they would do it soon.

Before anyone could mobilize to stop them.

They should already have been there, of course, to convert the captured Brakalons. He could only hope that they arrived in time to do so now that Jeltor had failed to entrap the admiral.

"No further orders," he told the soldier.

The soldier nodded and left, and Qarwit returned to his study of the portrait.

"What would you do?" he asked Grisor's picture. He began to pace. "I am as devoted to the cause as you are, Excellency, but I do not have your skill. I do not have your connections."

Whatever orders Grisor had given in the event of his death, Qarwit had been immediately installed as the leader of the Committee after Grisor's abduction. Some of the other senators had made snide comments, but the soldiers and scientists had not even commented on the change. Suddenly, Qarwit was "Excellency," and they deferred to his judgment in all things.

The other senators did not quite dare to push their luck.

Qarwit had the sense that he should be grateful for this change. After all, unlike many in the Committee, he truly believed in its mission. He knew that many of the others simply wanted to have power, while some sought riches and many just wanted to be a part of something secretive.

There were not many, it turned out, who truly had the clarity of vision Grisor'd had.

Qarwit should feel pleased and proud to be overseeing this critical stage of the Committee's plan. Things had begun to unravel when Huword was killed. Their plans had come into the light far earlier than they wanted, and they had to move now, before they were ready. But it was still possible to triumph, and the leader who did so would be remembered throughout the ages.

Qarwit, however, did not want to lead. He had not only believed in the mission of the Committee, but he had also believed in Grisor. He had watched Grisor's speeches for years, picking up on the subtleties other senators missed. He had noticed who Grisor's mentor had been.

He was not pleased to be taking Grisor's place, not when the former leader was likely being tortured somewhere—or was already dead, having been killed out of hand by a human who operated outside the law.

Vigilante. Qarwit shuddered with disgust. Other species produced such chaos. They sent people like this human all over the universe, enacting some warped vision of justice, when anyone with sense could see that calm, steady leadership was best for the universe.

Humans, he had learned, highly valued free will. They were quite fanatical about it, in fact. Even when their choices caused them hardship and pain, they clung to the concept. If they would simply surrender some of their free will, they would be like Jeltor: calm, certain of their place in the universe, and equally certain of their purpose.

It was a good life, being sure of such things. *Not* being sure about them caused such pain. Why could they not see that?

Screams echoed down the hallway and Qarwit turned to look. It seemed that the soldiers and scientists were obeying his command, and were converting their new target with as much speed as possible.

He might break, it was true, but it was no loss to them if he did. And if he did not, if he was able to be converted and put back on Jotuna quickly enough, they might be able to use him to acquire a far greater prize.

In the meantime, there was work to do. Qarwit gave one last look at the portrait. "I will do everything I can to build the universe you wanted," he told Grisor. "I would rather you were here, but I will not shirk my duty."

In the main control room, he nodded to each of the deputies in turn.

"Tell me the status of our projects."

"We have four machines ready to send to Kordinev," one of the scientists reported. "The original research team had trouble converting Brakalons, but we think we can see some of the places they went wrong, and we are confident we will be able to convert the necessary personnel quickly as soon as we arrive."

"If they're still in our possession," Qarwit said tightly. He looked at one of the generals. "Where do we stand after the attack?"

"We don't know," the general admitted. "We do know that our defensive networks were readying for an attack, but we have not been able to verify if the attack occurred, if it was successful, or who attacked."

Qarwit ruffled himself in confusion.

"There should not have been any military personnel stationed in the city," the general explained. "And no one should have known that the officials were trapped in those facilities. We kept any message suggesting such a thing from reaching its target. In order to attack, they would have needed to do so entirely outside any networks, and without their military. Or perhaps an outside force intervened."

Qarwit could think of one such outside force, and it was enough to make his blood pressure rise.

"No one should have been able to get word off-planet," he ground out.

"No," the general agreed, "but it is possible..." His voice trailed off and he gathered his courage. "It is possible that Grisor told the humans where we were planning to attack."

Qarwit shook with rage. "Grisor would *never* betray us," he spat. "Never."

"You should consider the possibility." It was the same scientist who had admitted the loss of the devices to Grisor. Qarwit remembered her. "Jeltor was also strong-willed and principled."

"His principles were—"

"Wrong, but he held to them strongly." She was undaunted. "We do not know what sort of torture the humans have at their disposal. After enough torture, anyone could break."

Qarwit thought this over. Every part of him was furious at the idea of calling Grisor a traitor, and yet he had to admit that this scientist might be correct.

If Grisor had betrayed them...

A plan was taking shape in his head, but he needed more information.

"Why do we not know how the attack went?" he asked.

The general looked at the scientist before answering him. "Our communications stream from Kordinev was interrupted before the attack began. We are not certain why. They apparently know our frequencies, however, and have blocked them."

"They clearly realized something was wrong," Qarwit said, half to himself. "And they were trying to stop us from knowing what was going on. The question, of course, is who 'they' are. It is possible that the personnel were able to shut something down from inside their bunkers."

He considered further and came to a decision.

"We will proceed with the plan," he ordered. "But we will be prepared to use alternate methods of persuasion. Plan for several strike teams to accompany our first landing force. These teams will find and capture the families of the officials we need. If their cooperation cannot be obtained via conversion, we will use their families to ensure it. And the first thing we will ask of them will be that they go into the conversion chambers."

The others nodded, pleased by this plan.

Qarwit could hear the mutters of the other senators in the background, and he turned to give them a long look. They shut up, although they glared at him.

"Do you have any suggestions?" he asked. He forced himself not to snap at them. They might not believe in the mission of the Committee, but they could still be useful—and they would be more likely to support this initiative if they felt they'd had a hand in planning it.

They shook their heads.

Qarwit was beginning to understand why Grisor had

been planning a round of assassinations. He turned back to the desk and considered what was in front of him.

"Make sure everything is ready," he said finally. "For the return to Jotuna, for the strike teams, and for the equipment. We will need to move quickly. Whatever is happening on Kordinev, we must get there as quickly as we can."

They nodded and left, and Qarwit went to one of the windows to look out.

So much of this operation had not gone as planned. Jeltor's conversion, which should have been smooth and seamless and given them early entry into the top brass, had been sabotaged. Huword's death had touched off meddling from the humans and exposed the Committee—and they, already involved in Jotun politics because of the debacle with the Yennai Corporation, had not simply walked away as they should have.

It was a nightmare. It would be easy to say that there was no way for them to win at this point.

But he refused to give up. He was here because he truly believed that the Jotuns were superior and that a world ruled by his kind—with peace enforced by conversion—would be better in all ways.

For everyone.

He would make this work.

Another idea came to him as he went to leave the room, and he turned. "Send Captain Jeltor as well," he said. "We all know that the human may be there, and he's shown himself to be weak where Jeltor is concerned."

The general gave a decisive nod. "Not to mention," he added, "that Jeltor has been aboard the human ship and knows some of the human's weaknesses. He will be a valuable asset to our strike teams."

Qarwit nodded. Jeltor had failed to bring them the admiral, but he could still be of use. The key to being a leader was to be adaptable, after all—and never to forget the weapons one had at hand.

CHAPTER TWENTY-TWO

Barnabas was impressed when they arrived on the surface of Kordinev. Not only had the Brakalons been efficient in freeing their leaders and planning a rescue operation, but they had also worked closely with Ferqar to determine any salient details about Jotun technology.

The Brakalons who had died in the rescue attempt were laid out under shrouds in one of the Brakalon temples, being overseen by several priests. Although Barnabas was not familiar with any part of Brakalon religion, some things transcended religion or species—and an elegy was one of them. The pure, raw sound of it made the hair on his arms stand on end, and he paused to say a silent prayer of respect before following Kelnamon into the makeshift headquarters of the resistance.

"General Vidrelor," Kelnamon said respectfully. "This is Barnabas, the human who helped—"

"I'm aware of his exploits," Vidrelor interrupted. Tall and stone-gray, he had an unmistakable set of scars and walked with the faint asymmetry of someone who had sustained injuries and long ago learned to live with them. His grip, when he shook Barnabas' hand, was warm and certain, and he made sure not to crush Barnabas' fingers. "I've read up on you," he explained to Barnabas. "Whenever someone shows up in the sector and starts wreaking havoc, it's good to know more about them. I've read a lot about your Etheric Empire—and about you, although some of it is clearly a load of horseshit. Did you know that some of the writing on you says you were a cleric once?"

"Er." Barnabas took his hand back and gave a polite smile. "Well, you can't believe *everything* you read, I suppose." The truth seemed too complicated in this case. "Rest assured, I hope to work *with* the Brakalons in this case, not on my own. I hope to work with the Jotuns, too," he added.

There was a pause as not only Vidrelor but also everyone else gave him a wary look.

"Not with the faction that is trying to conquer Kordinev, I assure you," Barnabas continued, "but with the portion of society that respects the rule of law, and which will oversee justice proceedings against this rogue faction."

"Heh." Vidrelor's snort was contemptuous. "You'll be disappointed, human. You have too much faith. I think perhaps your species has not spent long enough among others. When the crimes are against a different race, the society will excuse anything."

"That's one possibility." Barnabas refused to worry about that right now. "But we have more to deal with than that right now. Who is it we need to rescue?"

"General Fedranor," the general said promptly.

"And the Senate Majority and Minority Leaders," added Ferqar patiently.

General Vidrelor snorted again.

Ferqar was undaunted. "All three of them are valuable targets with a great deal of knowledge and power. The general can order troop mobilization, but the other two have knowledge of many classified things, and also of many aspects of Brakalon infrastructure that would be *very* useful for the Jotuns to know." He paused. "Is there something we can call this group other than the Jotuns? It's a bit awkward."

"They're the Infrastructure Revitalization Committee," Barnabas explained absently. "Apparently, their idea of infrastructure revitalization is to take over *other* planets' infrastructure and use their populations as slave labor." He considered. "That, or they just picked the most boring name they could in the hopes that no one would pay attention to them."

Everyone nodded in agreement.

"Very well," Ferqar agreed. "The Committee, then. Now, Brakalon protocol, if I understand it correctly, was that the highest-ranking military and political officials would relocate to a series of bunkers like this one. The top echelon would be removed to even more remote and secure locations."

"Interrupting for a moment," Barnabas interjected. "We're sure the Jotuns are not still in the system, right?"

"Very sure," Shinigami replied. "I found an old backup, wiped the entire system, and reinstalled. I was able to isolate the pieces that had been changed. From the programs I found on the turrets, I think they were dual-purpose. They likely started landing more than a week ago and made their way into the cities, embedding programming into everything they could find."

"And who are you?" General Vidrelor asked her dubiously.

"I'm Shinigami," she said, giving him Bethany Anne's patented "bureaucracy sucks" smile. "I'm not human."

She didn't elaborate further.

"Right," Barnabas said before anyone could ask more questions. He knew Shinigami well enough to know she would give accurate answers in the most unsettling way she could. "So, where are these people?"

"General Fedranor is in this facility, about fifty-five *jilwa* outside the city."

A jilwet is about five kilometers, Shinigami translated before Barnabas could ask. *I swear, their plural form makes no sense. It's worse than Latin.*

Thank you. You're invaluable. Also, Latin has its uses.

I know I'm invaluable, and no, it doesn't. She flashed him a smile.

"The facility is entirely locked down, but we've been able to recover traffic camera data and other assorted pieces of information that would *suggest* they're still alone in there," Ferqar reported. "Now, it's not a certainty, so we have a few people working on how we might determine if they've been converted."

"I can do that," Barnabas offered.

Everyone gave him curious looks.

You're in it now, chief, Shinigami told him.

I know, but I'd rather they know what I can do. Coming up, it's going to be damned useful.

And if the Committee finds out?
I'm not sure that would be bad, actually.

Barnabas looked around at the group and gave a somewhat guilty smile. "I can read minds," he explained. Hoping he could move through this explanation quickly, he added, "Part of the conversion is to create strong loyalty to Grisor and the Committee. A converted individual will likely know to say things that make them seem normal. They can lie and pretend just fine, but if we ask them about Grisor, their feelings about him will show the truth."

There was a long silence.

"You can read minds?" Ferqar asked delicately.

"Er, yes."

"So when you were aboard the *Srisa*," Kelnamon said, "investigating Huword's death..."

"Yes." Barnabas smiled tightly. "Jotun thoughts are difficult for me to read, but I knew from your thoughts, Kelnamon, what the scene had been in Huword's rooms—and there was no similar memory in Ferqar's head. What confused me, of course, was the strong feeling of guilt I was getting from Ferqar."

"What is the meaning of this?" Vidrelor rumbled. "Do we have a murderer here?"

"Yes," Ferqar admitted without preamble. "As you may know, the *Srisa*—Kelnamon's ship—was stopped after a fellow Jotun naval captain was murdered. Although I did not carry out the murder, I arranged for it and made sure Huword would be somewhere the Jotun government could not easily reach."

"What he's not telling you," Barnabas added a moment later, sighing, "is what Huword did. He was attacking remote alien colonies and torturing the civilians. Ferqar was disgusted by this and helped arrange for Huword's death so that he could not continue the practice. It was murder, yes, but there was an element of Justice to it."

"I see," Vidrelor said after a moment. "Humans and Jotuns are both eager to take the law into their own hands. Brakalons are not like that. We respect laws, even when they are inconvenient. Ferqar should have brought his colleague to stand trial, and *you*, human—you should have stayed out of it, or brought Ferqar to his government."

Barnabas hid his smile as he nodded. Now did not seem a good time to have a debate on the merits of vigilante Justice and wide-scale government corruption. He could tell from the general drift of Ferqar's thoughts that the Jotun was thinking the same thing.

"Shinigami," he suggested gravely, "can you assist General Vidrelor in coming up with a strategy to release the Jotun hold on the building where Fedranor is being held?"

"Of course," Shinigami replied demurely.

Barnabas knew her better than to think it was anything more than an act, but no one else here did.

They set about making a plan, and within an hour, they had finalized their strategy. Ferqar knew that Jotun auto-targeting had difficulty in both twilight and rain, and it was possible that they would get both this evening. Even if they were to attack at dusk, it would still give them an edge.

They didn't want to wait any longer than that.

"I will assemble the strike team," Vidrelor stated. He gave Barnabas an annoyed look, "As your crew member

Shinigami is an integral piece of this operation, I will allow you and she to assist."

Barnabas didn't want to push his luck, but his team had put too much effort into this not to be allowed to participate. "Two more members should be involved."

Vidrelor growled but nodded. "We leave two *eta* before dusk," he said shortly. "Be at the city gates, or we will leave without you."

"Well." Barnabas looked at Shinigami. "I think that went as well as could be expected, don't you?"

"Better, honestly." Shinigami lifted a shoulder. "I would have thought they'd be at each other's throats. Just when I think I have a handle on organic life forms, you all throw me another curveball."

"That's...accurate." Chuckling, Barnabas went to find Gar and Gilwar and tell them about the operation.

There was a lot he could not remember. Gorsik drifted in the tank of his biosuit and tried to go over the events of the last day. For some reason, any attempt to think about it made him nauseated. He remembered terrible pain but little else.

But why? What would have hurt so much?

He must have been in an accident of some kind. The answer came to him slowly. His mind wasn't working very well, after all. Yes, an accident. Perhaps his suit had malfunctioned.

Then why was he here in his offices, alone? Surely he should have medical personnel attending to him. He tried to make his suit work, but the effort was too much for him. He did not understand what was happening. He did not…

He fought the urge to vomit, tentacles rigid. It took longer than he wanted to get hold of himself, but eventually he was able to relax again.

And then he remembered his purpose. He remembered why he was here.

The admiral. He needed to bring the admiral to a certain location. They had told him this when they left him here in his office. They told him it should be easy for him to arrange. After all, he had been her aide for several years now. He knew what to say to get her off her guard.

And when they had her…

His heart filled with happiness. When the admiral was converted like he was, she would be happier. He wanted her to be happy. She had not been very happy lately. She would be happy, and Grisor would be happy, and the true work of the Committee could begin.

Although he was still in pain, Gorsik struggled to his feet and went in search of Admiral Jeqwar.

There was much to do. He could not afford to waste a single moment.

CHAPTER TWENTY-THREE

"Holy shit, boss, it's actually you." Tom Mears strode across the docking bay of Heavensward Station. Although he stood only 5'4", he radiated confidence and charm that filled any room he was in—up to and including the docking bay. He slung his bag over his shoulder and reached out to clasp Aliana's hand. "Kinda thought I'd never see you again."

"Likewise," Aliana replied honestly. She felt a stab of old hurt and pushed it away.

Tom saw it, though. He shook his head at her. "I'm so sorry for what happened. I didn't know at first, I swear. We just left port, and he said you had some business to finish up and you'd meet us a little later on. Then he said—"

"That he and I were breaking up and I'd given him the ship," Aliana finished. "I know. The others told me. I'm not mad at you, Tom. I shouldn't ever have been, I should have known he'd lie to you all, too."

Ria, of course, *had* known the truth, but she and Aliana had settled that.

"Well, I didn't fix it when I knew, did I?" Tom shook his head. "Figured it was all legal-like, tied up so neatly, and we've all had bad bosses afore, haven't we? Told myself I'd make it up to you if I ever saw you again, but that was dodging things and I knew it." He gave a sigh. "Say, how *did* you get the ship back?"

"You wouldn't believe me if I told you," Aliana promised him. "Suffice it to say, Lawrence is *not* happy about it, but the whole process *did* involve him spending about an hour trying to land an heiress, and that was fun for all of us to watch."

She meant that literally. Shannon had sent along the video later, and they'd all had a good laugh, throwing popcorn at the screen as Lawrence laid a bunch of smarmy pickup lines on the woman.

Aliana hadn't seen her wearing a recording device, but she must have had one embedded. She found herself fascinated by the woman. She didn't seem intimidated by anything, and last time Carter had mentioned Barnabas, he hadn't mentioned any stunningly attractive female members of his crew.

She had no idea that if Barnabas knew the general drift of her thoughts, he would have laughed himself sick.

Anyway, she told herself firmly, she was *not* jealous. Not jealous at all. She busied herself letting Tom into the ship and showing him to his old bunk with a flourish. Lawrence had been lazy enough that he hadn't cleaned out the cabins after he fired everyone, but since they were in port anyway for Ria to do the repairs, Aliana had busied herself cleaning the ship from stem to stern.

Consequently, every part of her ached and all of her clothes smelled like cleaning solution.

It had been worth it, though. She told herself that she'd scrubbed every last bit of Lawrence out of the *Melisande*. When they left port, the ship would be clean, and Aliana vowed to herself that she would never again think of him. It would be as if he'd never been on board.

They'd come to Heavensward specifically to find Tom since Aliana had spent the last few days tracking down every member of the crew that Lawrence had fired. All of them had been happy to sign on again, and with every one of them, Aliana had made the same deal: it was all water under the bridge as long as they'd tell her the next time someone tried to tell them to leave port without her.

They all promised they would—and more than one of them promised to give Lawrence a solid kick in the groin if they ever saw him again. Aliana had started to protest the first time someone had said that, then decided not to intervene. The crew had their own grudges with him.

He solidly deserved it.

She passed Ria in the hallway. The tiny woman seemed to be covered with grease smudges and the toolbox she was lugging was about half her size, but she was grinning from ear to ear.

"Engine upgrades have her purring like a kitten," she reported happily. "Just the gun turrets to do now. And did I hear Tom?"

"You did." Aliana pointed down the hall. "Same bunk. I think he's still unpacking."

"Awesome!" Ria dropped her tools with a clank and took off. "Tom! *Tom!* You're back!"

Aliana watched her go with a grin. Seeing the rest of the family come together again was helping her feel better about everything.

And she had to be honest—she had definitely looked the other way when a boss had done something unethical. She had given herself all sorts of excuses, like that it wasn't her business or that a paycheck was a paycheck.

She wasn't very impressed with her past self now.

She was humming an old Earth song when she heard a familiar voice nearby. With a frown, *sure* she must be mishearing, Aliana made her way to the front hatch of the ship.

"Sir, please." Tara was trying to block access into the ship. "Please just let me ask the captain if—"

"It's all right, Tara." Aliana gave a chuckle. "Zinqued. Fancy seeing you here. What business on Heavensward? I warn you, if you steal the flour transport job out from under us, I will be *very* put out."

Zinqued chortled. "Ah, we are rivals now! This will be fun. But this time, I am not here for the same job; do not worry. In actuality, I heard you had come to Heavensward, so I came here to see you."

"Me?" Aliana frowned. Then she guessed what he must be getting at and groaned. "You *can't* be serious, Zinqued."

"I don't know what you're talking about." Zinqued sniffed loftily.

"You know very well what I'm talking about." Aliana jabbed a finger at him and then sighed, lifting both hands in a helpless gesture. "But still, I know you better than to think I'll get you out of here without at least talking to you about this, so come on. I'll make tea."

"Tea!" Zinqued followed her happily. "The one that makes my nose go all cold and hot at the same time, yes?"

"Peppermint, yes, I remembered you liked that one."

She showed Zinqued into the main social room of the *Melisande*. He looked around appreciatively, and Aliana smiled as well. Handmade braided rag rugs covered the deck with circles of bright color, an old wooden table was worn shiny with use and topped with a pottery fruit bowl, and various comfortable chairs had been acquired over the years so that the whole crew could sit and relax together. Many nights, they did; there were game boards and a very scattered collection of old books, not to mention a few knitting projects.

The kitchen was one of Aliana's favorite parts, decorated with fading wallpaper that nonetheless had a pattern she liked, and with walls that could come down if someone burned something, and keep the smell from getting into the whole ship.

This large room was surprisingly cozy. The day might come when this place got old, but it wasn't going to be for a very long time.

Zinqued sat while Aliana got the tea and brought it over to the table. When he took the earthenware mug, his nose twitched in appreciation and he sneezed the next moment. Peppermint made the Hieto sneeze, which seemed only to make him enjoy the tea even more.

Aliana supposed humans did some pretty strange things, too.

"So." She took a sip of her tea and raised her eyebrows. "Make your pitch, then."

Zinqued took another sip of tea, sneezed again, and

smiled broadly. "This tea is good! And you know what my pitch is, surely. You are a human, and you have a good rapport with Barnabas. You can help me more than any other crew member I could get. So the question isn't what I want, it's what *you* want."

Clever of him. Aliana smiled and tucked her legs up.

She was surprised to find that she had no good answer to the question.

"I don't think I really *want* anything," she told him honestly. "I have my own ship, and I can go wherever I want. Usually, I don't have quite enough money for all the repairs, and I'm a little worried about where the next job will come from, but it's still the best life I can imagine. Perhaps it won't always be." She thought of Carter's bar on High Tortuga and the family apartments above it, with his twins shrieking as they played in the backyard. "For now," she added quietly.

Zinqued seemed to know that her mind was miles away. He waited, sipping his tea and sneezing occasionally until she looked at him again.

"I'll help you," Aliana said slowly. She saw his face light up and held up a finger. "But I'll only help you with a Barnabas-style plan."

Zinqued paused.

A smile was tugging at Aliana's mouth now. "Barnabas makes very clever traps," she told Zinqued. "You heard me speak to him about it. They're traps that only catch you if you do a foolish or immoral thing. I will set *that* kind of trap. Barnabas, of all people, should be able to evade it."

Zinqued might have complained that this was hardly useful, but he said nothing.

"I'll have to learn more about him," Aliana said, suddenly flushing as she looked down into her tea. "Anything I can find out. Do my research. And I'll make a plan. If he falls into the trap, it will be because he didn't watch himself."

"Mmm." Zinqued set his now-empty mug on the table. "I accept, then."

"You do?" Aliana was mildly surprised. "I'll, uh…well, I'll work on it."

"Do." He stood. "I'll wait to hear from you. Of course, this will likely mean you cross paths with him again."

Aliana's stomach did its damnedest to hop sideways. She recovered before she spilled her tea everywhere, set the mug down hastily, and managed a smile.

"I'm not worried about that."

It was a shame that she couldn't tell if she was lying. The thought of seeing Barnabas again was terrifying.

And yet…

CHAPTER TWENTY-FOUR

"Are you ready?" Barnabas asked Tafa as they walked down the corridor in the *Shinigami*.

"I think so." She looked at him. "Were you ever worried that you were going to...lose yourself? It's just the thought of getting in that Pod and coming out someone else."

"I wasn't changed in a Pod," Barnabas explained. "My upgrade process was a little less...refined, shall we say."

Understatement of the decade.

She was looking at him curiously, though, so he continued, "Yes, I did worry that I would lose myself. In fact, in the way I was first upgraded, there was a very strong voice in my mind telling me to give myself up to end the pain. But that won't happen to you. What's happening is that the Pod-doc—which *doesn't* have a mind of its own—will make the changes Shinigami has determined. There's no pain, and no voice."

Tafa relaxed a little bit.

"You're always changing, Tafa," Barnabas told her. "Everything that happens to you changes you. You're just choosing this change. And it's all right—if you decide you don't want to fight after all, you won't have to."

"I *do* want to fight," she insisted fiercely.

He smiled at her. Privately, he wasn't sure that Tafa would ever be a warrior, but he approved wholeheartedly of her reasons for this change.

In the med bay, Shinigami was waiting. She was already in her armor for the mission, but she had covered it with a white lab coat and had her hair pulled back neatly. She somehow radiated quiet confidence as she helped Tafa into the Pod-doc. Beside her, Gar was clearly worried, but Shinigami must have told him to keep a lid on it because he wasn't allowing himself to worry out loud.

"I'm going to close the top," Shinigami said, "but we'll all be here. If you don't like it in there, we can open the Pod-doc right back up, okay? But you'll probably fall asleep at once. You might dream, but it's more likely that you'll just wake up when you're ready to be taken out, okay?"

"And you'll be here if so?" Tafa looked worried again. "Even if the mission runs long—"

"If the mission runs long, we can get a Pod back up here within a minute or two," Barnabas assured Tafa. "And, remember, Shinigami *is* the ship. She can open the lid for you."

"Oh! Right." Tafa nodded. She gave Gar a tremulous smile and lay back as Shinigami closed the lid.

Not even two seconds later Shinigami reported, "She's out cold."

Gar let out a breath. "I don't know why this is so scary for me. I did this, and it was fine."

"It's always harder to watch someone else do it,"

Shinigami said with a surprisingly human dose of wisdom. "Come on now, get your armor on. We have to meet Vidrelor and the team at the city gates. He absolutely *will* leave without us, and you *know* he wants to."

"He doesn't trust us." Gilwar had appeared in the door. "I suppose he's right not to, at least in my case. I thought I might stay behind on the ship to make sure Grisor doesn't escape."

"There's no need for that," Barnabas replied easily. "We have a contingency plan."

"Oh, yeah." Shinigami smiled as she took off the white lab coat. "The second it looks like he might actually get out? We're ejecting that pod."

Gilwar gave a surprised chuckle. "Well, then. In that case, I'll probably stay in the capital city."

"Why are you so determined not to come?" Barnabas asked suspiciously.

"Well, you have Ferqar as a resource on Jotun technology, so you don't *need* me, and…well, I don't trust myself not to snoop if I'm in that bunker." Gilwar gave a mechanical shrug. "You see, I've been a spy for almost all of my life, and that bunker has the absolute best in terms of Brakalon technology. Even if I'm not trying to snoop, I'll hear them saying code words, and I'll see their security processes. I'd rather just stay behind. I can advise whoever's left on other technology they might see during the invasion."

"Let's hope we prevent that," Shinigami said.

Gilwar nodded, but his silence was not encouraging. "Of course," he added simply.

"Well, then." Barnabas made one last check of the Pod-doc controls and ushered them toward the shuttle bay. "Let's get down to the surface."

A scant ten minutes later they joined the strike team at the gates of the city. Vidrelor, as Shinigami had predicted, did not look entirely pleased to see them. Still, as a warrior with a warrior's honor, he had kept his word to wait until the assigned time; he wasn't going to resort to trickery to leave them behind. He gave a sigh and motioned them into the trucks, and the party set off toward the bunker.

Admiral Jeqwar sighed as she piloted her biosuit along the corridors of her office. She wished she could be in one of the tanks, floating happily among the seagrasses or hunting fish.

That, of course, was just a distraction. What she *really* wanted was to be in the middle of her fleet, unleashing the full potential of the Jotuns on—

Well, on other Jotuns, it seemed. She didn't like that; she had never enjoyed her desire for war. She was what she was, however, and that had proved invaluable to the Jotuns over the years. She had saved her people from destruction more than once.

She would do it again now. In fact, she did not intend to wait even one more day. She had made a decision: she was going to destroy the Committee, process and legalities be damned. Barnabas could carry out his theater with Grisor, but meanwhile, there would be no more of the vermin to carry out their plans in the shadows.

It was a perfect solution to her way of thinking. She did

not allow her enemies to stay alive and dangerous once she knew who they were.

She was surprised, when she rounded the corner, to see Gorsik hard at work.

"Gorsik." He had been taken ill very suddenly a day or so ago, and she could see from his movements that he was not feeling entirely better yet. "You should not be here. We've all been working too hard." How long since any of them had taken a night off?

You didn't *get* nights off, of course, when there was a plot within your government to violently overthrow multiple other species.

And after a time, it wore on you. After a time, even when there was so much to do, a person could take no more. She should have noticed the signs of burnout coming, she thought guiltily. Even sick, he was still here.

He looked up at her, however, and smiled. He was happy. He was calm, not frantic. That helped her feel somewhat better.

"Come see." He stood aside. "I've developed a plan to mobilize the fleet so that the Committee will not know. The navy is segmented, so that no matter where they have spies, they won't be able to respond quickly and interfere."

Intrigued, she came to stand beside him.

A few moments later she nodded approvingly. His plan was good in many ways. There were only a few things missing from it, pieces of the network that he would not realize existed. She wouldn't tell him that, not exactly, but she could make some changes to it.

"The only thing, of course," Gorsik said, "is that it will not be easy for the captains to communicate with one another. All of it would have to go through you as a central hub."

Jeqwar considered this. She began to pace, her tentacles thrashing. Gorsik was right; this was a dangerous plan. If something happened to her, the other captains would not be able to get in touch with one another. They might walk into a trap that they could otherwise avoid.

Was it worth it?

It depended, she supposed, on just how much the Committee could do to compromise them.

"It's not worth it," she decided finally. "There haven't been any other disappearances. Who can say if there are traitors in the ranks? There must be, so you are right to worry, but I don't think any of the captains are compromised, so not this plan. It is a good plan, Gorsik. It is a good way to move quickly without things being easily stopped, but there is no need to take such a risk yet."

Gorsik accepted this gracefully. "I think I will go walk out in the sun for a little while."

"That would be good. You've been working too hard. Not that I don't appreciate it, of course." She indicated her appreciation with a flutter at the base of her body.

"You work harder than I do," he pointed out. "Come walk with me. Surely some time out in the sun is not too much." When she wavered, he added, "You can see so clearly when others work too hard but not you?"

She laughed at that and nodded her biosuit's head. "Let us go take a walk, then. Some sunlight will be good for us both."

They emerged into one of the smaller gardens on the base, one meant only for walking in biosuits. There were no pools of water here, but she had always liked this place anyway. There were trees and shaded pathways as well as some in bright sunlight.

No benches. In their biosuits, the Jotuns did not need them.

They had just made their way into a copse of trees when the attackers stepped onto the path.

"Gorsik, run!" Admiral Jeqwar triggered the distress signal in her suit and threw herself into action.

Or she tried to. She could not move, however. Why could she not move? She thrashed inside her tank to look behind herself and saw Gorsik's hand moving away from the back of her suit's neck. He had immobilized her.

"Gorsik?" She felt horror creeping up on her. "What have you done?"

"What I needed to do," he told her, "in order to help you. To help all of us. Your talents are too precious to waste on their side. We need you, Admiral." To the others, he added, "Take her. We have a plan to put in motion once she is converted. Be quick about it."

CHAPTER TWENTY-FIVE

They went in to retrieve the general just before dusk. The bunker housing was built into the side of a mountain, so similar to some human structures that Barnabas did a double-take. This part of Kordinev even resembled the American Southwest in many ways, with rust-red rocks, scrub brush, and sand. The granite-gray mountain rose out of all of this, tenacious little trees clinging to its sides. The setting sun made it glow golden-red.

This would be a pretty place to walk around, Shinigami commented to Gar and Barnabas. When both of them looked at her curiously, she added, *I mean, obviously not during a battle.*

That's not what's confusing us, Gar explained.

Barnabas agreed with a nod. *I didn't think you noticed things like that.*

It wasn't part of my original programming, but I'm trying to learn. She met their eyes with a somewhat combative expression, then folded. *Fine, you got me. It was a total shot in the dark. I'm just trying to figure out what organics find pretty in a landscape.*

Barnabas snorted and shook his head when General Vidrelor looked over severely. The Brakalon was quite understandably worried about any lapse of discipline that might give them away.

Of course, to Barnabas' way of thinking, it wasn't necessary to be silent when they were approaching the bunker in plain sight. Their jeep-like vehicles were kicking plumes of dust into the air, and they weren't exactly *quiet.*

He didn't say any of that, however. Vidrelor was officially in charge of this mission, and Barnabas was telling himself that he was fine with that.

He wasn't, but he was telling himself that he was.

"Their turrets are beginning to power up," Shinigami reported a few moments later. "And it looks like the bunker's guns are hot, too."

General Vidrelor swore under his breath. He had hoped that the Jotuns would be unable to get into the bunker's defense systems, which Barnabas had known was a long shot. The Committee was already in the networks and had managed to block specific messages. It was objectively no more difficult to get into the turrets.

And *that* didn't even take into account the possibility that General Fedranor had been converted. That was Barnabas' true fear.

If he had been, what damage could he do while they attacked?

"Fighters, come in hot," Vidrelor ordered. "Target our guns."

Shinigami and Barnabas exchanged looks. She had, on

his orders, brought the *Shinigami* lower so that they could do a second pass if the Brakalon fighters were not able to handle things on their own. Now her fingers twitched slightly, and he knew she was eager to handle this herself.

He understood the urge all too well. It just felt *wrong* to be following someone else's orders.

The first wing of Brakalon fighters screamed through the air overhead. They had been circling high above, hopefully out of range of the bunker's scanners, and now they accelerated downward at harrowing speed. Even having leapt out of shuttles and off the edges of buildings, Barnabas felt slightly queasy.

On Earth, fighter pilots were partially selected to be as light as possible. The Brakalons hardly qualified by that metric.

Vidrelor had chosen his tactic well, however, and the pilots were clearly both skilled and well-trained. The guns at the bunker had been preparing to fire on the ground assault team and were not positioned well to deal with the death that came hurtling down at them from above.

General Vidrelor was keeping careful count of the guns disabled. He did not seem inclined to share that information, but Barnabas did not need it. Shinigami held up one finger as the first gun was destroyed. Then another finger went up, and a few moments later, a third gun was taken out of commission.

The guns are withdrawing, Shinigami told Barnabas and Gar a moment later. *They won't be able to get any more of them.*

A few moments later, General Vidrelor gave a grim look and ordered the trucks to speed ahead. Barnabas watched, pleasantly surprised, as Vidrelor kept the pressure on the bunker. If the guns emerged, they would be taken out by the fighters that regularly passed overhead.

That left only the turrets, and the strike team could see their red laser sights gleaming as they got closer.

Barnabas pulled out a rifle and took his place, standing to lay his weapon down on top of the truck. There was a small opening—in Brakalon terms, which meant that not only was it very roomy for Barnabas, but he also had to stand on one of the benches in order to see out of it.

He pushed away the feeling of ridiculousness.

You'll be in range...now. Shinigami's voice was certain.

Thank you. Barnabas began to fire, leveling quick bursts at the turrets and calling status reports to the other gunners. Marksmanship was not one of his innate talents, but he had trained in it for precisely that reason. He liked getting into a fight and using his own two hands, but not every fight could be won that way.

He didn't want the bad guys to win someday because he'd been lazy about learning new skills.

Between his reflexes and his training, he was able to take out two of the Jotun turrets, and the vehicles screeched to a halt for Shinigami to leap out and run for the doors with Ferqar.

The bunker's guns, meanwhile, all popped out at once. There was a terrifying moment while Barnabas tracked the missiles coming from the fighters overhead, then everyone threw themselves flat as the guns exploded.

"Perfectly timed," Vidrelor called over the radios, but Barnabas could hear him panting slightly, and all of them shared looks. Yes, they had planned well, but one mistake and they would have been very dead right now.

Shinigami gave a loud whistle as the doors opened and the strike team poured out and into the darkness. With Ferqar's knowledge of Jotun programming and Shinigami's innate abilities to hack it, they were able to make good progress down the eerily silent corridors.

"I don't like this," Vidrelor murmured once to Barnabas. Given that he hadn't wanted Barnabas along at all, the man took this as a sign of just how worried Vidrelor was.

At last, they made their way down the main corridor to a series of heavy blast doors. Shinigami opened the keypad and gave a few commands, bending her head close as if to listen.

"He's in there," she reported. "Or a Brakalon I can't distinguish from him. Alive. Held motionless in the center of the room somehow."

Vidrelor nodded. "Take your places," he told the strike team.

They had brought light, durable barriers that they erected now to give themselves cover, and everyone had their weapon primed and ready before Shinigami gave the command to open the doors, and sprinted back to cover alongside Barnabas.

The hallway seemed to explode with gunfire. Turrets lined the room at the heart of the bunker, all stalking forward so that they were between the strike team and General Fedranor.

Barnabas squinted at the center of the room. The general did not seem to be restrained, but he sat motionless and silent as the turrets attacked his strike team and they fought back. He did not even dive for cover, as he should in order to give his team a clear shot.

Are you thinking what I'm thinking? Shinigami asked Barnabas.

Take two barriers, get into the room, and shred them in the crossfire?

Awwww, we really have *started to think alike!*

With a glance at each other and a yell for a temporary ceasefire, they burst into motion and into the room, Shinigami tackling several turrets along the way. As soon as they were out of the direct line of fire, the rest of the strike team started firing again.

Several turrets tried to stop them, one even managing to send a shot so close to Barnabas that it singed his coat. He and Shinigami both got their barriers up, however, and managed to take out the turrets without having the general in their line of fire.

Then, as quickly as it had begun, it was over. Vidrelor gave Barnabas a resolute nod, and the Brakalon's fingers tightened around his rifle.

He was ready to do what needed to be done, and although Barnabas prayed it didn't come to that, he was disconcerted by General Fedranor's silence.

He stood up from behind his barrier and walked out into the open room, stepping carefully over the fallen turrets.

"General Fedranor?" he asked.

"Yes." The general stood then and looked at the strike team. "Why are they not moving? Am I accused of something?"

"I will explain shortly." Barnabas allowed himself to get

a feel for the general's thoughts. There was worry, yes. He *was* worried that they might accuse him of treason.

"I gave them nothing," Fedranor said fiercely. He laughed. "Of course, there was only one message, and that was recent—to come in here and stay in that chair without moving. I had been there for a day and a half when you arrived."

To Barnabas' surprise, his thoughts bore this out.

"Ah," he said contemplatively. "And tell me—what do you know of Senator Grisor or the Committee for Infrastructure Revitalization? How do you feel about the Jotuns ruling this sector?"

There was no mistaking Fedranor's revulsion for all three, and Barnabas gave a smile as he turned.

"He hasn't been converted."

There were a few quiet cheers, and Vidrelor's shoulders sagged in relief. "Thank all the gods," he said. He stood and slung his weapon over his back, then came to clasp Fedranor's hand. "We'll explain everything. We've recovered everyone we can; there are only a few who remain at these high-tier bunkers."

"The Jotuns were behind this?" Fedranor demanded. "What is their endgame?"

"We're not sure yet," Vidrelor replied. "Come, speak. We have much to coordinate." His eyes traveled to Barnabas. "And many allies we have yet to decide whether to trust."

Barnabas looked at Shinigami. He had argued passionately for the Brakalons to trust Admiral Jeqwar, but he could not be sure they would listen to him. As much as it frustrated him, he could easily see why that was.

He looked through the wreckage, Shinigami at his side, and shook his head.

The Committee was backed into a corner, but as far as Barnabas was concerned, that didn't make them *less* dangerous. It made them *more* so.

And he was very sure this wasn't the last of their plan. He wasn't sure if the senators were the key to it or if there was something else coming—but he knew there would be more.

Pain. Pain over pain over pain, multiplying until she could do nothing but let it flow through her, erasing any trace of who she'd been.

Or at least, that was what she prayed for. Admiral Jeqwar had tried to cling to sanity for what felt like days, hours, weeks. Now she tried just as hard to shed it. She could not bear sanity any longer.

She thought that Jeltor came to taunt her, telling her of the principles she must hold to, but she could not see him. Perhaps she had imagined it.

She knew what they were trying to do, and she was powerless to stop it.

The whispers they put into her head were laughable at first but became harder to ignore as the pain went on. Every time she thought she found a pocket of reprieve, the pain seemed to intensify and layer upon itself.

She was going to go mad, and madness would be all she wanted and more.

The calm, when it came, was blinding.

She would remember that moment forever, she thought—the moment when it all became clear and the pain fell away. She understood now. She had been held captive by fear and doubt, but there was no doubt any longer, and no chaos.

No, she was a shining light in the darkness—a warrior who would help her people bring order.

She floated to the top of her tank, and when she was lifted out and placed in her new biosuit, she met Gorsik's eyes.

"You have given me new life," she told him.

"I know." His tone told her he knew exactly how she felt. "We will change the world. We will save them all. And we must go now. There is much to do.

CHAPTER TWENTY-SIX

The Brakalons decided to first speak to Ferqar and Gilwar and then to confer by themselves for the rest of the night. Barnabas told himself that he understood this, yet he found himself incredibly frustrated by this turn of events.

Shinigami had landed the ship nearby, and she found him in the med bay sometime later.

"How's she doing?" she asked him.

"About a third of the way there," Barnabas said before realizing that Shinigami was surely already aware of Tafa's status. He gave her a look.

"I wanted your assessment." She lifted a shoulder. "I feel less confident now that I have a body of my own."

Barnabas looked at her curiously.

"I might have a body," she explained, after a moment, "but it doesn't work like yours. It's difficult not to make assumptions that aren't accurate."

Barnabas gave a nod, considering, and tilted his head to indicate the corridor. They stepped outside and strolled in the general direction of the bridge. Neither of them seemed to have a proper direction or any desire to speak, and at the blast doors, Barnabas headed outside on a whim.

It was a beautiful night. They must be in a warm season on Kordinev, he thought, because the air had the soft, perfect feel of energy right before a summer storm.

As he watched, lightning began to play across the horizon.

"Do you think you'll ever want to settle down?" he asked Shinigami finally.

She gave him an incredulous look. "I'm an AI. What would that even mean?"

"I don't know. Stop living in a ship, live in a…building? Space station? Same place, different types of problems to think about. I don't want to say there'd be no danger, but you see what I mean."

"Oh." She considered this. "I really don't know. I have never thought about it. I've spent my whole life doing this sort of thing."

"I always forget how young you are. You seem older."

"Yeah, well, I have a lot of accumulated knowledge to work with." She smiled at him. "And it turns out being part of an interspecies, universe-wide war really helps you grow up quick." She caught sight of his expression. "Oh, don't feel guilty. It was a joke."

"I know." Barnabas wandered over to a rock and sat.

"Do *you* ever want to settle down?" Shinigami asked him dubiously. She leapt onto a nearby rock and began to do balancing exercises.

"Hard to say, honestly." Barnabas shrugged. "I never thought it was an option. Now I see Carter and I wonder. I can't say it's too late, since I'm practically immortal and I'm still in my prime."

"That's what *you* say, Grandpa."

"Don't talk back to your elders," Barnabas told her in mock severity. He watched as she did a cartwheel and paused at the top, taking one hand away to balance.

"The real question is," Shinigami continued, "what you *want*. I asked before, and you just talked about what was possible. But it is possible, so all you have to do is decide you want it."

"That's how you think human brains work?" Barnabas gave her a bemused smile. "Bless you, child, but you have a lot to learn."

Shinigami let her legs down with a thump and glared at him. "I am not a *child*, thank you very much."

"Yes, yes, you're a very fearsome AI with excellent marksmanship skills."

"And a killer uppercut." Shinigami made a fist and blew on it dramatically. "I don't think I understand the difficulty, though. If you know what you want—"

"Taking steps to acquire what you want means that you have the possibility of *failing* to acquire it," Barnabas explained.

Shinigami stopped. She was silent for so long that Barnabas thought he might have broken her, but she finally said, "All right, I've run this calculation every way to Sunday—as Tabitha would say—which doesn't take that long because it's *only two options*, but I still don't get this. You have two options, right? You want a thing. Option A, you try to get the thing, maybe you fail, and maybe you don't. We don't know the probabilities.

Option B, you don't try to get the thing, so you definitely don't get it."

"It might fall into my lap by accident," Barnabas pointed out wickedly. He knew exactly where she was going with this and she was right, but he was going to have some fun in the meantime.

Shinigami gave him a pained look. "You can't *plan* on that! That's a terrible way to do things! I don't even get it. *Surely* that's less likely? You *know* it has to be less likely, don't you? It's—ohhhhh." She narrowed her eyes. "You were fucking with me."

"Little bit," Barnabas admitted. He dove behind his rock the next moment as a boulder came sailing at him. "Hey! Not all of it was artifice! Some of it was real!"

"Okay." Shinigami appeared over the top of the rock and looked down at him. Apparently, she could make her eyes glow red. "Tell me which part of this fuckery is real?"

Barnabas looked up at her vengeful face and prayed that they hadn't made a huge mistake in giving her a body. She had, after all, a very short temper for illogic. "All I can tell you is the *truth*." He stood up and adjusted his coat before sitting down gracefully. He would accept his death elegantly, he had decided. "It can feel worse to devote all your energy to something and fail than not to get it because you never tried."

Shinigami stared at him for a long moment, then slowly her eyes faded from red and she gave a somewhat surly nod.

There was silence.

"Oh, I hate this," she said finally.

"What about it?" Barnabas frowned.

"It makes sense," she explained, sounding annoyed, "but I can't figure out *why* it makes sense because it makes *no* sense! Do you see?" She patted her body absently. "I hope I'm not going to burst into flames when all of my circuits melt down."

Barnabas laughed. "A little illogic never hurt anyone."

"You're not an AI. You're not *built* on logic!"

"Think of it as a learning opportunity," Barnabas suggested. "If you can crunch this, you can crunch anything. I *know* you've been trying to work instinctive leaps into your algorithms, so why not this too?"

"Easy for you to say." She sat down next to him on the rock with a harrumph. "What if I told you to just *learn* how to calculate based on saving the most lives without any hope of saving who you loved specifically? You wouldn't like to learn it. New ways of thinking are hard. If you don't think the same way, are you even the same person anymore?"

"Sure," Barnabas said immediately.

"You didn't think about that at all."

"No, I meant…" He laid back. "Now seems as good a time as any for a philosophy discussion. This is the sort teenagers usually have, of course, but I've found that if you get a bunch of old white-haired philosophers in a room, they actually don't make any more sense than the teenagers."

Shinigami gave a sudden bark of laughter. "I wasn't sure how to tell you that most of your human philosophers were full of shit."

"I wouldn't go *that* far. They had some good points."

"Wrapped in a lot of pompous bullshit. I'm standing by my assessment."

"It's hard to argue, really." Barnabas sat back up again. "I wish they'd finish their planning. I hate having nothing to do."

Shinigami snickered. "You hate not being in charge."

"That's not right," Barnabas denied, prickly. "I'm perfectly fine not being in charge."

"Lies. Lies and deceit. You believed wholeheartedly in Bethany Anne's mission and leadership, and you were *still* more comfortable off running your own missions. It's not wrong." She patted his hand as if comforting a small and particularly dumb dog. "It's just how you are, sweetie."

"Call me sweetie again," Barnabas murmured contemplatively, "and I'll take your hand off."

"And he's deflecting! *There's* the man we know and love." Shinigami grinned. "Doing the right thing isn't always easy, chief. I think you're right that they need to do this on their own. It's just maddening."

"Yes." Barnabas nodded. "And I wish we'd had word from the Admiral. I know she has a lockdown on information since she doesn't want anyone finding out what's going on and what she knows, but it's hard to make any sort of good plan without knowing when and if she'll be willing to mobilize the fleet—or if she's found the fleet the Committee has."

"I'm telling you, they want to use the Jotun Navy."

"And *I'm* telling *you*, that is way too big a gamble. Plus, Jeqwar has things locked down. None of the captains can disappear without someone knowing. They identified Jeltor's disappearance before we did."

"Yes." Shinigami looked uneasy. "Because Gil and Wev held up his conversion as long as they dared."

Barnabas shrugged.

There was a shout nearby and a young Brakalon loped over, occasionally using his knuckles to push off. He was barely panting when he reached them, but he looked worried.

"General Vidrelor says you're to come at once, both of you."

Barnabas and Shinigami exchanged a worried look before following the Brakalon back to headquarters. They arrived to find the place in chaos, with some Brakalons yelling and others setting up charts and maps.

"What's going on?" Barnabas asked.

Vidrelor gave him an unfriendly look. "We're receiving reports that the Jotun fleet is mobilizing and there's a strike team set to land within the next hour as part of the advance force."

"The Jotun…Naval fleet? Under the command of Admiral Jeqwar?"

"I don't have a clue," Vidrelor replied brusquely, "and I don't care. There's no word to say they're allies, so they're enemies."

"They're not enemies," Barnabas countered heatedly. "The Navy is on your side."

"Really?" He gave Barnabas a look. "Then explain why they're on their way, hmm?"

Barnabas unfortunately had no answer for that. He looked at Shinigami, then at Vidrelor again.

"Put us in the response to the strike team. Hopefully, I'll

be able to learn enough about their plan to help you put a stop to it."

Vidrelor looked at him for a moment. "And if they're here to kill us?"

"Then I'll protect the civilians," Barnabas promised without hesitation. "We've faced down fleets before, General. We'll do it again if need be."

That, at least, seemed to satisfy the Brakalon. He gave a nod. "Get ready, then. We have a hopper waiting to head to the suspected drop site."

CHAPTER TWENTY-SEVEN

The shuttle door opened, shuddering with the force of the atmosphere around it, and the Brakalon captain waved the response team out urgently.

"Go, go, go! Their strike team is already on the ground!"

Brakalon fighters laid down cover fire to keep the Jotun strike team pinned as the response team leapt in ones and twos. Barnabas, Gar, and Shinigami were waved out in the middle of the group, Gar giving what Barnabas could only think of as a roller coaster scream.

He missed roller coasters, he thought philosophically as he plummeted toward the ground. Humanity *had* come up with the occasional good idea.

The Jotuns had already surrounded the second bunker and were trying to batter their way inside. The two top-ranking Brakalon senators, however, were resourceful enough to have figured out how to keep the doors locked. From what Barnabas could see, they must have powered down the entire bunker to keep the Jotuns from taking over the system.

If the response team didn't clean this up fast, of course, the senators would suffocate, but Barnabas approved of the plan in any case.

Some of the Jotuns were hastily improvising explosives to try to get through the blast doors, making use of the lower-powered grenades and munitions they had brought, while others turned to mount a concerted defense against the Brakalon response team.

The best defense, of course, was a good offense, and the Brakalon team had barely had time to get to their feet before the Jotuns were charging at them in a spear formation, two wide flanks spreading out to the sides and ready to close.

"Geronimo!" Kelnamon yelled as he ran to meet them. He flashed Shinigami a smile, and she waved a thumbs-up in his direction.

"Now you're getting it!" she called back.

Barnabas grinned privately. Human culture had its flaws, but he enjoyed the way Shinigami went around stealth-bombing little pieces of it into this sector.

Then the Jotuns raised their arms and began to charge explosive rounds, and he didn't have time to think about that anymore. He dropped and went into a skid, bringing his arm up with a panel of his coat. Between his armor and the engineered fabric of his coat, as well as getting out of the way of the first rounds, he should be safe for a few more seconds.

That was all he needed to get to the Jotuns. He rolled and came up, dropping into a place of instinctive action so that he wouldn't shrink from the hulking metal body, fairly bristling with weapons and sharp edges.

It wasn't exactly pleasant to slam into, but the Jotun hadn't had the first idea what force Barnabas could summon. It hadn't altered its course at all, likely thinking it could simply throw Barnabas out of the way and keep moving. That was a fatal mistake; Barnabas' fist shot out as he tackled it, and the glass of the Jotun's tank cracked.

It yelled and tried to get away, but Barnabas had the upper hand now. Knocked onto its back on uneven terrain, the Jotun flailed and tried to get purchase to stand while Barnabas slammed his fist down over and over until the tank cracked. He wasn't taking any chances. He grabbed the Jotun body out of the tank and threw it as far as he could into the brush nearby.

Ice cold, Shinigami told him. When he looked up to locate her, she was grabbing another Jotun out of its ruined tank and flinging it away. She shrugged at him. *What? I said it was ice cold, not that it wasn't a good idea.*

With a snicker, Barnabas took stock of the situation—and felt his stomach drop.

The response team hadn't spread its formation wide enough, and the Jotuns were getting ready to close their flanks. With the rifles in their arms, they could easily catch the Brakalons in a crossfire as they closed.

"*Vidrelor!*" His voice was a roar, as loud as he could make it.

To his credit, Vidrelor saw what was happening. He gave a sharp look around and spoke urgently into his radio.

He says to wait as they start to close, Shinigami said, *and then send two groups out to either side to fire on their backs.*

Do they know the weak points in the suits? Barnabas

demanded. *Jotuns aren't easy to cut down by scattering fire at their backs.*

I know that. She wasn't even pausing as she leveled kick after punch after shot at the Jotuns around her, each motion made with military precision and deadly grace. *But it's probably our best shot anyway.*

I don't like this. He stooped to grab a Jotun by the ankles, yanked it into the air, and winged it sideways into another one, producing a satisfying crash. All of the nearby Jotuns turned to look at him. *But we'll finish this conversation later. Busy now!*

You just keep getting their attention, Gar broke in. *We'll handle cleanup.*

With a laugh, Barnabas obliged. He threw himself this way and that, wreaking havoc wherever he landed. More tanks cracked as his hands and feet pummeled the Jotuns, and several times he was able to slide one of his knives into a gap in the armor, using his faster-than-average reflexes to catch the brief moments of vulnerability.

He lost count of the Jotun blades that sliced near him or, more than once, caught him with a searing line of pain down an arm. Deadly in their sharpness, imbued with some kind of current, the knives were able to part the fabric of his coat.

But with so many of them trying to attack him, they were in each other's way and had no good plan for who would attack at any given time. He could—and did—use that to his advantage. He made sure that any moment of hesitation cost them, and he did the most outrageous things he could think of to make sure they were always hesitating, always unsure what he might come up with next.

Barnabas! Shinigami's warning came an instant too late. An explosive round caught him full in the back and he thudded to the ground, pain blotting out any other thoughts for a long moment.

Between his armor and his healing ability, he could recover from this if he only had the time to do so.

He saw a flash of shadow as Gar went hurtling overhead to latch onto a Jotun's biosuit. The Luvendi ripped the head off and threw it, then began stuffing little static grenades into the open neck of the biosuit while the Jotun flailed and tried to pull him off. Several others, horrified, ran to their fellow soldier's defense, and Gar, laughing maniacally, made a game of evading them as he took shots with his Jean Dukes and set the static grenades off one by one.

Shinigami, meanwhile, was nearly a blur. She was racing back and forth in Barnabas' field of vision as he pushed himself up to his hands and knees, drawing labored breaths into his lungs.

Your vital signs are good, she told him. *I'm getting readings off the charts in terms of pain, but you're healing just fine, and there's no sign of internal bleeding or any lasting injury.*

That gave him the push he needed. Knowing that he was not risking serious damage, Barnabas was able to launch himself into motion once more. The pain made him gasp as he lashed out at the Jotuns, but he knew it would pass.

There was the high trill of a whistle, and four groups of Brakalons exited the fight at high speed. They must be executing Vidrelor's plan, Barnabas thought. He noticed explosions going off behind him at the blast doors and knew they had to wrap this up quickly. The two senators had very little time remaining, and the information they knew was too valuable to fall into Jotun hands.

Break their line, he told Shinigami and Gar. *Get to the bunker. Give them nowhere to retreat.*

Then he turned and charged into the thick of the Jotun forces, the compressed spear formation that could still retreat toward the bunker and their friends. Instead of retreating toward the explosions and rushing the bunker, the Jotuns were distracted into the fight.

Another explosion went off nearby, and Barnabas looked up in time to see a Jotun stagger away from the bunker and collapse to its knees.

Strange, but he had no time to think about that right now. He lashed out in an ever-widening circle, clearing his enemies with single-minded precision. One by one, they fell. Streaked with blood and with rips and blackened holes in his clothing, Barnabas knew he presented a fearsome sight. He should be dead by now, and the fact that he wasn't, was terrifying to them.

Reinforcements! Shinigami's cry could have been ambiguous but for the frustration in it.

Shit. Barnabas kicked his speed up a notch. *Tell Vidrelor he needs to stop fucking around and get back to the bunker.*

Roger.

There was no immediate response after that, however. In fact, Shinigami was silent for a long enough time that Barnabas looked over to see what was going on and picked out both her and Vidrelor in the chaos. Both were stealing glances at the bunker.

It would be deadly to split his focus further, but this was the sort of riddle Barnabas could not resist. He looked up—

Just in time to see an RPG of some sort go streaking up from near the bunker. It hit the Jotun landing craft and sent it cartwheeling through the air, trailing black smoke. With most of the battlefield watching open-mouthed, it tumbled out of control into the side of a nearby hill.

For a moment Barnabas thought the doors would open and soldiers would come pouring out, but some self-destruct must have activated. The whole thing went up in a flash so bright he saw stars, and chunks of red-hot debris shot up into the air.

What the hell is going on? he demanded of Shinigami.

Vidrelor wants to know the same thing. Almost absent-mindedly, she grabbed a Jotun by the neck and shook it violently until the tank popped out of the body and went rolling over the ground. She didn't even spare it a glance. *He thought we were the ones up by the bunker.*

What?

Well, someone *clearly is. Someone who's on our side. Heads up, I think we've got all of them if we move now.*

In unison, the three crew members of the *Shinigami* pulled out their Jean Dukes, and each took out two of the remaining Jotuns in their little knot. Then, without a word, they took off for the bunker.

Debris and Jotun bodies littered the area so that they had to scramble up over little hills in order to see the doors. When they did, Barnabas' jaw dropped.

"How did you—"

"They sent me with the strike team," Jeltor said. He looked at all of them. "And in all the confusion, no one thought to make sure I was still converted."

"Jeltor." Barnabas wanted to believe, but he could not be sloppy about this. He looked into Jeltor's mind. "Senator Grisor—"

There was a surge of something tired and too simple in Jeltor's mind, followed almost instantaneously by revulsion, both for the conversion and for Grisor.

"He's a traitor," Jeltor said. "You were right, Barnabas. My own thoughts and experiences showed me the truth once, and they did it again. I know you thought you failed back at the estate—that you couldn't convince me. But you did. You saved my life—and I'm here to help you make sure they can't use the people in this bunker or anyone else for their purposes."

CHAPTER TWENTY-EIGHT

"He's not converted." Barnabas felt a prickling in his eyes. "Shinigami, tell them. He's not converted." He took two steps and pulled Jeltor into a hug, laughing. It was ridiculous to hug a biosuit, but he did not care. This was his friend. Now that Jeltor was here and safe, Barnabas admitted to himself that he had never expected to see Jeltor again.

Worse, he had expected that they would come face to face as enemies and Barnabas would have to kill the Jotun.

"Barnabas." Jeltor's voice was grave. "There are more coming. We need to get the Brakalons out of the bunker. But—please. Jelina. The children. They're all right?"

At the thought of Jeltor's family, Barnabas' tears made his vision blur. He blinked them away as he nodded.

"They are," he said. "They'll be glad to see you."

How much the children knew, he wasn't sure, but he did know that Jeltor's wife hadn't ever expected to see her husband again.

Purpose flowed through him, and he strode to the edge

of the hill. "Quickly!" he called. "Clean up there and get this bunker open. We need to get the senators out before reinforcements arrive!"

The Brakalons went to work with a will, and the Jotuns, seeing their forces nearly wiped out by one of their own, fought with desperate rage but little hope. They fell one by one as Barnabas watched grimly.

When Jeltor came to stand beside him, he looked at him curiously. "Are you sure you want to see this?"

"They chose violence and death," Jeltor replied. "Not because they were tortured. They came here willingly. Whenever I doubt what we're doing, and if it's worth it, I want to remember this: those soldiers trying to blast their way into a bunker to capture politicians and torture them into becoming agents. And these fighters, too, knowing there's no hope of them surviving, simply wanting to make their enemies hurt as much as possible so they'll be weak when the fleet arrives." He paused. "There's something you should know about that."

Barnabas looked at him wordlessly.

"They converted Admiral Jeqwar," Jeltor told him. "I tried to stop it, Barnabas. I really did. I went in and tried to give her hope, telling her to cling to her principles. I should have killed her, I know that—but I couldn't bring myself to."

Luckily, Barnabas had Shinigami nearby, and her smile told him that she remembered their conversation.

"She of all people might yell at you for not killing her," Barnabas told Jeltor, "but you know how the crew of the *Shinigami* works. We don't write people off. Not our friends."

What might have been a touching moment was ruined by a stray rocket-propelled grenade that shot overhead, making all of them duck. They turned to watch as it thunked harmlessly onto the side of the bunker.

"Are anyone else's ears ringing?" Gar asked dubiously. "It's just explosion after explosion this time, even when they aren't *doing* anything. Normally, there's more hand to hand combat." He smiled at Jeltor. "It's good to see you again. Tafa will be glad you're well."

"She's safe, then?" Jeltor sounded relieved.

"Safe and—well, we'll explain later." Barnabas didn't want to go into the subject of Tafa's upgrades right now.

Vidrelor came scrambling up the hill toward them. He looked at the bunker but seemed to decide the politicians were safe enough for now. He jerked his head at Jeltor. "Who's this?"

"Captain Jeltor of the Jotun Navy." Jeltor introduced himself with a slight bow. "I come with the very good news that the mind-control the Committee has is not permanent. As you can see," he added drily, gesturing at the Jotuns around him.

"You killed your own comrades," Vidrelor said. There was distaste in his voice.

"Perhaps you would have preferred to have them kill your troops?" Jeltor asked bluntly. "No, I don't think you would have. There are more pieces of this plan coming, General. Your forces need to be as strong as possible. We can discuss ethics later."

"*Finally*," Shinigami exclaimed. She came over to loop her arm around Jeltor's shoulders. "Someone else who understands that right in the middle of a fight is not the time to moan on about ethics and moral philosophy."

Barnabas took the hit with an eye roll. "General Vidrelor, Jeltor has told us that there are more reinforcements incoming. We should get the senators out of the bunker as quickly as we can and—"

"*STATE YOUR NAMES.*" An automated voice blared out of the speakers near the blast doors.

Everyone jumped.

Jeltor recovered first. "I am Captain Jeltor of the Jotun Navy. As you can see from my actions during the battle, I oppose the invasion of Kordinev."

"*NEXT,*" the voice blared.

"General Vidrelor," the Brakalon called. "I am leading this rescue mission to free the Senate Majority and Minority Leader."

"*THE HUMAN NEXT.*"

"It means you," Shinigami told Barnabas.

"I am Barnabas," he said. "I was once a Queen's Ranger in the Etheric Empire, and participated in the rescue of the Brakalon ship *Srisa*." That was playing somewhat fast and loose with facts, but it was close enough. "This is Venfaldri Gar, of my crew, and Shinigami, another of my crewmates."

There was a silence.

"*BRAKALON. WHO DO YOU SERVE?*"

"Senators." General Vidrelor looked impatient. "I assure you, I am loyal to you. I too was imprisoned until very recently, and just hours ago we freed General Fedranor. There are Jotun reinforcements coming, and the Jotun fleet is inbound. We need to get you somewhere safe, where the Jotuns have not compromised the controls of the building."

There was a pause, then the doors slid open one by one. Two Brakalon walked out, both immediately going to stand on opposite sides of the group.

General Vidrelor leaned close to murmur in Barnabas' ear, "They're famous enemies. Frankly, it's a wonder they didn't kill each other while they were in there."

"The touching thing about all this is how it's brought us together," Barnabas replied blandly.

General Vidrelor chuckled quietly before looking at Jeltor. "You, Jotun. You say there are reinforcements coming?"

"Yes." Jeltor raised one arm and scanned the horizon, then pointed.

The general took note of the heading and gave an order, sending two wings of the circling fighters streaking off.

"We should get back to the city," he told them all. "We have injured soldiers, and need to mobilize the Army and formulate a plan."

"Yes," Jeltor said. "I think the first piece we should include is a strike team to infiltrate the Jotun flagship and rescue the admiral."

"We'll discuss it," Vidrelor said opaquely. "Let's get to the shuttles for now."

As they walked, Barnabas reached over to clasp Jeltor's shoulder. "I'm glad you recovered," he said quietly.

"So am I." Jeltor heaved a sigh. "Not that there weren't benefits to being converted, I can tell you that much. Life is back to being more complicated. It was easy when all I had to worry about was Grisor's orders." He shuddered inside his tank. "He was a nasty piece of work."

"Mmm." Barnabas wasn't sure yet how he wanted to broach the topic of Grisor's current imprisonment on the *Shinigami*. "Him and all of them. Let's make our plan and get this show on the road. I take it we don't have very long until they get here?"

"Six hours," Shinigami said.

"Six hours." Barnabas sighed and rotated his shoulders, grimacing. "Not a lot of time to plan a planet-wide defense against a famous admiral, but if anyone can do it, we can."

With a laugh, the others followed him into the shuttle.

On the *Shinigami*, Tafa stirred and opened her eyes.

"Shinigami?"

"Hello, Tafa." Shinigami's voice was surprised. "Why did you wake up? You still have some of your upgrades to go."

"I'm not sure why I woke up." Tafa felt pleasantly drowsy, as if she had run a long race and sparred a lot—although she wasn't as sore as she would be in that case, she was sure.

"Ah, I see the issue," Shinigami told her. "Your system processes the anesthesia much more quickly. Once I knew what I was looking for, I could see why. Are you ready to go under again?"

"Yes. Wait." Tafa tried to sit up. "Oh, my bones feel like lead. It's nice, though. It feels all right, just…very tired."

"Your body is doing a lot of work to heal and grow," Shinigami explained. "What did you want me to wait for?"

"How are things?" Tafa asked. "Did the mission go all right?"

"It went just fine," Shinigami soothed her. "We were able to get the Brakalon captives out, and you'll never guess who showed up! Jeltor. Barnabas checked his thoughts. He's no longer converted. He said that Barnabas' words to him at Grisor's estate helped him shed the conversion. He's safe, Tafa. Rest. You'll see him when you wake up."

Tafa gave a smile and settled back. As unconsciousness took her again, she knew only a feeling of profound contentment. Jeltor was back, the team was safe, and she could feel the changes in her bones and muscles.

She knew now what Barnabas had meant when he said that these changes were not to be feared. She could tell that she was more durable now, and stronger, but she also knew that she was the same person at heart.

All would be well.

The Jotun flagship hurtled through the black, and Admiral Jeqwar paced around her quarters. She was behind. The Committee had mismanaged their time and resources, and she was being brought in—as was normally the case—far too late in the process.

Luckily, any commander worth their position knew how to account for that. It was still frustrating, however, and even more, she had to deal with her present visitor.

"Do you have qualms?" Senator Torsen asked her delicately.

"What? No." She gave the female Jotun an impatient look. "Surely you're familiar with my history?"

"That was against another fleet," the senator pointed out. She had been sent as the Committee's main representative within the fleet to ensure that the Committee's orders were followed.

Admiral Jeqwar understood the necessity. After all, she had recently been the Committee's enemy. Still, the senator's insistence on having long discussions about feelings was tiresome and time-consuming.

They had an invasion to plan. That was no small thing.

"I do what I need to do in order to keep the Jotuns safe," Admiral Jeqwar told the senator, trying not to show her frustration with this conversation. They had gone through it multiple times. "We are, of course, trying to bring peace and order, not death. I will hardly kill civilians for the sake of it. Hopefully, the Brakalons will see the wisdom of letting us rule, and this can be accomplished easily, with minimal Naval involvement."

The senator looked at her suspiciously.

"What we *need* to do," Admiral Jeqwar said, running out of patience, "is make sure that the other captains do not realize what is happening. We have only one chance to take control of the fleet *and* enact our maneuvers before they realize who they are serving."

"You sound disapproving." The senator clearly did not think much of this.

"You could have waited until you had more captains converted," Admiral Jeqwar pointed out. "You say you have agents on some of the ships, but they can't pilot them, and I can't pilot the whole fleet indefinitely. You're rushing things. I still say we should pause once we get to Kordinev and bring the captains here in ones and twos to be converted. It's safer, and will eliminate some of the messiness down the line."

Senator Torsen got up to pace. She was delicate, and seemed to have compensated for that by making her suit bigger and bulkier than it needed to be.

She was, however, inflexible when it came to the Committee's orders. Her loyalty was absolute, and she had been hand-picked by Qarwit to come on this mission.

"There may be something to that," she admitted finally. "I will speak with His Excellency. After all, it's not as if the Brakalons have a *fleet*, right?"

"Exactly," Admiral Jeqwar replied. "I understand the need to move quickly, but we must not leave ourselves open. Better to take time where you need it."

Five stories under the surface of the capital city of Kordinev, an elevator opened to allow its passengers out. They strolled onto a broad semicircular deck and Shinigami gave a low whistle.

The cavern was massive. It was so big that Barnabas could not begin to guess its volume.

The problem was, things like carriers were so out of scale with a human body that the eye could barely encompass what it was looking at. He had to look twice, three times, even four times, before he accepted what he was seeing. It was still difficult to believe.

"The Brakalons *have* a fleet?" he asked.

"Yes." General Fedranor was amused by Barnabas' expression, but more amused by the mute astonishment of Ferqar and Jeltor. "Assembled in secret and hidden here, where even fairly detailed scans would miss them under the activity of the city."

Shinigami whistled again.

"And you've just been waiting for when you needed to use them," Jeltor said quietly, in awe. "Well, now's the right time."

"Agreed," Fedranor said. "If not now, when? When the Jotun fleet arrives, we'll have a surprise for them."

CHAPTER TWENTY-NINE

"Barnabas." Shinigami appeared in the hallway as a projection.

"You're looking particularly bloody-minded," Barnabas observed. She was wearing red armor several shades darker than blood, and somehow managed to be more menacing because of it. A cape fluttered from her shoulders in an unseen wind, held up by gold wolfs'-head clasps on her pauldrons. She held a helmet under her arm.

"Good. I'm feeling particularly bloody-minded." She got a glint in her eye, and Barnabas reflected that with most people, the glint would be figurative. With her, it was not. It was a literal glint, and it was red.

"You realize you don't *need* the helmet," he pointed out.

"Do I get on your case about how you dress while you're on the ship?"

"No." Barnabas gave her an unrepentant smile and picked an imaginary speck of dust off one sleeve. "But I dress irreproachably."

"Oh, *really?*" Shinigami cracked her knuckles. "One second—let me just limber up before absolutely annihilating you."

"Wasn't there something you had wanted to talk to me about?" Barnabas asked a bit hastily. He liked this suit. He was not prepared to have Shinigami tear it to figurative shreds just to make a point.

"Oh. Right." She nodded. "Three things: there's a planning meeting on the surface, Tafa is ready to come out of the Pod-doc already, and Jeltor says he needs to talk to you before you go down to the surface."

"Hmm. Let's start with Tafa."

"You got it, Al Capone."

"Hey!" Barnabas scowled as Shinigami sauntered off down the hall, snickering. He caught up with her a few moments later. "I am a *lot* better looking than Al Capone."

"Okay, I *will* give you that." She reached to open a door for him, the motion so smooth and effortless that he was through the door before he realized she'd timed her projection perfectly with the ship opening the door.

"That was impressive."

"Wasn't it? What must it be like to only be in one place at once, with no cool toys to play with?" She flexed her holographic hand, clearly pleased, and then made a giant flaming sword appear. "Oooh, I like this."

"You're wearing red armor and have a flaming sword, and you're getting on my case about my suit?"

"It's definitely not as cool as a flaming sword."

"Clothing should be about being neat," Barnabas admonished her severely. "Not being flashy."

"Oh, don't sell yourself short. You look very dapper."

"Thank you," Barnabas replied cautiously. He found himself more than a little worried that this was a trap of some kind.

He was right. "I'm sure Aliana would approve," Shinigami added, smiling beatifically.

"Listen here, now is no time to be talking about that. There is a fleet on the way which is commanded by an exceedingly capable admiral, and we have a planet-wide defense to plan." Barnabas stared Shinigami down and waited.

She didn't say anything.

He cracked. "Do you really think she would like the suit?"

Shinigami cackled.

"What *are* you two talking about?" Tafa broke in.

Both Barnabas and Shinigami jumped and looked at her.

"I'm so sorry, Tafa," Barnabas said after a moment. "We were, uh—"

"Arguing about clothes," Tafa finished. She swung her legs over the side of the Pod-doc, pushed off with her arms in an attempt to jump down, and managed to launch herself halfway across the room. "Oh, God! What the *hell*?"

"I should have mentioned," Shinigami murmured. She cleared her throat. "You're…a little stronger than you're used to right now. Be careful with it."

"Yes, that…*would* have been good to know before I threw myself on the ground." Tafa got up, moving very slowly and carefully.

"How do you feel?" Barnabas asked her.

"Well, I would say that I felt better before I got all bruised, but..." Tafa checked herself, "the bruises are already gone."

"Yes, that part *is* nice." Barnabas smiled. "Otherwise you feel good, though, yes?"

"Yes." Tafa smiled. "Remarkably good. I think...is my *vision* better?"

"Ah, yes." Shinigami smiled. "I made several adjustments in addition to strengthening you. Your vision and hearing have improved, the bones in your wrists and elbows were moved very slightly so that you'll get fewer tendon issues in the future, and your allergy to lactose is gone."

"I can have ice cream now?" Tafa demanded. She had been overjoyed to discover the human treat and crestfallen when it made her sick.

"You can have ice cream now," Shinigami confirmed. "In fact, I'll make a bowl for you in the kitchen. With whipped cream, which you didn't even get to try before."

"I'm going to go right now! I'm so hungry." Tafa took off at high speed, clipped the door frame, and ran into the wall on the opposite side of the corridor. "Oops! Still learning!" Her voice echoed back as she ran.

Barnabas was laughing as he looked after her. "I was worried about her being too timid. I didn't guess she would go full Gar on us."

"What?" Gar stuck his head around the door. "I heard my name. Also, I thought Tafa was here."

"Tafa is in the kitchen eating ice cream," Barnabas told him. "Unless she's managed to punch through a wall by accident."

"Speaking as the one with the ship-wide diagnostics, she's given it a couple of good shots," Shinigami said, rolling her eyes.

Barnabas laughed.

"I'll go find her," Gar said. "Unless...do you need me for anything?"

"I'll be going down to the surface for a planning meeting shortly," Barnabas told him. "I just need to speak to Jeltor first. I suspect we won't be able to bring everyone. They probably don't even want me there, but I want to make sure I know what's going on *and* that they're taking Ferqar and Gilwar's advice."

"Good call," Shinigami agreed. "Should we go talk to Jeltor first?"

"Yes." Barnabas nodded and flashed Gar a smile. "Keep an eye on Tafa for now. You know how disorienting it can be to suddenly have that much strength."

Gar headed off with a nod, and Barnabas and Shinigami made their way through the ship to Jeltor's quarters. The door slid open for them before they even knocked, showing that Jeltor had given them a tacit invitation to come in, but as they walked into the room, they heard the sound of crying.

"It isn't what I wanted," Jeltor was saying. "I didn't want any of this, Jelina. But my regret—it's for you. It's for the children. You didn't deserve to get caught up in this."

"*You* didn't deserve to get caught up in this!" Jelina's voice, even the mechanical voice from the biosuit, was wracked with pain. "Haven't you suffered enough? You've been tortured, Jeltor, and you didn't know who you were, but you found your way out. Haven't you done enough? Haven't you helped enough?"

Jeltor said nothing.

Almost in a whisper, Jelina asked, "Isn't there anyone else?"

"No." In that one word there was certainty. "Jelina, there isn't anyone else, I swear. If there were…"

"If there were, you would still do this because of your damned honor!" She flared, angry. "You'd say it was your responsibility. I know you." There was a long pause. "And it's part of what I love about you," Jelina whispered finally, defeated. "Jeltor, I understand. I know why you're doing this. I just…wish things were different."

"I know. So do I." Jeltor sounded devastated. "I would give anything for it to be different, but the Admiral needs to be turned back, or I don't even know how many lives will be lost. And I'm the only one who's been there and come back."

"I know." Jelina sounded like she was going to cry again. "At least you're dying as you, Jeltor, not as what they tried to make you."

"Yes." He sounded grateful. "Yes. I am glad we got to speak again."

Barnabas had heard enough. He strode into the room, and Jeltor swung to face him. On the monitors, Jelina looked over.

"*No one* is going to die for this," Barnabas announced. He held up a hand when Jeltor would have spoken. "No, you listen. We didn't get you back so you could throw yourself away in a Pyrrhic victory. I agree that Admiral Jeqwar needs to be re-converted, and I agree that you should be involved, but that's no reason to do things... Shinigami, what's the polite way to say this?"

"Don't be polite," Shinigami advised. She looked at Jeltor. "You're doing this the stupidest way possible," she explained. "Don't do that."

Barnabas threw up his hands and looked heavenward for patience.

"What? The fleet's arriving in five hours, so we don't have the time to be all pretty and flouncy."

Barnabas shook his head and looked at the screen. "Jelina, I am so sorry to cut this short, but would you mind if we spent some time planning with Jeltor? Please believe me when I say that I will find a way to have him help without putting him in undue danger. I give you my word."

Jelina hesitated, then nodded. "Jeltor, I love you. Listen to Barnabas."

"I...I will. I love you. Tell the kids I love them." Jeltor seemed ready to break down.

"I will." She, at least, seemed reassured by Barnabas' words. She ended the call.

"All right," Barnabas said briskly when Jeltor sat staring blankly at the black screen. "I know you were sure you were going to die and that would be the last time you would see her, but I'll be damned if I let that happen. And frankly I've been closer to being damned than most people, so I know what I'm talking about."

Jeltor gave a weak laugh.

"That's better." Barnabas pulled chairs over for him and Shinigami, and sat on one, smiling as she perched on the other. Fake cloaks apparently did not get snarled up on chairs. "So, what was your plan?"

"To infiltrate the flagship," Jeltor said miserably. "I thought I would try to appeal to her, call her back..." When his voice trailed off, Barnabas realized what Jeltor was hinting at and why he was so miserable.

He was prepared to kill Admiral Jeqwar if he needed to.

"It won't come to that," he assured the captain. "We'll find a way to cut her off from the fleet if we need to. And I wonder...is there a way to get you inside her head without being present on the ship?"

All of them pondered this for a few moments.

"There might be," Shinigami said finally. "So much is going through the system when an admiral takes control of the fleet. It shouldn't be difficult to sneak a few more signals in, in a way that they won't be able to find them for a while. With some help from our Jotun friends, I should be able to learn enough about the mechanisms to do that. The catch..."

"Yes?" Barnabas lifted an eyebrow.

"I'd have to be in the middle of the battle," Shinigami said. "I don't think I can do it from the ground."

Barnabas chewed his lip, but Jeltor laughed. "That sounds like old times," he said. "We faced down the Yennai fleet, and we can do this. At least I know this fleet well."

"That's the spirit," Shinigami said encouragingly. She cocked her head to the side. "Barnabas, the team on the ground has a plan, and General Vidrelor has offered to brief you on it."

Barnabas groaned and got to his feet. "He just hates having me involved, doesn't he?"

"He does," Shinigami confirmed. "He hates it *so much.*

But think of it this way: the fact that he's still including you is an incredible measure of respect for your abilities."

"I suppose there's that." Barnabas looked at Jeltor, then Shinigami. "So you have a plan, then? A way to get to the admiral without putting Jeltor in too much danger?"

Shinigami hesitated, then laid her plan out for him. It was dangerous, Barnabas had to admit that, but it was also very sound—and safer than Jeltor's plan. He looked at Jeltor.

Jeltor nodded once. "It's no more dangerous than being in any part of that battle," he said, "and good people, sailors and captains, are involved now. You're right, I don't have to do this the stupid way…but I'm not going to sit it out either. Tell Vidrelor what we'll be doing."

"I will," Barnabas assured him. He considered. "All right. I'm going to take Tafa and Gar, and I'll send the people you need back in a Pod. I'll see you all after the battle."

Shinigami gave him a salute that somehow managed to be ironic and serious at the same time, genuine respect showing under her mischievous smile. Jeltor nodded deeply to Barnabas.

"You keep saving my life," he observed. "I'll have to repay you for that."

"You can buy me some juice at Aebura's when we're done," Barnabas told him with a grin, and he made his way out of the room to get dressed for the battle.

He was whistling as he went, an old tune he'd long since forgotten the name of, and it occurred to him to wonder how he could be so happy on the eve of a battle.

He knew why, of course. Still, he told himself it was the fact that all of this would be done soon. The Committee was finally outflanked and outplayed. They had no idea they were going to face down a Brakalon fleet when they arrived. The Committee would be ended, and the long process of justice could begin.

Yes. That was why he was so happy.

CHAPTER THIRTY

Senator Torsen insisted on being on the bridge when the Jotun fleet arrived at Kordinev. It made Admiral Jeqwar want to beat her body against the wall of her tank, but she floated motionless in the central canister, her biosuit standing nearby, lifeless. From her position on the bridge, she could see everyone, and they could see her.

A large series of connections at the top and bottom of the tank gave her input from each of the ships in the fleet and allowed her to send signals back. If she tuned out the sensory data she received from her own body, she could *feel* the fleet around her—little pinpricks with different signatures, showing her which were accelerating and which were decelerating, which were arming missiles, and which were in communications with other ships. In a battle, she would be able to sense this not only about her own fleet but about the enemy ships that could be seen by their sensory arrays.

Because of this, she was the first one to notice the other fleet.

It was only by a split-second, of course. Almost instantaneously, the klaxons blared to life and the bridge descended into carefully-channeled chaos.

There was a moment, however, when she was the only one who knew, and she saw the game shift and change before her eyes. This had been almost dishonorable before, arriving at a planet that had no hope of defending itself. Now there was another fleet.

She knew the disappointment of a thwarted plan and the exhilaration of the coming fight.

Then she swung into motion. While Senator Torsen was still ducking—to get away from what? the admiral wondered contemptuously—and bobbing stupidly in her tank, Admiral Jeqwar took control of the fleet seamlessly and without hesitation. The formation spread into two wings at the sides, with contingents of fighters both above and below the flagship and a single spear thrusting toward Kordinev.

"Admiral Jeqwar!" Senator Torsen was babbling something about plans and Qarwit and all manner of useless rules and checklists the admiral had no time for.

"Let them come," she said, and because she was hooked into the entire system, her words boomed throughout the room and the fleet. "This is why you brought me here. This is what I do. Let us show not only the Brakalons but all species that they can try to stand against us, but they will be cut down."

Shinigami had established contact with the Jotun flagship as soon as it was in range of her scanners—which was to say, considerably before *it* saw *them*.

The idiots hadn't even thought to send scout ships. They'd been so damned certain that they knew what was waiting for them, they'd just launched their fleet through space with no plan as to what would happen if anyone stood up to them.

The admiral, at least, had reacted quickly. The formation of the Jotun fleet changed before their eyes, and Shinigami watched from the bridge of each Jotun and Brakalon ship as the two fleets readied for battle.

As General Vidrelor had asked, she had fed the admiral's words to each of the Brakalon captains. She was pleased to see that none of them seemed worried.

She had been worried when she listened to their plans through Barnabas' ears. How could a fleet that had never been in combat have a hope of defeating a famed admiral? She had thought it was a bad bet, indeed.

Then they had shown her the drills they ran with data pulled from every known battle of every alien species. The Brakalons had not simply built a secret fleet, they had trained extensively to use it.

And, much like the admiral had experience on her side, they had the element of surprise.

It hinged, in Shinigami's assessment, on how the Jotuns intended to use their fleet. After all, the Jotuns did not have much in the way of infantry, so their gambit must surely have been to put the major cities of Kordinev in the crosshairs and demand compliance.

Well, they had *probably* intended to have converted agents within the government who could order troop deployment before anyone knew what was going on, but now their plan would have to be enacted by force.

She did a quick scan of the Brakalon fleet to make sure no Jotun signals were interfering with operations, then checked in with Barnabas.

How are things going on the surface, chief?

Well enough, Barnabas reported. *We're all just waiting.*

The Brakalon action plan had been to ready troops and station them at various strategically-important jump points, getting ready to respond quickly to any ground assaults. With a Pod at his disposal, Barnabas had offered to be part of the first response team, and he and Gar were ready to go whenever the alert came.

Tafa was in the Pod as well, but Barnabas had absolutely forbidden her from stepping foot outside it. As soon as he and Gar were out, it would withdraw to a safe distance. Tafa wasn't happy with this, but even she had to admit that a two-species planet-wide showdown involving fleets, an entire army, and specialized strike teams wasn't exactly "baby's first battle" material.

How are things on your end? Barnabas asked curiously. *I see the admiral is preparing for confrontation.*

She's glad of it, Shinigami replied. *She's an honorable opponent. She didn't like the idea of steamrolling the Brakalons.*

I hope we get her back, Barnabas remarked soberly.

The way she reacted tells me that we should be able to. What kind of honorable opponent works for the Committee?

You ask that, but a great many people with well-developed

systems of honor have fought for deeply dishonorable causes over the years.

Give me this one. Shinigami began her quick dance through the Brakalon fleet. In order for their plan to work, they needed to be invisible to the Jotuns and moving quickly. Thankfully for her, she had experience with Jotun scanners and several Jotuns to work with to develop her strategy.

Then the main cannons began arming in the flagship and she felt herself settle into cold anticipation.

It's beginning. I'll update you as I can.

Godspeed, Barnabas said, and she caught both the worry and the affection in his tone.

You too, chief.

The Brakalon fleet had not only spread out into a maneuverable, difficult formation to take on, more ships kept arriving around the curve of the planet.

Where had they been *hiding* these ships, godsdammit? Admiral Jeqwar felt a stab of what might almost be called sympathy for Senator Torsen, who was pacing up and down and muttering to herself. She was clearly worried about what would happen to her if they failed in this mission.

And while politicians got, in the admiral's estimation, exactly what they deserved, she had to admit that this particular development could hardly be laid at the senator's door. No one had known this fleet existed.

There was no time for surprise, however. She needed to

show them what battle was. If no one had seen this fleet before, it meant that they had trained in simulations.

And in simulations, people didn't die. Her opening gambit would be to make them feel the losses and get their first taste of fear. She went for two of their support ships first, the repair-and-rescue ships that would zoom through the battle to any wounded ship. She had identified them early.

Take out your enemy's support and they had only one charge. Give them a taste of fear, put death nipping at their heels, and they would begin to make mistakes. They would take desperate risks, too emotional to hold the line and wait for their opportunity.

She would be ready.

The rescue ships went tumbling out of formation, and the countermeasures the flagship had launched, assuming that *it* was in the crosshairs, shot harmlessly into the void between the two fleets.

Admiral Jeqwar felt a wave of satisfaction. *Yes,* she thought. *Now it begins. Now you see.*

Then the words started in her head.

Admiral Jeqwar. She knew that voice, although she had never heard it inside her head. She could not place it.

Who is this?

A reminder of your conscience. There was humor now. *I am Gilwar. You do not know my name, but you have seen my work. It was my assassins who found Huword.*

A cowardly act, she shot back. She readied another spread of missiles, keeping her attention on the flagship, and then had the ships at the flanks set *their* missiles loose and begin to swing inwards.

No, the cowardly act was to abduct civilians and torture them. The cowardly act was to pretend that the Jotuns were superior. If we were superior, it would be so clear that other species would welcome our leadership. Now, even our own people do not. They must be brainwashed.

She felt bile swirl within her. She was not brainwashed. She hated that accusation. It filled her with strange panic. She shot wildly, succumbing to her own emotions before calming herself.

I was not brainwashed, she told her opponent. *I was freed. I was given clarity to accept my own thoughts on the matter.*

Oh? said a new voice, one that was much more familiar. *I thought the same once, Yeneda. But those thoughts—the thoughts that we were superior—they were thoughts I had already rejected, and I rejected them again.*

Traitor. Admiral Jeqwar listened to the words coming from her mind and felt a strange sense of dislocation. She had never been one to spit insults at people, and yet, here she was. She meant the insults, too. It felt good to say them. Jeltor *was* a traitor; he had turned his back on Qarwit and Grisor.

Unfortunately, he also knew her well.

It isn't like you to say something like that, he observed. *Yeneda. I remember how this feels, how uncomplicated it feels to love the Committee and hate who they hate. But it doesn't sit right in your mind, does it? You know it's false. It feels wrong.*

Frozen in her tank, Admiral Jeqwar missed a round of missiles, and her captains had to seize control of their ships to get out of the way in time.

"What's going on?" Senator Torsen hissed.

"There's a signal, and they've gotten it into her tank."

One of the communications officers was stabbing keys desperately. "As soon as she started communicating, I found it, but I can't shut it down. I'm doing everything, I swear."

Senator Torsen snarled in fury, but she knew better than to make an example of the people who were working to interrupt this. She paced a few steps, then swung around to look at the commanders clustered around the battle table.

"Find out where that signal is coming from."

"Yes, ma'am. We're working on it."

"You're 'working on it?'" she asked dangerously.

"Yes, ma'am. It's moving very quickly, as we know the *Shinigami* is capable of doing. They're moving and bouncing the signal off the Brakalon ships."

Senator Torsen considered this. "Send in a squadron of fighters. Take. Them. Out."

"Yes, ma'am."

As the fighters accelerated into the black, Shinigami snickered to herself. Then, the sleek form of her ship lying flat in a shadowed groove atop the Jotun flagship, she continued her work of opening one of the exterior hatches for Jeltor, Gilwar, and Ferqar to sneak aboard.

As the hatch opened silently, Shinigami caught another command: "And land the strike teams."

Barnabas.

Hmm?

You're a go. Strike teams are leaving. I'll keep you all updated on their trajectories.

Thank you.

This senator is practically shitting herself, by the way. Almost no one knows that this is a fake mission, and she can't afford to let them find out. Don't worry, I'm taping it. We can have some popcorn and watch the highlights reel later.

So good of you to keep me in mind.

Don't be snide. This is comedy gold right here.

CHAPTER THIRTY-ONE

"General." Barnabas activated the communications unit in the Pod, which had been tied into the Brakalon network. Shinigami had stress-tested it and rigged it to shut down if there was even a possibility the line was being tapped. "The strike teams are on their way. My Pod will intercept automatically, and I will keep you apprised of locations."

"Understood." General Vidrelor's voice was calm. "I envy you, you know," he added.

A piece of the puzzle snapped into place and Barnabas smiled. Part of General Vidrelor's ill-temper, it seemed, had been because he was jealous that Barnabas would be in the thick of things and he would not.

Barnabas approved of that. He had no use for military leaders who were afraid to get their hands dirty.

All he said was, "Do Brakalons speak of tempting fate, General? You may get your chance."

The general rang off with a good-natured laugh that

said he would not be sad to do so, and Barnabas smiled in anticipation as the Pod began to move.

Two strike teams, Shinigami reported. *Verified by my scanners, the Brakalon scanners, and what the bridge crew is tracking. They're going to the two sites where the top-level officials were quartered. It appears they are not sure what happened there. Our cutoff worked.*

It's going to be pretty obvious when they get there, Barnabas responded wryly. *But we'll pin them down and take them out before they can go wreak havoc anywhere else. Which team should we go to?*

The heavier team is heading for the military site. They seem to be assuming that a military leader would be more able to launch a defense if necessary.

Solid thinking. Too bad they're behind the curve.

Yeah, couldn't have happened to nicer people.

Barnabas smiled and relayed Shinigami's words, telling the Brakalons that he and Gar were heading to the military site. Gar was elated, while Tafa frowned and fidgeted.

"Next battle, you'll get to participate," Barnabas told her.

"I'm not worried about that. What if someone senses Grisor?" She looked worried. "What if he manages to create problems?"

"Ah." Barnabas held up one finger. *Shinigami, could you project an image of Grisor's cell into the Pod for Tafa?*

Sure? Shinigami's doubtful tone aside, she did so with alacrity. *There you go.*

Thanks. "See?" Barnabas said to Tafa. "Entirely cut off from any signals and still trapped."

"Aren't we going to...use him somehow?" Gar asked doubtfully. "I'm with Tafa on this one."

Barnabas gave an evil smile and sat back, stretching out his legs. "Actually, I had a rather different idea. We don't need him to head off this plan, at least not yet, and it's driving him *crazy* to be held captive and not even be interrogated. He doesn't have a self-destruct on his suit, and he's a coward about death. He made sure everyone else had them, but he doesn't, so he has no way to get out of this. And once the battle's over?" His smile was very cold. "I'll go down and tell him about it. Tell him that while he was rotting in that cell, the Committee fell to pieces and he had no idea it was even happening. Then I'll take him back for his trial."

There was a moment of stunned silence, then Gar whistled. "You're *cold*."

"I learned from the best." Barnabas grinned as he thought of Bethany Anne.

Barnabas, you're arriving at the site. You've beaten the strike team. I suggest hiding behind the bunker. All of the decoys are in place to draw them in.

Good, Barnabas said. The decoys had been a rather ingenious Brakalon idea that they had perfected with Ferqar's help. They would emit signals indicating that the lost data showing what had happened at these sites could be found inside the bunker.

The Pod let Barnabas and Gar out, and both of them smiled at Tafa before leaving. She waved at them bravely, but Barnabas could see she was worried for them. Then the Pod shot back into the sky, invisible to the naked eye and Jotun scanners.

Barnabas and Gar hid behind the bunker, settling a large cloak of stiff fabric over them that confused most scanning technology and hid their biosignatures.

Not long now, Barnabas thought, and he felt the familiar rush of anticipation. He had fought the Committee for so long from the shadows. He was glad to be fighting them out in the open at last.

He jumped when something rustled nearby, then started laughing.

"Hello," Kelnamon greeted him. "They said that after my service and injuries I couldn't be allowed to fight in this battle. Didn't matter that I told them you'd patched me up, so I picked a place I was pretty sure would see some action, and here I am."

"Glad to have you." Barnabas clasped his hand in greeting. "Couldn't ask for a better fighter at my side."

Captain Qrevar of Strike Team 4 was a sturdy, thick-bodied Jotun who wielded his biosuit like a tank, always ready to charge into the action headlong rather than hide away and snipe at his enemies.

In his years doing various black ops work for both the Senate and the Navy he'd learned a healthy dose of respect for the fighting capabilities of various species, but he had never lost his conviction that the Jotuns were superior to all others. After all, the Jotuns could adapt themselves to any environment or opponent, their grasp of technology was incredible, and they were, of course, more intelligent than other species.

That was just fact. People could deny it, but they knew they were lying. He was confident.

"Get ready," he barked at his team. He did not tolerate sloppiness or emotion on the battlefield, and some of them seemed shaken by the first images they were seeing of the other bunker. The scattered Jotun bodies there had been Team 2, and the teams had fought together. "We're going to extract every piece of information we can from this bunker and go find their leaders. Speed is of the essence. You want to cry, you can quit right now. We'll be better off without you."

Everyone readied their weapons without a word. When their shuttle touched down, they were leaping out before it had stopped and charging into the bunker on heavy, mechanized legs.

"Spread out!" Qrevar ordered. He was heading up the rear as they went into the darkness, so he was poised to advance in the first wave.

Or that had been the plan.

There was a faint hint of motion behind him, and he swiveled sharply in his tank but saw nothing. He sent out a brief pulse of scanning, sensed no life forms, and sighed internally. He was being superstitious. The building had been heavily damaged by the bombing; of *course*, it was creaking oddly.

He swiveled back around and shot backward to slam against the wall of the tank in shock.

His biosuit's sensors had not picked up the alien, but there it was, staring at him with its head tilted to the side as other species did to indicate curiosity.

And its eyes were glowing red.

"Hello," it said pleasantly.

Qrevar's arm was already coming up out of sheer instinct, rifle primed and loaded, but he felt the stab of pain a moment later, haptic controls embedded in his suit and telling him that the connections were being severed one by one. His body went rigid, unsure of the input he was sending it, then thudded to the ground when the power went out.

Qrevar was still floating helplessly in the tank as a Luvendi stepped over his body and disappeared into the darkness without another glance—heading for Qrevar's team, none of whom knew that there were enemies inside the bunker.

The captain was taken out quickly and efficiently, and Barnabas and Gar continued into the darkness silently, Kelnamon leading the way like a giant, hulking shadow.

Ahead of them, the Jotun strike team was calling to one another as they spread out. They weren't being sloppy, which Barnabas appreciated—but their loyalty was in a very unfortunate place, and he could not let that go unpunished.

At the opening of the main cavern, he gave Gar and Kelnamon a nod and disappeared into the rafters, leaping lightly and climbing his way up. He had communicated his plan to them while the strike team was landing.

That plan was shock and awe. The Jotun might have heard of Barnabas before, but it was almost certain that they considered stories of his exploits to be overblown.

They were about to learn how wrong they were.

Barnabas waited until one group had advanced to the center of the room, checking the main command desk for clues, and then he activated the first line of defense. Around the room, what had looked like inert and destroyed turrets came to life in jerky motion, swinging themselves to their spidery feet and each locking on a target: one of the Jotun soldiers

Which was when Barnabas dropped out of the ceiling onto the team below.

He hit the desk with a thud that spread a crack all through it and looked up, baring his teeth at them. They weren't human, not born of Earth, but some things were universal, and one of those universal things was a fear of sharp, pointy claws and teeth. Given two shocks in a row, the team froze for one critical, deadly moment.

A moment, of course, was all Barnabas needed. He swung into action at once, grabbing the closest Jotun and flipping it over his head to bring it crashing down on the corner of the table. The tank in its biosuit cracked and was partially dislodged, and he picked it up to slam it down again before ripping one of the legs and one of the arms off, doing the same with the head, and flinging all of the pieces in opposite directions. He bared his teeth at the other three in the group and hissed.

Around the edges of the room, the other soldiers had been pinned by the turrets. The laser sights made it clear that if they fired they would be picked off one by one. Still, in an admirable display of loyalty, they tried.

They failed on two counts. First, because the turrets truly *were* an outstanding piece of technology, and

Shinigami had easily been able to reprogram them; and second, because they had failed to realize that Gar and Kelnamon were also in the room.

The turrets and the other members of the team set to work methodically, working their way through the Jotun strike team as holo of the event was beamed back to the Jotun fleet.

Meanwhile, in the middle of the room, Barnabas dodged the strikes and weapons of the Jotun team as they launched themselves at him in a fury.

The Jotun strike teams were well-trained in hand-to-hand combat, but none of them came close to matching Barnabas. The Jotuns tended to rely on their technology, using reaction time and brute strength to overpower their foes.

Their tactics were weak, and Barnabas was easily able to exploit them. One after the other, he punched through their tanks, ripped off their limbs, and destroyed both the suit and the Jotun within.

When it was over, and the room was finally silent, he looked up to where the cameras were observing.

"You spent so much time thinking you were superior," he told the Jotun, "that you never even bothered to check if you were right. *And you were wrong.*"

That got their goat, I'll tell ya. Shinigami was chortling in Barnabas' mind. *They're pissed as hell.*

Good. Any progress on your mission?

Coming along. She sounded a bit worried now. *I'll let you know, however we end up having to do this. There's a small chance we may just initiate the pod ejection into space for her tank and snatch her that way.*

Mmm. Let me know.

On Jotuna D, Qarwit paced and threw glances at the screen in increasing worry.

This wasn't how this was supposed to be unfolding. The strike teams had been used dozens of times in his memory, and he had *seen* them in action. They were unstoppable, a deadly force that infiltrated, found intel, and spread outwards until all targets had been eliminated.

And now two of his teams had easily been wiped out. Not only that, the Brakalons had a damned *fleet*.

He sensed the other Committee members watching him, judging him, and he drew himself up.

"One strike team is nothing," he said dismissively. "And if the Brakalons have anyone as good as Admiral Jeqwar, I'll eat my biosuit."

CHAPTER THIRTY-TWO

The Jotun fighters wove through the Brakalon fleet at top speed, splitting to arc over and under the enemy ships, coalescing and bunching like birds in flight. They had to avoid not only the Brakalon turrets aboard the ships but also their own missiles, which were hurtling toward the Brakalon fleet at unpredictable intervals.

There had been some disturbance aboard the flagship. They were aware of that, but firing had resumed and they were not going to waste their time wondering what was going on.

They had dangerous quarry to catch, after all: the *Shinigami*, elegant and maneuverable, not to mention absolutely deadly. Many of the pilots here had been part of the confrontation with the Yennai fleet weeks ago, and they had seen the *Shinigami* then.

It wasn't clear to them why the *Shinigami* had been their ally in that fight, only to become their enemy now, but there was broad support for the admiral. Unlike many who rose high, she had earned her place with brilliant tactics and a breathtaking command of the entire fleet.

If she said that the Brakalons and the *Shinigami* were their enemies, the pilots were not going to question her.

The thing was…

"Blue Leader to flagship," Captain Horutan radioed back finally.

There was a pause.

"Yes?" The communications officer sounded somewhat harried.

"Are you *sure* the *Shinigami* is over here?" Horutan asked.

"Yes. That's where the signal is coming from. Why?"

"Because we should have seen it by now," Horutan insisted. She calibrated her scanners for the eighth time. "If not on our scanners, then with the naked eye. And we can't find them anywhere."

A new voice came over the line, snapping at them furiously:

"This is Senator Torsen. You find that ship and you take it out *now*, do you understand? They are trying to attack the admiral!"

What that meant, Horutan did not know—nor did she understand why there was a senator on board the flagship. But a threat to the admiral was something she took *very* seriously.

"Blue team, spread out," she instructed. "They're trying to hurt the admiral, and we're *not* going to let them."

There was a round of wholehearted agreement. No one was going to touch the admiral. They would make sure of it.

"This is dangerous," Jeltor murmured to Gilwar as they strode down the corridors. "I shouldn't have come. Too many of them know me by sight."

"Anyone who knows you is likely to be an ally," Gilwar pointed out. "We have video evidence of what the Committee has done, and they'll know something happened to you."

"If they sound an alarm, though…" Jeltor was worried. "They're good sailors. They don't deserve to die for the Committee."

"That's why we're sticking to side corridors," Gilwar told him soothingly. "I can incapacitate them if I need to. We just need to be able to drag them into a corner if necessary without too many people seeing." He looked at Jeltor. "I think you've waited long enough, by the way. Try again."

The infiltration team of Jeltor, Gilwar, and Ferqar was advancing through side corridors, making for the bridge while Jeltor periodically established contact with the admiral.

After the first disturbance, she had not been so vulnerable. She had taken back command of the fleet with a single-minded intensity and was making fast, daring maneuvers that left the Brakalons scrambling to mount a defense.

With such danger, they hadn't yet been able to mount any sort of offense, and Jeltor feared they might be running out of time. Sooner or later, someone would slip. They would fail to get out of the way in time.

He knew exactly what was going through Admiral

Jeqwar's head. He had been there, after all, with his conversion fighting his true thoughts and memories. He understood that although his questions to her were gently prying away the conversion, each round of questions spurred an instinctive defense and rush of loyalty.

In order to turn her back to their side, he would need to allow each rush of loyalty to burn itself out, leaving only the questions and doubt behind. So, between each round of questions, he had waited several minutes.

His fear was that, as the rushes of loyalty took over, the admiral might do something truly terrible. When Jeltor had been faced with the same trial, he hadn't been hooked into an entire fleet. He'd been alone in his prison.

This one, he thought, had to count. This one had to finish it.

Admiral.

You again! Her voice sounded fearful. *Where are you? My fighters can't find you.*

Yes, I see them. He wasn't above fooling her. *They're looking for the wrong thing.* As she dropped out of his mind for a moment, no doubt giving them orders to search for a different ship, he said gently, *What are you afraid of when you hear my voice? You're afraid of not supporting the Committee anymore...aren't you?*

Get out of my head! The voice was horrified, pleading. *I'm doing what must be done.*

Slow down and think for a moment, Jeltor advised her. *You don't want to, do you? What they did to you makes you not want to think. Because if you did, you'd want to know why you have to attack the Brakalons.*

We need an army, she said at once.

Yes. They told me the same thing.

She had no answer to that.

So, tell me this, Jeltor asked her. Their small group walked past another group running in the opposite direction, and they saluted. His heart pounded, but the others did not recognize him. *They say that we need an army, that the only way to outmaneuver the other species is by taking them over one by one.*

It's true, she said at once.

Admiral, it is no flattery to say that you are the greatest tactical mind in generations. If that were true...why wouldn't you have thought it, yourself?

There was a long silence.

Boom, Shinigami said softly in Jeltor's mind.

You were listening?

Of course. Every time you start talking to her, she starts firing like crazy and then it trails off. I'll try to give the Brakalon fleet a heads up.

Smart.

You literally just described an AI.

Jeltor managed a trembling smile. Since this had begun, he'd been gripped by fear.

They had made their way through two more turns and were approaching the bridge when Admiral Jeqwar spoke again. Her voice was hushed and fearful.

Jeltor, I am afraid to think of it. Me! I am afraid to think.

Jeltor tried to come up with something inspirational to say, something that would stir her to battle, and then he realized that was not what she needed. *I am here,* he told her. *I was afraid, too. Step through the fear. Think the thoughts it doesn't want you to think. I am here.*

She said nothing for a long time and their group hesitated, out of sight of the bridge doors. They couldn't stand for much longer without attracting attention.

Admiral—

They will kill me when they see that I have turned back. Her voice was tight. *Have I—did I kill any of the Brakalons?* She seemed to remember, then. *I did. All gods forgive me, I took out their rescue ships.*

Right now you must focus on ending this battle, Jeltor said urgently. *Can you send a message to the captains without the senators on board knowing?*

Better, she said after a moment, and there was a flash of the commander she had been, capable and confident. *I can shut down their ships remotely and broadcast a message about what is going on. But Senator Torsen and her thugs—*

Leave that to us, Jeltor said. To the other two, he said quietly, "We need to move *now*."

They burst out of the shadows and began running for the doors to the bridge. The senator's personal guard leapt into action at once, leveling their rifles.

"Stop!"

"Urgent message for the senator!" Jeltor called back. He wasn't sure this would work, but he didn't really mind either way. Of all the people on this ship, he wouldn't mind killing these two. They were trying to prevent any news from getting onto the bridge.

"What message?" one of the guards called suspiciously. "Slow down and approach with your hands up or we *will* take this as a sign of aggression."

I need you on the bridge now! Admiral Jeqwar told Jeltor.

"Aggression it is, I guess," Jeltor murmured.

Gilwar gave a snort.

All three raised their weapons and shot in unison. Jeltor used a technique he'd seen Shinigami and Barnabas use and brought his back leg up to kick out as he reached the door. The force of his kick lifted one of the guards and threw him against the metal.

Or it would have. Shinigami obligingly forced the doors open at the correct moment, and the guard went sailing into the room.

The lights dimmed and a voice boomed out, projected to the whole fleet.

"The senators aboard your ships are traitors. There is no reason to attack the Brakalon fleet. I have been freed from their control and tell you to seize each one aboard their ships. Evidence will be sent to the bridge of each ship."

"Shut off that message!" Senator Torsen screamed.

But she had been right to worry. The Jotuns on the bridge turned, stunned, to where the admiral had forcibly taken command of the fleet and decommissioned all the guns.

"Just as Jeltor was taken captive by rogue agents in the government, so was I," she told them. "There, my mind was altered to produce loyalty to a rogue faction of our government. They sought to take *your* service and turn it to their own ends!"

"If you won't do it, I'll do it myself!" Senator Torsen grabbed a gun from one of her personal guards and leveled it at the admiral's tank. "Traitor! I knew you were wavering."

She didn't get the chance to shoot.

"Bridge left shoots!" one of the commanders yelled. "Bridge right, duck!"

Those on the right of the bridge dropped to the floor as those on the left pulled out their sidearms and shot. Sensory panels exploded across the room, and in the center of it, the senator and her guards were caught in the fire of dozens of weapons.

When the echoes died down, there was a long pause.

"Well done," the admiral said drily. "But next time let's not destroy *quite* so much equipment, shall we?"

There was a laugh and a ragged cheer, and Jeltor felt the tension in his body relax. He floated happily in his tank.

I'll tell Barnabas, Shinigami said. A moment later, she added, *Actually, do you three want to stay there? Barnabas and I have a rabbit to catch.*

Eh? Gilwar asked.

Seconded, Ferqar said. *I'm confused.*

Qarwit and his personal guard saw what happened on the surface and what happened here, Shinigami reported, with relish. *They're running.*

We'll stay here, Jeltor said after checking with the others. *Good hunting.*

Thank you, Shinigami said. *I'll make a highlights reel, don't worry.*

CHAPTER THIRTY-THREE

The *Shinigami* was racing through the darkness when Barnabas made his way down to the brig.

Grisor turned to stare at him, and Barnabas didn't have to know Jotun mannerisms to feel the hatred emanating from the senator.

"Did you think solitude would turn me?" he asked viciously. "I am as devoted to my cause as I ever was."

"That's nice," Barnabas said blandly. "Did you know that Qarwit took over in your absence?"

"I instructed that he should," Grisor said stiffly. "If you hope to make me turn on him out of jealousy, you will be sadly disappointed."

"You really don't know me at all." Barnabas leaned in the doorway, arms crossed. "No, you see, I wasn't looking for anything from you. I just came here to give you some facts."

Grisor paused in his pacing. There was wariness in his thoughts now, piercing the absolute certainty he'd had before.

"The Jotun people will support me," he asserted finally. Barnabas had seen his assessment: that the Jotun people must know about the Committee by now.

"Oh, that's good to hear," Barnabas commented. "For you, I mean. I personally doubt it, but I guess we'll see what happens when they find out, won't we?"

There was fear in Grisor's mind now. "What have you done?" he asked, his voice thick with anger.

"Oh, I hardly think you should be allowed to get angry on that score. Do you?" Barnabas could feel his own anger beginning to stir. "You're the one who abducted civilians, naval captains, and Lord only knows how many of your own species and others, to torture them into compliance. You're the one who made plans to forcibly take over other planets. I don't think you get to ask me what I've done, as if I've gone and done something rash; something ruinous."

You're getting poetic, Shinigami commented.

I like words, so sue me. I deserve some dramatic flair now and again.

Uh-huh.

"Qarwit knew there wasn't much time," Barnabas said. "He did something quite clever, really. He abducted the admiral's personal aide, Gorsik. Once converted, Gorsik was able to lure the admiral into a trap as well, and they set off for Kordinev at once. Of course, when they got there..." He allowed himself a chuckle. "They found out that all of the captives on the ground were already free, and not only *that*, the Brakalons had a fleet! Who knew?"

Pure shock came from Grisor. "You're joking."

"I assure you, I am not." Barnabas offered a small olive branch. "It was a surprise to me, too."

Grisor seemed very far from appreciative. "Get on with it, then. The fleet took losses?"

"Oh, no." Barnabas was chuckling now. "No, it turns out that *Jeltor* actually shed his conversion, so he was one of the ones who took out a strike team on the ground, and then he sneaked aboard the flagship and un-converted the admiral, so there were only a couple of ships lost on either side. Whoever the senator was on the flagship, *she's* dead, and her guards, and a few of the senators on the other ships…and the Committee's files have all been sent to the Senate while I take *you* back to stand trial."

Grisor stared at him.

"That was it," Barnabas finished. "Qarwit got away, so you're probably going to take the fall for the invasion—which *is* fair, really, since you *did* plan it. Your technology has been destroyed. Only the results of the experimentation have been kept, so no one can rebuild it. You spent decades on this, didn't you? Now it's all gone."

He gave a smile, pushed himself away from the door, and headed away.

He had gotten five steps before he won his bet with Shinigami.

"Wait! What if I knew where Qarwit went?"

Ha-Ha! Barnabas was triumphant. *I told you he had no loyalty to anyone.*

Earlier, you said that people could be honorable and do dishonorable things!

Sometimes. Sometimes they're cowardly little shits.

It's your fault for confusing me with organic illogic.

Mmhmm. Barnabas strolled back to the door and peered at Grisor. "How would that help me?" he asked.

"How would it— I planned the invasion, but he carried it out!" Grisor was practically spitting nails, or would have been if he'd had a mouth. "They'll hang me out to dry, but he should pay too."

I hate this kind of person, Barnabas told Shinigami wearily. *If they suffer, everyone else has to as well.*

To Grisor, he said, "I don't know. I'm willing to see you hang for it. Seems like you want this more than I do."

"You *hate* letting people get away!" Grisor was defiant. "I know you do, don't pretend. And I don't want much. I'll tell you everything—as long as you don't let them give me the death penalty."

Barnabas stared at him for a long moment. There was no resolve left in Grisor, no principle or even the memory of it. He was all desperation, and he was going to tell the truth.

"All right," Barnabas agreed easily. "Where's Qarwit?"

"You won't let them give me the death penalty?"

"I won't let them give you the death penalty."

Grisor sagged with relief. Barnabas thought that if he were human, he might have wet himself. "Thank all the gods. Qarwit is on a ship shuttling between two moons." He turned and projected the coordinates on the wall. "There's extensive interference from the sun and the nebula, so it's almost impossible to find, and the ship is stocked for years. He'll be able to hide out until long after people have stopped looking for him, and then he'll have the money to go start a new life." He sounded resentful.

"You always knew you might fail," Barnabas said. He waited.

"Yes," Grisor admitted finally.

"You feel like that money should be yours."

"Yes."

"Mmm. Well, since I can tell you told me the truth, we'll go take care of Qarwit. In fact, we'll do what you want to do to him for failing you. We'll kill him."

Grisor sensed the danger. He looked up.

"Then we'll take you back to stand trial," Barnabas said. "And you'll take whatever punishment they give you."

"You promised me!" Grisor yelled.

"I don't make bargains with people like you," Barnabas told him. He shook his head. "And I will not interfere in the Jotun process of Justice." He turned to leave, then stopped. "Do you know," he said conversationally, "it might not be a bad idea to let you live. Let you live with your failure, knowing that the Jotuns didn't support you after all. That might not be a bad idea at all."

He was smiling as he left the brig.

The coordinates Grisor had provided lay not too far from Jotuna, so it was only a matter of hours before the *Shinigami* reached Qarwit's ship. In that time, Barnabas ate, showered, and changed his clothes. Then he changed his clothes again.

Then he changed into a loose-fitting black outfit and did every martial arts form he knew. When he was finished, he showered again and re-dressed himself in a brown suit that complimented his coloring. He was fastidious about the fit, the lay of his shirt, and the part in his hair.

Shinigami, meanwhile, sent word that the Jotun Navy and Senate had put aside their differences long enough to seize every known member of the Committee, freeze their assets, and lock down their properties, guards and all. All technology found was confirmed to have been destroyed at once.

None of it calmed him.

He found himself wishing he had someone to talk to, but when he thought about just who he *wished* were there, any shred of calm evaporated.

So he paced.

Finally, there was a knock at his door, and it slid open to reveal Shinigami. She was wearing a positively restrained outfit of jeans and a black blouse.

"We're coming up on his ship," she told him gravely. "I thought you might like company for your walk to the bridge."

"Am I being as obvious as that?" Barnabas joked. He grabbed his suit jacket and put it on as he accompanied her out. "Thank you," he added, a few moments later.

"Anytime." She looked at him curiously. "Why are you so nervous about this one? This will tie it all up in a neat bow."

Barnabas only nodded.

Shinigami looked annoyed for a moment, but then her face cleared. "Do you…do you not *know* why you're anxious?"

Barnabas gave her a quiet nod.

"Man, humans are *weird*."

"You're telling *me*."

Shinigami laughed then. "Well, whatever's going on in

your head, boss-man, I'm glad to have run this mission with you. I don't think anyone else could have tracked them down quite like you did."

The doors to the bridge slid open, and Barnabas came in to find Tafa and Gar already in their seats. They nodded to him.

"You look nice," Tafa told him.

"Thank you." Barnabas sat in the captain's chair. "What am I—ah, I see it, now." In the static, he was able to see the faint image of a ship.

"Yes," Shinigami said, taking her place. "Even our scanners have trouble with it, but not so much that we can't shoot them down—if that's still the plan."

"It's still the plan." Barnabas wrapped his fingers around the arms of his chair and considered. "I'd like to do it."

Shinigami blinked in surprised but she nodded, and a moment later, a control panel rose out of the floor.

"Press the button when you're ready," she instructed. "We're already locked on to its trajectory. We can barely see it...and it shouldn't be able to see us at all."

Barnabas lifted his hand and paused. Part of him thought he should bring Qarwit back to stand trial, but part of him recognized just how dangerous the Jotun male was. Outmaneuvered, lacking critical resources, he had nonetheless stepped out of the shadows and confidently ordered an entire fleet to go take over the Brakalon homeworld. When opportunity came for him, he had not wavered.

Instead, he had ordered death, destruction, and slavery—and now he had the remaining prototypes with him on that ship. Barnabas had no doubt about that, while Grisor argued and pleaded for his life, betraying himself and his cause, Qarwit would play the reformed senator and escape to try the same thing over again.

His eyes locked on the ship. Sometimes you had to go with your instincts.

His hand came down on the button and a missile raced away. A few moments later, the ship in its sea of static spun out of control and disintegrated.

There was no warning. Qarwit didn't deserve one.

EPILOGUE

"I *wish* you hadn't killed Qarwit," Admiral Jeqwar stated testily a few days later.

"Really?" Barnabas asked skeptically.

She gave him a look. "No," she admitted finally. "The bastard deserved it. He was a nasty piece of work. The more we dig, the more we find. I'm sure you'll be unsurprised to learn *that*. But it does make it difficult to run the trials...and leave you out of them. You said you were going to let this be a Jotun process, if I recall correctly."

Vigilantes gotta vigilante, Shinigami commented over the Etheric comm. She flashed Barnabas a smile from her chair on the other side of Jeqwar's office.

I cannot begin to think how I'd translate that. Barnabas hid his answering smile. "It was a matter of self-defense. As I said, he *did* fire on our ship."

That was the lie they'd chosen, anyway. Admiral Jeqwar just looked at him wordlessly, and something about her flutters told him that she knew the truth.

"Also, he had the rest of the prototypes," Barnabas said. "I wanted them destroyed."

At last, Jeqwar seemed to agree. She made a soft sound. "You might have told me that sooner."

"We didn't have any time without listening ears," Barnabas countered. He hesitated. "I'm willing to let the punishments be determined by the Jotuns. Perhaps I will not agree with them, but there are limits to what I can do as a vigilante. I meant what I said when I argued that it was not my place to determine the course of an entire society, but I was not willing to let that technology exist. It was made to torture and to implant false thoughts. It was evil. As long as I have reason to believe there are those who support the Committee, I could not let those machines exist."

"I understand." Admiral Jeqwar did not waste time playing devil's advocate, though he could tell she'd thought about it.

He appreciated her restraint. Now he stood. "I will leave you to your work, Admiral."

"Mmm." She watched him. "Are you sure you won't stay to watch the trials?"

"Quite sure. They would only raise my blood pressure to unhealthy levels." Barnabas nodded pleasantly. "Admiral. I hope we will meet again under far more pleasant circumstances."

"Agreed," she said at once. She held out a metal hand for him to shake and offered the same to Shinigami. "If you're ever agreeable to an exchange of technology, we have some upgrades you might like for that cybernetic body."

Shinigami looked surprised, and the admiral laughed.

As they walked out into the Jotun sun, crossing the

sandy beach to their landing pad, Shinigami looked at him curiously.

"I have to ask... You said at the start that maybe this wasn't a mission for a vigilante, but I can't imagine you being easy with that."

"Neither could I," Barnabas admitted, "until I realized that it's not a *limitation.* It means I get to hightail it out as soon as the fun part is over and the bureaucratic mess begins."

Shinigami laughed. They headed up the ramp and she stopped in the hallway, frowning. "So where are we hightailing it *to?*"

"Amarell Station." Barnabas smiled. "I got a message and need to meet up with the person who sent it."

"*You* got a message?" Shinigami stood still as she sorted through her data banks. "What message?"

"You're not the only one who can be sneaky, you know," Barnabas retorted with a grin, then sauntered off without explaining himself.

Amarell Station wasn't close, and Shinigami, in an effort to make Barnabas cave and explain himself, took the slowest route she could. It was three days before they reached the station, and he was fairly sure that she guided them into the dock with all the speed of a drunken sloth.

He didn't cave. He also expressly forbade any of the crew to follow him off and into the station. He left them huddled in a desperately anxious group and made his way into the bustle of the remote station, whistling as he went.

Not long after that, he was sitting in a booth at one of the shadier bars, staring dubiously at a mug of beer.

"It's legit," Aliana told him. "I checked."

Barnabas took a cautious sip, unsure if she was messing with him, and was pleased to find that the beer was decent.

Aliana watched him as he drank, smiling slightly, then said, "So, rumor has it you can read minds."

Barnabas spat out a mouthful of beer. When he looked up, she was sipping her own beer, one eyebrow raised.

"Yes," he agreed. "I...*can.* If I want to." At the moment, he was doing his best not to read hers, but she was making him *very* curious.

"You probably should." She looked like she was going to start laughing at any moment. "Otherwise, how will you know why I brought you here?"

"Oh, I didn't say I've *never* read your mind," Barnabas told her blandly. "Your first thoughts upon meeting me were particularly illuminating."

She laughed, throwing her head back, her whole body shaking with mirth. "Ah, I'll bet. I remember one endless string of profanities."

"Mmhmm." Barnabas, absurdly pleased to have made her laugh, took another sip of his beer. "So you're not going to *tell* me why we're here?"

"Nope." Aliana shook her head, setting her brown ponytail swinging. She gave him another look as she drained her beer, then leaned forward with a smile. "Last chance."

Barnabas gave her a slow smile and was pleased to see her blush. He lifted his shoulders. "What can I say? I like a mystery."

"Huh." From the look on her face, she hadn't expected that, but she pushed herself up from the table and gave him a mischievous grin. "Until next time, then."

"Until next time," Barnabas agreed. He watched her thread her way between the tables and head out into the station, and he raised his glass to his lips. "Let the games begin."

FINIS

AUTHOR NOTES - NATALIE GREY

DECEMBER 16, 2018

Thank you so much for reading Protector. I can't tell you how much I've loved working on Barnabas's story. Though he and Shinigami were an amazingly unlikely pair of friends, they gave each other exactly what they needed—for her, a sense of the gravity of her actions, and for him, the ability to trust his own judgement. She helped him unbend, he helped fire up her sense of morality.

As their ragtag group grows, I've enjoyed each new character, world, and storyline. I can't wait to bring you more of Barnabas's story!

I want to send my thanks out to all the usual suspects: my beta reading team, the JIT group, all of LMBPN Publishing, and, of course, Michael. Thank you to T & M, the cutest coworkers (curled up by my feet right now), B & L (who make everything tick), and the numerous friends who put up with me jumping up and leaving the room to write down story ideas.

If you're looking for more to read before the next Barnabas stories come out, I encourage you to check out The Dragon Corps or Bound Sorcery, and definitely check out the new LitRPG series Michael and I are collaborating on!

-Nat

AUTHOR NOTES - MICHAEL ANDERLE

DECEMBER 16, 2018

THANK YOU for not only reading this story but these *Author Notes* as well.

(I think I've been good with always opening with "thank you." If not, I need to edit the other *Author Notes*!)

RANDOM (*sometimes*) THOUGHTS?

I'm now fifty-one years old, and yet I can remember the impatience I would have for Christmas to approach.

Then, it was something different when I went out on my own (as our younger sons are doing now) and then different yet when I had young kids of my own.

It was at THAT stage of their lives (very young to … now practically) that Christmas became a lot more challenging to enjoy.

Why? Because I have to admit something which is kinda embarrassing.

I SUCK AT BEING SANTA CLAUS.

there, I said it. I admit it (and I'm not just talking about the fact that I don't have white hair (and until rather recently) didn't have the big stomach.

No, I suck at being Santa Claus because I always wait until the last moment to get gifts. Before the last couple of days, I just don't want to be bothered with the effort. Then, I rush to the stores to go through the shelves which have already had people who get up early to do Christmas buy everything.

ENTER GIFT CARDS

You would think that I could handle the simple five minute effort to get gift cards on time. But, I can flat out screw that up to.

ENTER GC CARDS THAT EMAIL

Finally, a product has come to market that I can use. Emailable gift cards. I like giving them, and I am happy receiving them.

Unfortunately, feeling this way makes me think of myself as a closer cousin of the Grinch than St. Nick.

I like the decorations, the food, the lights (although going on 'a family drive' to see lights bugs me... see, *Grinch*!)

I could probably go on and on about Christmas. I would like to blame getting older. But, I think it is really just that I'm too lazy for the season.

I am going to have to work on my 'Ho Ho Ho!' At some point for the grandkids...

Oh Geez, I hope that isn't for another decade!

HOW TO MARKET FOR BOOKS YOU LOVE

We are able to support our efforts with you reading our books, and we appreciate you doing this!

If you enjoyed this or ANY book by any author, especially Indie-published, we always appreciate if you make the time to review a book, since it lets other readers who might be on the fence to take a chance on it as well.

AROUND THE WORLD IN 80 DAYS

One of the interesting (at least to me) aspects of my life is the ability to work from anywhere and at any time. In the future, I hope to re-read my own *Author Notes* and remember my life as a diary entry.

12/16/2018 at Las Vegas Mccarran Airport - American Express Lounge.

I'm sitting on a little chair with a footrest, near the front of the lounge (I can see out the front doors to the "techonthego" store across the way.)

I should be landing in Dallas/Fort Worth right now but our flight was oversold. The lady behind the American Airlines desk placed a call saying she was willing to compensate up to 6 people willing to move to the 1:30 AM flight and they would voucher us $900.00 a ticket.

I'm not too proud. I can be bought for $900.00 a ticket.

So, now that I have extra time, I've spent the last few hours working on the 6th book in the Soldiers of Fortune and Fame Series. Specially, the book 06 beats. Once I finished those I figured I'd better get the author notes for this book done (they are due tomorrow night.)

I have a certain feeling I'm going to be wiped out.

I don't do too well with flights that early in the morning. Red eye for me means Michael is a cranky person the next day.

For those who I have meetings with me tomorrow, I'd like to offer my apologies in advance.

However, $900.00 a ticket was too much of the green stuff, I just couldn't pass it up.

FAN PRICING

If you would like to find out what LMBPN is doing and the books we will be publishing, just sign up at http://lmbpn.com/email/. When you sign up, we notify you of books coming out for the week, any new posts of interest in the books and pop culture arena, and the fan pricing on Saturday.

Ad Aeternitatem,

Michael Anderle

BOOKS BY NATALIE GREY

Shadows of Magic

Bound Sorcery

Blood Sorcery

Bright Sorcery

Set in the Kurtherian Gambit Universe

Bellatrix

Challenges

Risk Be Damned

Damned to Hell

Vigilante

Sentinel

Warden

Paladin

Justiciar

Defender

Protector

Writing as Moira Katson

Shadowborn

Shadowforged

Shadow's End

Daughter of Ashes

Mahalia

BOOKS BY MICHAEL ANDERLE

For a complete list of books by Michael Anderle, please visit

www.lmbpn.com/ma-books/

All LMBPN Audiobooks are Available at Audible.com and iTunes. For a complete list of audiobooks visit:

www.lmbpn.com/audible

CONNECT WITH THE AUTHORS

Natalie Grey Social

Email List

https://landing.mailerlite.com/webforms/landing/w0k9j4

Follow Natalie on Amazon

https://www.amazon.com/Natalie-Grey/e/B01MYG7K8P/

Facebook

https://www.facebook.com/Natalie-Grey-393234677682987/

Michael Anderle Social

Website: http://lmbpn.com

Email List: http://lmbpn.com/email/

Facebook:
www.facebook.com/TheKurtherianGambitBooks

www.ingramcontent.com/pod-product-compliance
Lightning Source LLC
LaVergne TN
LVHW041621060526
838200LV00040B/1385